Amanda Minnie Douglas

A little girl in old New York

Amanda Minnie Douglas

A little girl in old New York

ISBN/EAN: 9783337414030

Printed in Europe, USA, Canada, Australia, Japan

Cover: Foto ©Andreas Hilbeck / pixelio.de

More available books at **www.hansebooks.com**

IN

OLD NEW YORK

BY

AMANDA M. DOUGLAS

AUTHOR OF "LOST IN A GREAT CITY," "SHERBURNE BOOKS,"
"IN WILD ROSE TIME," ETC.

———————

NEW YORK
DODD, MEAD & COMPANY
1896

To

DOROTHY MOORE,

A LITTLE GIRL OF TO-DAY,

FROM

HER MAMMA'S FRIEND,

AMANDA M. DOUGLAS.

NEWARK, 1896.

CONTENTS

A LITTLE GIRL IN OLD NEW YORK.

Chapter One.

THE LITTLE GIRL.

"How would you like to go to New York to live, little girl?"

The little girl looked up into her father's face to see if he was "making fun." He did sometimes. He was beginning to go down the hill of middle life, a rather stout personage with a fair, florid complexion, brown hair, rough and curly, and a border of beard shaved well away from his mouth. Both beard and hair were getting threads of white in them. His jolly blue eyes were mostly in a twinkle, and his good-natured mouth looked as if he might be laughing at you.

She studied him intently. Three months before she had been taken to the city on a visit, and it was a great event. I suspect that her mother did not like being separated from her a whole fortnight. She was such a nice, quiet, well-behaved little girl. Children were trained in those days.

Some of them actually took pride in being as nice as possible and obeying the first time they were spoken to, without even asking "Why?"

The little girl sat on a stool sewing patchwork. This particular pattern was called a lemon star and had eight diamond-shaped pieces of two colors, filled in with white around the edge, making a square. Her grandmother was coming to "join" it for her, and have it quilted before she was eight years old. She was doing her part with a good will.

"To New York?" she repeated very deliberately. Then she went on with her sewing for she had no time to waste.

"Yes, Pussy." Her father pinched her cheek softly. The little girl was the most precious thing in the world, he sometimes thought.

"What, all of us?" You see she had a mind to understand the case before she committed herself.

"Oh, certainly! I don't know as we could leave any one behind."

Then he lifted her up in his lap and hugged her, scrubbing her face with his beard which gave her pink cheeks. They both laughed. She held her sewing out with one hand so that the needle should not scratch either of them.

"I can't—hardly—tell; and her face was serious.

I want to explain to you that the little girl had

not begun with grammar. You may find her making mistakes occasionally. Perhaps the children of to-day do the same thing.

"Would we move everything?" raising her wondering eyes.

"Well, no—not quite;" and the humorous light crossed his face. "We couldn't take the orchard nor the meadows nor the woods nor the creek." (I think he said "medders" and "crick," and his "nor" sounded as if he put an *e* in it.) "There are a good many things we should have to leave behind."

He sighed and the little girl sighed too. She drew up her patchwork and began to sew.

"It is a great deal of trouble to move;" she began gravely. "I must consider."

She had caught that from Great-Aunt Van Kortlandt, who never committed herself to anything without considering.

Her father kissed her cheek. If it had been a little fatter she would have had a dimple. Or perhaps he put so many kisses in the little dent it was always filled up with love.

I don't know whether you would have thought this little girl of past seven pretty or not. She was small and fair with a rather prim face and thick light hair, parted in the middle, combed back of her ears, and cut square across the neck, but the ends had some curly twists.

Certainly children are dressed prettier nowadays. The little girl's frock was green with tiny rivulets of yellow meandering over it. They made islands and peninsulas and isthmuses of green that were odd and freaky. Mrs. Underhill had bought it to join her sashwork quilt, and there was enough left to make the little girl a frock. It had the merit of washing well, but it gave her a rather ghostly look. It had a short, full waist with shoulder straps, making a square neck, a wide belt, and a skirt that came down to the tops of her shoes, which were like Oxford ties. Though she was not rosy she had never been really ill, and only stayed at home two weeks the previous winter at the worst of the whooping-cough, which nobody seemed to mind then. But it must have made a sort of Wagner chorus if many children coughed at once.

"I had a very nice time in New York," she began, with grave approbation, when she had considered for some seconds. "The museum was splendid! And the houses seem sociable-like. Don't you suppose they nod to each other when the folks are asleep? And the stores are so—so—" she tried to think of the longest word she knew—"so magnificent? Aunt Patience and Aunt Nancy were so nice. And the cat was perfectly white and sat in Aunt Nancy's lap. There was a little girl next door who had a big doll and a cradle and a set of dishes, and we had tea together. I'd like to have some dishes. Do you think Uncle Faid is coming back?" she asked suddenly.

"I believe he is, this time. And if we get very homesick we shall have to come back and live with him."

"I shouldn't be homesick with you and mother and the boys, and Steve and Joe. It would be nice to have Dobbin and Prince, but the stores are on the corners instead of going to the village, and its nice and queer to ride in the omnibuses and hand your money up through the roof. The drivers must have an awful sight when night comes."

They even said "awful" in those far-back days, they truly did.

Father Underhill laughed and squeezed the little girl with a fondness she understood very well.

Just then a voice called rather sharply: "'Milyer! 'Milyer!" and he sat the little girl down on the stool as carefully as if she had been china. He put another kiss in the little dent, and she gave him a tender smile.

His whole name was Vermilye Fowler Underhill. Everbody called him Familiar, but Mrs. Underhill shortened it to 'Milyer.

The little girl's name was Hannah Ann. The school children called her Han and Hanny. One

grandmother always said Hanneran. But being
the youngest, the most natural name seemed "little girl."

There were three sons to lead off, Stephen
Decatur, Joseph Bennett, and John Fowler.
Then a daughter was most welcome, and she was
called Margaret Hunter after her mother, and
shortened to Peggy. They used nicknames and
diminutives, if they were not as fanciful as ours.

After Margaret came George Horton, Benny
Franklin, and James Odell. The poor mother
gave a sigh of disappointment, she had so longed
for another girl. When Jim had outgrown babyhood altogether and was nearly five, the desired
blessing came.

There was a great discussion about her name.
Grandmother Hunter had married a second time
and was a Van Kortlandt now. She had named
her only daughter after her mother and was a bit
offended that Margaret was not named for her.
Now she came with a fairy god-mother's insistence, and declared she would put a hundred dollars in the bank at once, and remember the child
in her will, besides giving her the old Hunter
tablespoons made in London more than a hundred
years ago, with the crown mark on them.

Grandmother Underhill's name was Ann. She
lived with her eldest son at White Plains, who had
fallen heir to his grandfather's farm. When a

widow she had gone back to her girlhood's home and taken care of her old father. David, her eldest son, had come to work the farm. She had a "wing" in the house, but she never lived by herself, for her son and the grandchildren adored her.

Now she said to the baby's mother: "You put in Ann for a middle name and I'll give her a hundred dollars as well, and my string of gold beads that came from Paris. And I'll make her a nice down bed and pillows."

So Hannah Ann it was, and the little girl began life with a bank account. She was a grave, sweet, dainty sort of baby, with wondering eyes of bluish violet, bordering on gray. I think myself that she should have had a prettier name, but people were not throwing away even two-hundred-dollar chances in those days. Neither had they come to Ediths and Ethels and Mays and Gladys. And they barbarously shortened some of their most beautiful names to Peggy and Betsey and Polly and Sukey.

Left to herself the little girl went on with her patchwork, and recalled her visit to the city. There were so many aunts and cousins and so many wonderful things to see. She must find out whether there would be any snow and sleighrides in the winter. As for fruit and vegetables and eggs and poultry the farmers were always sending them in to the city, she knew that.

The prospect of a removal from Yonkers, where they had always lived, was not so new to the elders. Stephen was in New York nearly all the week now. Joseph was studying for a doctor. John was not in love with farming and had a great taste for mechanical pursuits. Margaret, a tall, fair girl of seventeen, was begging to be sent away to school another year, and learn some of the higher branches people were talking about. Joe thought she should. Her father was quite sure she knew enough, for she could do all the puzzling sums in "Perkins' Higher Arithmetic," and you couldn't trip her up on the hardest words. She went to a very good school in the village. And the village was quite primitive in those days. The steamboat-landing was the great focus of interest. It was all rock and hills and a few factories were plodding along. The farm was two good miles away.

The young people thought it a most auspicious turn in affairs that Uncle Faid was coming back. His real name was Frederic. Since David had his grandfather's farm, this had been divided between the two remaining sons, but Frederic had been seized with the Western fever and gone out to what was called the new countries. His sons had married and settled in different places, one daughter had married and come East to live, and Uncle Faid was homesick for the land of his youth.

Mrs. Underhill had declared at first, "She wouldn't stir a step. 'Milyer could buy out his brother's part in the house"—the two hundred acres had been already divided. But people had begun to complain even then that farming did not pay, and John wanted to learn a trade. And if three or four went out of the old home nest! Steve wanted his father in New York. If they were not satisfied they could come back and build a new house. And presently she began to think it best even if she didn't like it.

The little girl finished her block of patchwork, pinched and patted down the seams, and laid it on the pile. Her "stent" for that day was done. There were nine more blocks to make.

There was a wide half closet beside the chimney and she had the top shelf for her own. It was so neat that it looked like a doll's house. Her only doll had been a "rag baby," and Gip, the dog, had demolished that.

"Never mind," said her mother, "you are too big to play with dolls." But the little girl in New York was almost a year older, and she had a large wax doll with "truly" clothes that could be taken off and washed. If she went to the city she might have one.

She piled up her patchwork with a sense of exultation. She was extremely neat. There was a tiny, hair-covered trunk grandmother Van Kortland had given her full of pretty chintz and calico pieces. She kept her baby shoes of blue kid that were outgrown before they were half worn out, so choice had her mother been of them. There were some gift-books and mementos and a beautiful Shaker basket Stephen had given her at Christmas. It was round, so she imagined you put something in it and shook it, for she had no idea the Shakers were a community and made dainty articles for sale, even if they discarded all personal vanities.

She went through to the next room, which was the kitchen in winter and dining-room in summer. She took down her blue-and-white gingham sunbonnet, and skipped along a narrow path through the grass to the summer kitchen. This was a short distance from the house, a big, square room with a door at each side, and smoky rafters overhead. The brick and stone chimney was built inside, very wide at the bottom and tapering up to the peak in the roof. There was a great black crane across it, with two sets of trammels suspended from it, on which you could hang two kettles at the same time. If you have never seen one, get Longfellow's beautiful illustrated poem, "The Hanging of the Crane." A great many old country houses had them, and they were considered extremely handy.

The presiding genius of the kitchen was a fat

old black woman, so old that her hair was all grizzled. When she braided it up in little tails on Saturday afternoon Hannah Ann watched with a kind of fascination. She always wore a plaid Madras turban with a bow tied in front. She had been grandmother Underhill's slave woman. I suppose very few of you know there were slaves in New York State in the early part of the century. Aunt Mary had sons married, and grandchildren doing well. They begged her now and then to give up work, but she clung to her old home.

"Aunt Mary," inquired the little girl, "is the chicken feed mixed?"

"Laws, yaas, honey, lem me scoop it in de pail. You's got such little claws o' han's. Don't seem 's if dey ever grow big ernough fer nothin'."

She ladled out the scalded meal, mixed with bits of broken bread. The little girl laughed and nodded and crossed the small bridge that spanned the creek. The spring, or rather the series of them, ran around the house and down past the kitchen, then widened out into quite a pond where the ducks and geese disported themselves, and the cows always paused to drink on their way to the barn.

She went down to the barn. On the carriage-house side in the sun were some chicken-coops. Pretty little chicks whose mothers had "stolen their nests;" thirty-two of various sizes, and they belonged to the little girl.   She rarely forgot them.

There were plenty of chores for Ben and Jim. They drove the cows to pasture, chopped wood, picked apples, and dug potatoes.   You wondered how they found any time for play or study.

Jim "tagged" the little girl as she came back with her pail.   She could run like a deer.

"Here you, Jim!" called Aunt Mary, "you jes' take dis pail an' git some of dem big blackbre'es fer supper steder gallopin' roun' like a wild pala- kin ob de desert!" and she held out the shining pail.

A "palakin of the desert" was Aunt Mary's favorite simile.   In vain had Margaret explained that the pelican was a bird and couldn't gallop.

"Laws, honey," the old woman would reply, "I aint hankerin' arter any ob dis new book larnin'. I's a heap too old fer 'rithmertic an' 'stology.   I jes' keeps to de plain Bible dat served de chillen of Isrul in de wilderness.   Some day, Miss Peggy, when you's waded tru seas o' trubble an' come out on de good Lord's side an' made your callin' an' 'lection sure, you'll know more 'bout it I done reckon."

"Come with me, do, Hanny," pleaded Jim. "You can walk along the stone fence and pick the high ones and we'll fill the kittle in no time."

Jim thought if he had made a spelling-book, he would have spelled the word that way. Jim would have been a master hand at phonetics.

The little girl crossed two of her fingers. That was a sign of truce in the game.

"No play till we come back," said Jim.

The little girl nodded and ran for her mitts of strong muslin with the thumb and finger ends out. The briars were so apt to tear your hands.

They ran a race down to the blackberry patch. Then they sat on the fence and ate berries. It was really a broad, handsome wall. There were so many stones on the ground that they built the walls as they "cleared up." The blackberry lot was a wild tangle. There were some hickory-nut trees in it and a splendid branching black walnut. Sometimes they found a cluster of hazel-nuts.

The great blackberry canes grew six or seven feet high. They generally cut one path through in the early summer. The long branches made arches overhead.

The little girl pinned a big dock-leaf with a thorn and made a cup. When it was full she emptied it into Jim's pail. They were such great, luscious berries that they soon had it filled. Then they sat down and rested. Everybody knows that it is harder work to pick berries than to play "tag."

Jim had a piece to speak on Friday afternoon

at school.   They had these exercises once a month, but this was to be a rather grand affair, as then school closed for a fortnight.   That was all the vacation they had.

Jim was rather proud of his elocutionary gift. He stood up on a big flat stone and declaimed so that the little girl might see if he knew every word.   It was extremely patriotic, beginning:

> "Columbia! Columbia! to glory arise,
>   The queen of the world and the child of the skies!"

"Oh, you say it just splendid!" declared the little girl enthusiastically.   She never laughed and teased him as Peggy did.

She was learning some verses herself, but she wondered if she would have courage enough to face the whole school.   They were in her "Child's Reader" with the "Little Busy Bee," and "Let Dogs Delight to Bark and Bite."   She thought them beautiful:

> "The rose had been washed, lately washed in a shower,
>   Which Mary to Anna conveyed."

It puzzled her small brain a good deal as to why the rose needed washing.   But Peggy showed her one day how dusty the leaves and flowers grew in a dry time, and she learned that the whole world was the better for an occasional washing. She asked Mary afterward why the clothes were not put out in a hard rain to get them clean.

"Laws, honey, dey need elbow-grease," and the old woman laughed heartily.

"I do wish my name was Anna," she said, with a sigh.

"Well, you just need to put another *a* to the Ann," said her brother confidently.

"And I don't like being called Han and Hanny."

"I'd a heap rather be called Jim than James. When pop calls me James I think it's time to pick myself up mighty spry, I tell you!" and he laughed.

"It's different with boys," she said, with a soft sigh. "Girls ought to have pretty names, and Hanneran is dreadful."

"I'd stand a good deal for two hundred dollars. And it doubles in fourteen years. And seven again! Why you'll have more than five hundred dollars when you're grown up!"

She did not know the value of money and thought she would rather have the pretty name. Yet she wasn't *quite* sure she would choose Anna.

"You stay here while I run after the cows," said Jim. "It will save another journey."

Boys are often economical of their steps, I have noticed. Perhaps this is how they gain time for play. The little girl jumped down presently and looked over at the wild flowers. There were clusters of yarrow in bloom, spikes of yellow snapdragons, and a great clump of thistles in their purple glory. She must tell her father about them, and have them rooted out. Would it hurt them to be killed? She felt suddenly sorry for them.

A squirrel ran along and winked at her as he gave his tail an extra perk. Nothing was ever afraid of the little girl. But she ran from the old gobbler, and the big gander who believed he had pre-empted the farm from the Indians. She generally climbed over the fence when she saw old Red, who had an ominous fashion of brandishing her long horns. But she didn't mind with Jim nor Benny.

Jim came now and took up the pail. The cows meandered along. She was rather glad Jim did not see the thistle. She would not tell him about it to-night.

Chapter Two.

GOOD-BY TO AN OLD. HOME.

WHEN they reached the barn they saw Aunt
Mary carrying a great platter of corn up to the
house. The little girl washed her hands and her
face, that was quite rosy now, and followed. How
delicious it all looked! White bread, corncake,
cold chicken, pot-cheese in great creamy balls, and
a hot molasses cake to come on with the berries.

The little girl always sat beside her mother, and
Margaret on the boys' side, to help them. There
were four boys and two hired men.

Mrs. Underhill was a notable housekeeper.
She was a little sharp in the temper, but Mr. Underhill was so easy that some one had to uphold
the family dignity. She complained that 'Milyer
spoiled the children, but they were good-natured
and jolly, and quite up to the average.

After supper the cows were milked, the horses
fed and bedded, Margaret and her mother packed
up the dishes in a big basket, and the boys took
them down to Mary. Mrs. Underhill looked after
the milk.

The little girl went out on the wide porch and

studied her lessons.   There were two long lines in Webster's elementary spelling-book to get by heart, for the teacher "skipped about." The children went up and down, and it was rare fun sometimes. The little girl had been out of the Baker class a long while. They call it that because the first column began with that easy word. She was very proud of having gone in the larger class. Her father gave her a silver dollar with a hole punched through it, and Steve brought her a blue ribbon for it. She wore it on state occasions. She studied Peter Parley's geography and knew the verses beginning:

> "The world is round and like a ball,
>   Seems swinging in the air."

How it could be puzzled her. She asked her father, for she thought he knew everything. He said he believed it was, but he could never make it seem so.

Aunt Mary strenuously denied it. "Sta'ns to reason de folks would fall off w'en it went swirlin' round.   De good Lord He knows His business better'n dat.   Jes don't mind any sech foolin', honey! Its clear agin de Bible dat speaks ob de sun's risin' an' settin', an' de Lord nebber makes any mistake 'bout dat ar Bible."

The little girl studied her lesson over four times. Then Jim came up and they had a game of tag.

Dave Andrews and Milton Scott sat out under the old apple-tree smoking their pipes and talking politics. One was a Whig and the other a Democrat who believed that we had never had a President worth mentioning since Andrew Jackson, Old Hickory as he was often called.

When her father came round the corner of the house she stopped running after Jim and held out both hands to him. Her cheeks were like wild roses and her eyes shone with pleasure. They sat down on the step, and he put his arm about her and "cuddled" her up to his side. She told him she had gone up three in saying seven times in the multiplication table, and four in spelling "tetrarch." Then when Charley Banks was reading he said "condig-en" and the class laughed. She also told him she had been studying about Rhode Island and Roger Williams, and all the bays and inlets and islands. She made believe comb his hair with her slim little fingers and once in a while he opened his lips like a trap and caught them, and they both laughed.

Presently Mrs. Underhill, who sat by the window knitting in the twilight, said: "'Milyer, that child must go to bed."

She felt she had to issue this mandate two or three times, so she began early.

They hugged each other and laughed a little. Then he said: "All the chickens right?"

"Yes, I counted them. They're so cunning and lovely."

"I hope they'll get their feather cloaks on before cold weather," said her father.

"'Milyer, that child *must* go to bed! I don't see why you want to keep her up all hours of the night."

They hugged each other a little closer this time and did not laugh, but just kissed softly. It was beginning to grow dusky. The peeps and crickets and katydids were out in force. The katydids told you there would be frost in six weeks.

When her mother added in a dignified tone, "Come, Hannah Ann," the little girl took one last hug and came into the room. Margaret had lighted the candles in their polished brass candlesticks. One stood on the hall table, one on the stand in the middle of the room. Mrs. Underhill had knit past the seam in her stocking and pulled out a few stitches. Then she laid it down and unfastened the little girl's frock and said, "Now run to bed this minute." Margaret was reading, but she glanced up and smiled.

The candle made a vague yellowish light on the stairs. There were people who burned lamp-oil, as the oil from whales was called. The little girl held it in curious awe, associating it with the story of Jonah. Mrs. Underhill despised the "ill-smelling stuff" and would not have it in the house. She made beautiful candles. Oil-wells had hardly been thought of, except that some one occasionally brought a bottle from Pennsylvania for rheumatism.

The little girl had slept in her mother's room, which answered to the back parlor, until this spring when she had gone up to Margaret's room. There were four large chambers on the second floor and a spacious clothes-room with a closet for bedding. Up above was an immense garret with four gables. The three younger boys and the two hired men slept there.

The little girl didn't mind going to bed alone, but her mother generally found some good reason for going upstairs. On cool nights she was afraid the little girl wasn't well covered; and to-night she looked in and said:

"I hope you're not bundled up in a blanket this hot night, Hannah Ann! Children seem to have such little sense."

"Oh no, I have only the sheet over me." But the little girl raised up and held out her arms, and her mother gave her a soft squeeze and patted the pillow and said:

"Now you must go to sleep like a good little girl;" quite as if she was in the habit of being bad and not going to sleep, but they both understood.

You may think the little girl's life was dull with lessons and sewing and going to bed at dusk. But she found no end of fun. Now and then a host of cousins came, and they climbed trees, ran races, waded in the brooks, went off to the woods and swung in the wild grape-vines. Sometimes they walked out on the end of a wide-spreading branch, holding to the one above, and when they began to "teeter" too much they gave a spring and came down on the soft ground. The little girl could go out a long way because she was so light and fearless. They never broke their necks or their limbs. They laughed and shouted and turned summersaults and ran races. No day was ever long enough.

The school was a good mile away, but on very stormy days they were taken in the covered wagon. They studied with a will, just as they played, and you heard nothing about nerves in those days.

Some of the parents came that last day at school. Jim acquitted himself creditably in his "Ode to Columbia," and the little girl recited with a rose in her hand, though Margaret had quite a trouble to find one for her. Roses didn't bloom all the year round as they do now. When the children were dismissed they went out and gave some deafening hurrahs for the two weeks' vacation. Oh, what throats and lungs they had!

When the little girl reached home she found a houseful of company. When families have lived from one to two hundred years in one section of the country, they get related to almost everybody. And though Aunt Becky Odell was a second cousin of her mother's, she was aunt to the little girl all the same. She had come up from West Farms to spend a few days and brought her two little girls. Some other relatives had come from Tarrytown.

The little girl greeted everybody, took off her Sunday white frock that had a needleworked edge that her mother had worn twenty years and more ago. Then she took the little girls out to see the chickens and hunt some eggs and have a good play on the hay in the barn.

"Oh, ain't you just crazy to go to New York to live?" cried Polly Odell. "The stores are so beautiful! When I go down I just don't want to come back!"

"You was homesick at Aunt Phœbe's, you know you was," said her sister, with small regard for her tense.

"Well, I didn't like Aunt Phœbe one bit. She's old and cross, and she isn't our own aunt either. She won't let you stand by the window les' you breathe on the glass, and she won't let you rock on the carpet nor run up and down stairs, nor touch a book, and makes you get up at five in the morning when you're so sleepy. She wanted me to stay 'cause she said 'I was handy to wait on her.' And it wasn't truly New York but way up by the East River. I wouldn't have stayed for a dollar. I just jumped up and down when poppy came, and she said, 'For goodness' sake! don't thrash out all my carpet with your jouncin' up an' down.' You can just go yourself, Janey Odell, and see how you like it!"

"I'm sure I don't want to go. But you just jumped at it!"

"Well, I thought it would be nice. But oh, Hanneran, it's just splendid here! And to-morrow Uncle 'Milyer's going to take us out riding. He said so. Oh, Hanneran, wasn't you awful 'fear'd to speak a piece before all the folks at school?"

Polly Odell looked at her in amazement.

"Well—just at first——"

"I wouldn't dast to for a dollar!" cried Janey.

They went on with their play, now and then stumbling against a discussion that never really reached the height of a dispute. Margaret came to hunt them up presently that they might have their tousled heads smoothed and their hands and faces washed.

The little girl was always interested when they had a high tea in the sitting-room. The best old blue china was out, the loaf sugar, and the sugar-

tongs that the little girl watched breathlessly lest
her mother should lose the lump of sugar before
it reached the cup.

The men and boys were having supper in the
other room, but the little girls waited on the
porch. They were so quiet and kept so tidy that
Mrs. Underhill gave them a lump of sugar in each
glass of milk, and took it up with the sugar-tongs,
to the little girl's great delight.

She couldn't help hearing the talk as they all
sat out on the porch. Uncle Faid had really sold
his farm, stock, and crops, and was to give possession in September. Then they would visit their
two sons and some of Aunt Betsey's people in
Michigan, and get on about Christmas.

"It's a shame to have to give up the house," declared Cousin Odell. "Can't you keep it, 'Milyer?"

"A bargain's a bargain. Faid did a fair thing
when he went away, and I can't do less than a
fair thing now. If he'd died, his share in the
house would have been offered to me first. I dare
say we could put on an addition and live together
without quarrellin', but the boys want to go to
New York, and they couldn't all stay here and
make a living. The young folks must strike out,
and I tell mother if she don't get to feeling at
home I'll come back and build her a house."

"It'll never be like this one," said Mrs. Underhill sharply.

"The world is full of changes," declared the Tarrytown cousin.

The little girl sat in her father's lap and listened until she went soundly asleep. Janey Odell leaned against the porch column and almost tumbled over. Mrs. Underhill sprang up.

"Mercy on us! These children ought to be in bed. Wake up, Hannah Ann!"

"I'll carry her upstairs," said her father, and he kissed her tenderly as he laid her on the bed. Her mother undressed her and patted down her pillow. She flung her arms about her mother's neck.

"Oh, mother!" she cried softly, wonderingly, "do you want to go to New York?"

"Child dear, I don't know what I want," and there was a muffled sound in her voice. "There, go to sleep, dear. Don't worry."

They inspected the pretty knoll the next day where Mrs. Underhill was to have her new house built if they didn't take root in New York. Were not her children dearer to her than any spot of ground? And if they were all going away——

The children had a very jolly time. On Monday the Odells went home, and the little girl hated to say good-by. Cousin Famie Morgan, her real name was Euphemia, wanted to go to White Plains to visit a while with Aunt Ann and David, and Cousin Joanna would stay a few days longer and go to New York to do some shopping. Margaret would go with Cousin Famie. The little girl wanted to go too, and take her patchwork. She had only six blocks to do now.

Grandmother was very glad to see her, and praised her without stint. Uncle David and Aunt Eunice had some grandchildren. Two sons and one daughter were married, and one son and daughter were still at home. Aunt Eunice was a very placid, sweet body, and still clung to her Quaker dress and speech, though she went to the old Episcopal church with her husband. Her folks lived up in Putnam County.

Grandmother would have spoiled the little girl if such a thing had been possible. She would help her with the patchwork, and then she brought out some lovely red French calico that was soft and rich, and began to join it. They had some nice drives, and one day they took Cousin Morgan home and stayed to dinner. There were three single women living together in a queer rambling house that had been added to, and raised in places. Mr. Erastus Morgan and his wife lived in Paris, and once a year or so there would come a package of pretty things—china and ornaments of various kinds, odd pieces of silk and brocade for cushions, gloves, and fans and laces and silk for gowns, as if they were still quite young women.

Uncle David had the "Knickerbocker History of New York," which everybody now knew was written by Mr. Washington Irving, and various members of the family were settled about Tarrytown, and many others in the Sleepy Hollow graveyard. The very next day the little girl began to read the history, for she wanted to know about New York. They had a delightful visit with grandmother and Aunt Eunice. Uncle David was seven years older than her father. The little girl concluded she liked him very much.

When she and Margaret went home everything was going on just the same. The little girl was somewhat amazed. No one said a word about moving. She had expected to see everything packed. The children started for school as usual. Then Mrs. Underhill went down to the city and stayed a fortnight and came home looking worn and worried. The impending change weighed upon her. But the little girl was so interested in Mr. Dederich Knickerbocker which she was reading aloud to her father that changes hardly mattered.

Early in December Mr. Frederic Underhill with his wife and daughter came to hand. He was thin and stooped a good deal, and looked older than Uncle David. Aunt Crete's name was Lucretia, and the little girl was amazed to learn that. She was tall and thin and wore a black lace sort of cap to cover the bald spot on her head. Then she had a false front of dark hair. Her own was very thin and white. She had been a great sufferer from 'ager,' as she called it, and the doctors said only an entire change of climate would break it up. And goodness only knew how glad she was to get back East.

Lauretta—Retty as she was called—was about twenty-two, a good, stout, commonplace girl who made herself at home at once. She had a lover who was coming on in the spring when they would be married, and he expected "to help Pop farm. Pop was pretty well broken down with hard work, and he'd about seen his best days. He'd been awful anxious to get back among his own folks, and she, Retty, hoped now he'd take things kinder easy."

Grandmother and Uncle David's family came down to welcome them. All the country round seemed to turn out. And just before Christmas, with all the rest of the work, the little girl's quilt was put in. Some of the older people came the first day and had a fine supper. Next afternoon it was the young people's turn.

The little girl had a blue-and-white figured silk frock made from a skirt of her mother's. The tops of the sleeves were trimmed with four or five ruffles and there were two ruffles around the neck. She wore her gold beads, and Margaret curled her hair. Everybody praised her and she felt very happy. Some of the young men came in while they were taking the quilt out of the frame, and oh, what a tussle there was! The girl who could wrap herself first in it was to be married first. Such pulling and laughing, such a din of voices and struggle of hands—you would have thought all the girls wild to get married. The little girl looked with dismay, for it seemed as if her quilt would be torn to pieces.

Retty wound one corner around herself, and two of the young men rolled Margaret and several of the other girls in the other end amid the shouts of the lookers-on.

Then grandmother shook it out and folded it.

"There!" she exclaimed, "to-morrow I'll put on the binding. And, Hannah Ann, you have a good beginning. Not every little girl can show such a quilt as that, pieced all by herself before she was eight years old!"

"But you helped, grandmother——"

"Nonsense, child! Just a piece now and then! And I've a nice pair of wool blankets I'm saving up for you that I spun myself. You'll have a good many things saved up in a dozen years."

What fun they had afterward! There were two black fiddlers in the hall; one was Cato, Aunt Mary's grandson, a stylish young fellow much in demand for parties. They danced and danced.

Steve took his little sister out several times, and John danced with her. Her father thought her the very prettiest one in the crowd. Her mother let her stay up until eleven.

"I'm so sorry you are going away," said Retty, the next morning. "I never did have such a good time in my life. I don't see why we can't all live together in this big house!"

In the new year the real business of changing began. It was hard to select a house. Joe said all New York was going up-town, and that before many years the lower part of the city would be given over to business. Bond and Amity Street, around St. John's Park and East Broadway were still centres of fashion. The society people had come up from the Bowling Green and the Battery, though there were still some beautiful old houses that business people clung to because they wanted to be near to everything. Harlem and Yorkville were considered country. Up on the east side as far as Eightieth or Ninetieth Street there were some spacious summer residences with beautiful grounds. A few fine mansions clustered about University Square. City Hall Park was still covered with fine growing shade-trees. There was such a magnificent fountain that Lydia Maria Child, describing it, said there was nothing to equal it in the Old World.

Still, the unmistakable trend was uptown.

Grace Church was agitating a new building at Tenth Street. Rows of houses were being put up on the new streets, though down-town people rather scoffed and wondered why people were not going up to Harlem and taking their business places along.

After much discussion the Underhills settled upon First Street. Stephen made the decision, though he had great faith in "up-town." This was convenient. Then they could buy through to Houston Street, and there was a stable and sort of storehouse on the end of the lot. And though you wouldn't think it now, it was quite pretty and refined then, from Avenue A out to the Bowery. They were in a row of nice brick houses, quite near First Avenue, on the lower side of the street. Opposite it was well built for quite a space, and then came the crowning glory of the block. About a dozen houses stood thirty or so feet back from the street and had lovely flower-gardens in front. Stephen would have liked one of these, but the houses were not roomy enough. And in their own place they had a nice grass-plot, some flower-beds, and several fruit-trees, beside a grape-trellis. He thought his mother would be less homesick if she could see some bloom and greenery.

It was the last of March, 1843, that the little girl came to New York. Mrs. Underhill believed it only an experiment. When the boys were grown up and married, settled in their own homes, she and 'Milyer would go back to Yonkers on their part of the farm and have a nice big house for their old age and for the grandchildren. In her motherly heart she hoped there would be a good many of them. She couldn't have spared any of her eight children.

The house in First Street seemed very queer. It had a front area and two basements, two parlors on the next floor with folding-doors and a long ell-room, rather narrow, so that it would not darken the back room too much. Up-stairs there were three large chambers and one small one, and on the fourth floor, that did not have full-size windows, three more. That there was no "garret" caused endless lamentation.

They could not bring old Mary, indeed she would not come, but they had a rather youngish countrywoman whose husband had deserted her, and who was looking for a good home. Mary thought she would stay a while with the "new folks" and get them "broke in," as she phrased it, and then go and live with her son.

The little girl stood on her own front stoop looking up and down the street. It was queer the houses should be just alike—six brown-stone steps, and iron side railings, and an iron railing to the area, that was paved with brick. You would always have to be thinking of the number or you might get into the neighbor's house. Oh, no. Here was a sure sign, the bright silver door-plate with black lettering—"Vermilye F. Underhill." She looked at it in amazement. It made her father suddenly grand in her estimation. Could she sit in his lap just the same and twist his whiskers about her fingers and comb his hair and read out of her story-books to him? And where would she go to school? Were there any little girls around to play with? How could she get acquainted with them?

While she was considering this point, two girls went by. Both had straw gypsy hats with flowers and ruffled capes of black silk. They looked up at her. She was going to smile down to them in the innocent belief that all little girls must be glad to see each other. One of them giggled— yes, she absolutely did, and said:

"Oh, what a queer-looking thing! Her frock comes down to her shoe-tops like an old woman's, and that sun-bonnet! Why she must have just come in from the backwoods!"

Chapter Three.

FINE FEATHERS FOR THE LITTLE WREN.

THE little girl stood still a moment as if transfixed. There came the passionate desire to run and hide. She gave the door-bell a sharp pull.

Martha Stimis answered it.

"Goodness sakes, is it you, ringin' as if the world wouldn't stand another minnit? Next time you want to get in, Haneran, you jest come down the *aree!* And me a-mouldin' up the biscuit!"

The little girl walked through the hall with a swelling heart. She couldn't be allowed to ring the door-bell when her own father's name was on the door!

The ell part was her mother's sleeping chamber and sitting-room. No one was in it. Hannah Ann walked down to the end. There was a beautiful old dressing-case that had been brought over with the French great, great grandmother. It had a tall glass coming down to the floor. At the sides were several small drawers that went up about four feet, and the top had some handsome carved work. It was one of Mrs. Underhill's choicest possessions. In the mirror you could see yourself from "top to toe."

The little girl stood before it. She had on a brown woollen frock and a gingham high apron. Her skirt *was* straight and long. Her laced shoes only came to her ankles. Her stockings were black, and she remembered how she had watched these little girls coming down the street, their stockings were snowy white. Of course she wore white yarn ones on Sundays. A great piece of their pantalets was visible, ruffled, too. Yes, she did look queer! And the starch was mostly out of her sun-bonnet. It wasn't her best one, either.

She sat down on a little bench and cried as if her heart would break.

"Oh, Hanny dear, what is the matter?"

Margaret had entered the room unheard. She knelt by her little sister, took off her sun-bonnet and pressed the child in her arms. "What is it, dear?" in a soft, persuasive voice. "Have you hurt yourself?"

"No. I—I——" Then she put her little arms around Margaret's neck. "Oh, Peggy, am I very, very queer?"

"You're a little darling. Did Martha scold you?"

"No. It wasn't—some girls came along——" She tried very hard to stop her sobbing.

"There, dear, let me wash your face. Don't cry any more." She laid aside the bonnet and bathed the small face, then she began to brush the soft hair. It had not been cut all winter and was quite a curly mop. Stephen had bought her a round comb of which she was very proud.

"It was two girls. They went by and they laughed——"

Her voice was all of a quaver again, but she did not mean to cry if she could help it.

"Did they call you 'country'?"

Margaret smiled and kissed the little girl, who tried to smile also. Then she repeated the ill-bred comment.

"We are not quite citified," said Margaret cheerfully. "And it isn't pleasant to be laughed at for something you cannot well help. But all the little girls *are* wearing short dresses, and you are to have some new ones. Mother has gone out shopping, and next week cousin Cynthia Blackfan is coming to fix us all up. But I *do* hope, Hanny, you will have better manners and a kinder heart than to laugh at strangers, no matter if they are rather old-fashioned."

"I don't believe I ever will," said the little girl soberly.

"Now come up in my room. Mother said I might rip up her pretty blue plaid silk and have it made over. I came down to hunt up the waist."

She found it in one of the drawers, pinned up in a linen pillow-case.

"And you can have on a white apron," the elder said when they reached the room.

This had long sleeves and a ruffle round the neck. The little girl was ever so much improved.

And I think she would have felt comforted if she could have heard the rest of the talk between the two girls.

"I do wonder if she belongs to the new people," said the girl who laughed. "They can't be much. They came from the country somewhere."

"But they've bought all the way through to the other street. And ma said she meant to call on them. Some one told her they owned a big farm in Yonkers, and one of the young men is to be a doctor. Maybe the little girl doesn't really belong to them. I wish you hadn't spoken quite so loud. I'm sure she heard."

"Oh, I don't care!" with an airy toss of the head. "Mother said the other day she shouldn't bother about new neighbors. Calling on them is out of style."

Hanny looked out of the window a long while. Then she said gravely: "Margaret, are all those old Dutch people dead that were in the history? And where was their Bowery?"

"It is the Bowery out here, but it has changed. That was a long, long time ago."

"If I'd lived then no one would have laughed

about my long frock. I almost wish I'd been a little girl then."

"Perhaps there were other things to laugh about."

"I don't mind the laughing *now*. But they must have had lovely gardens full of tulips and roses. There doesn't seem any room about for such things. And lanes, you know. Did the new people drive the Dutch away?"

"The English came afterward. You will read all about it in history. And then came the war——"

"That grandmother knows about? Margaret, I think New York is a great, strange, queer place. There are a good many queernesses, aren't there?"

Margaret assented with a smile.

"Oh, there's father in the wagon!" The little girl was all a tremor of gladness. He caught her eyes and beckoned, and she ran down. But she couldn't manage the night-latch, and so Margaret had to follow her.

"Bundle up my little girl," he said. "I've got to drive up to Harlem and I'll take her along."

Hanny almost danced for joy. Margaret found her red merino coat. The collar was trimmed with swan's down, and her red silk hood had an edge of the same. True, some ultra-fashionables had come out in spring attire, but it was rather cool so early in the season. Hanny looked very pretty in her winter hood. And as they drove down the street the same girls were standing on a stoop; one was evidently going away from her friend. The one who laughed lived there then. But neither of them would have guessed it was the "queer" girl, and they almost envied her.

"I've never been down to this corner," said Hanny. "And the streets run together."

"Yes, First Street ends and Houston goes on over to the East River."

The little girl looked about. There was a great sign on the house at the junction—"Monticello Hotel,"—and on the edge of the sidewalk a pump, which the little girl thought funny. They dipped the water out of the spring at home—they had not given up saying that about the old place. There was no need of a pump, and at grand-mother's they had a well-sweep and bucket.

Then they turned up Avenue A, where he had an errand, and soon they were going over rough country ways where "squatters" had begun to come in with pigs and geese. They seemed so familiar that the little girl laughed. And if some one had told her that she would one day be driv-ing in a beautiful park over yonder it would have sounded like a fairy tale. It was rough and wild now. Dobbin spun along, for the sun was hurry-ing over westward.

"We have some old cousins living beyond there on Harlem Heights." he said, "but it's too late to hunt them up. And it'll be dark by the time we get home. There was a big battle fought here. Their brother was killed in it. Why, they must be most eighty years old."

The little girl drew a long breath at the thought.

"We'll look them up some day." Then he stopped before a hotel where there was a long row of horse sheds, and sprang out to tie Dobbin.

"I had better take you out. Something might happen." He carried her in his arms clear up the steps. A lady came around the corner of the wide porch.

"I'll leave my little girl in the waiting-room a few moments. I have some business with Mr. Brockner," he said.

"I will take her through to my sitting-room," the lady replied, and holding out her hand she led Hanny thither. She insisted on taking off her hood and loosening her coat, and in a few moments she seemed well acquainted. The lady asked her father's name and she told it.

"There are some old ladies of that name living half a mile or so from here," she said. Then remembering they were very poor, and that poor relations were not always cordially accepted, she hesitated.

"Father spoke of some cousins," cried the little girl eagerly. "He said sometime we would hunt them up. We only came to New York to live two weeks ago."

"Then you have hardly had time to look up any one. They would be glad to see your father, I know. He looks so wholesome and good-natured."

The little girl was not an effusive child, but she and the lady fell into a delightful talk. Then her hostess brought in a plate of seed cookies, and she was eating them very delicately when her father entered.

"We have had such a nice time," she said, "that I'd like you to bring your little girl up again. Indeed, I have half a mind to keep her."

"We couldn't spare her," said her father, with a fond smile, which Hanny returned.

"I suppose not. But it will soon be beautiful around here, and when she longs for a breath of the country you must bring her up."

"Thank you, madam."

"And oh, father, the cousins really are here. Two old, old ladies——"

Mr. Underhill inquired about them, and learned their circumstances were quite straitened. He promised to come up soon and see them.

Mrs. Brockner kissed Hanny, quite charmed with her simplicity and pretty manner. And she had never once thought about the length of her old brown skirt.

It was supper time when they reached home. Steve and Joe and John were there. The three younger boys had been left at Yonkers. Indeed, George had declared his intention of being a farmer. Mrs. Underhill said she didn't want any more boys until she had a place to put them.

Afterward Joe coaxed the little girl to come and sit on his knee. They were talking about schools.

"Seems to me, Margaret better be studying housekeeping and learning how to make her clothes instead of going to school," said Mrs. Underhill shortly. "She can write a nice letter and she's good at figures, and, really, I don't see——"

"She wants to be finished," returned Steve, with a laugh. "She's a city girl now. I've been looking schools over. There are several establishments where they burnish up young ladies. There's Madame Chegary's——"

"I won't have her going to any French school and reading wretched French novels!"

Steve threw back his head and laughed. He had such splendid, strong, white teeth.

"My choice would be Rutgers Institute. It's going to be the school of the day," declared Joe.

"Exactly. I was coming to that. There would be one term before vacation."

"I call it all foolishness. And she'll be eighteen on her next birthday," said her mother. "If she wasn't a good scholar already — and what more *do* you expect her to learn?"

They all laughed at their mother's little ebullition of temper.

"The world grows wiser every day," said Joe sententiously.

"And what are you going to do, Pussy?"

Steve reached over and gave the little girl's ear a soft pinch.

"I am going to look up a nice school for her myself. Don't begin to worry about a child not yet eight years old," said their mother sharply.

"Eight years. She'll soon be that," remarked her father with a soft sigh. And he wished he could keep her a little girl always.

They went on discussing Rutgers Institute, that was one of the most highly esteemed schools of the day for young ladies. Steve looked over at his fair sister—she was *almost* as pretty as Dolly Beekman. Dolly had some dainty, attractive ways, played on the piano and sang, and Peggy had a voice blithe as a bird. Steve was beginning to be quite a judge of young ladies and social life, and there was no reason why they should not all aim at something. They had good family names to back them. Family counted, but so did education and accomplishments.

Mrs. Underhill gave in. Steve would have his way. But then he was such a good, upright, affectionate son. So when he announced that he had registered his sister, Margaret's pulses gave a great thrill of delight.

There was so much to do. True, Martha was a good cook and capable, and there was no milk to look after, no churning, no poultry, and the countless things of country life. Miss Cynthia Blackfan came the next week and remodeled the feminine part of the household. She was a tall, slim, airy-looking person, with large dark eyes and dark hair that she wore in long ringlets on either side of her face. She always looped them up when she was sewing. She had all the latest quips of fashion at her tongue's end—what Margaret must have for school dresses, what for Sunday best, what lawns and ginghams and prints for summer.

But when she went at the little girl she quite metamorphosed her.

"You must begin to plait the child's hair and tie it with ribbons [people generally used the word instead of 'braid']. And her frocks must be made ever so much shorter. And, Cousin Underhill, *do* put white stockings on the child. Nobody wears colored ones. Unbleached do wear stronger and answer for real every day."

"They'll be forever in the wash-tub," said the mother grimly.

4

"Well, when you're in Rome you must do as the Romans do," with emphasis. "It looks queer to be so out of date. Everybody dresses so much more in the city. It's natural. There's so much going and coming."

Even then people had begun to discuss and condemn the extravagance of the day. The old residents of the Bowling Green were sure Bond Street and the lower part of Fifth Avenue were stupendous follies and would ruin the city. Foreign artistic upholsterers came over, carpets and furniture of the most elegant sort were imported, and even then some people ordered their gowns and cloaks in Paris. Miss Blackfan's best customer had gone over for the whole summer, otherwise she would not have the fortnight for Cousin Underhill. She uttered her dictum with a certain authority from which there was no appeal. And she charged a dollar and a half a day, while most dressmakers were satisfied with a dollar.

So the little girl had her hair braided in two tails—they were quite short, though, and her father liked the curly mop better. Little girls' dresses were cut off the shoulder, and made with a yoke or band and a belt. In warm weather they wore short sleeves, though a pair of long sleeves were made for cool days. There were some tucks in the skirt to be let down as the child grew.

The little girl was most proud, I think, of her pantalets. There were some nankin ones made for every day. And she had a real nankin frock that Margaret embroidered just above the hem. It was used a great deal for aprons, too. Aprons, let me tell you, were no longer "high-ups" with a plain armhole. They were sometimes gathered on a belt and had Bertha capes over the shoulders trimmed with edging or ruffles. And every well-conditioned little girl had one of black silk.

"She'll have to hem her own ruffles," declared Mother Underhill almost sharply. "And how they're ever to get ironed——"

"There's hemstitching and fagoting, but I don't know as it's any less work than ruffling. And all the little girls are knitting lace. I'm doing some myself, oak-leaf pattern out of seventy cotton, and it's as handsome as anything you ever see."

"I don't know how any one is going to find time for so much folderol!"

"Oh, pshaw, Cousin Underhill, we did lots of it in our day. I worked the bottom of a party dress a good quarter up, and Vandyke capes, and those great big collars. And we tucked up to the waist. There's always something. And those old Jewish women had broidery and finery of every sort, and 'pillows' in their sleeves as we wore years ago. See what a little it takes to make a pair of sleeves now! We must have looked funny, all sleeves and waists up under our arms."

When you consider that sewing-machines had not been invented, it was a wonder how the women accomplished so much. But they always had some "catch-work" handy. The little girl was provided with a pretty work-basket, six spools of cotton, a pincushion, a needle-book, a bit of white wax, and an emery, which was a strawberry-shaped cushion topped off with some soft green stuff she knew afterward was chenille. This was to keep her needles bright and smooth. Then she had three rolls of ruffling, yards and yards in each piece. One was cambric, one was fine lawn or nainsook, and one of dimity. She had done some overseam in sheets, she had hemmed towels and some handkerchiefs, and sewed a little on the half-dozen shirts Margaret had made for father last winter. But the stitches had to be so small, and oh, so close together! Then they looked badly if they were not straight. She liked the dimity the best because the stitches seemed to sink in, and it ruffled so of itself.

But the little girl didn't sew all the time. She wiped dishes for Martha. And one day, when she saw a little girl up the street sweeping the sidewalk, she begged to do that. She could dust a room very nicely. There was much running up and down, and she was always glad to wait upon Steve. Indeed, she ran errands cheerfully for anybody. But she *did* miss Benny Frank and Jim.

Margaret had felt quite diffident about her new school, and at first rather shrank from the young ladies, much as she desired to be among them. But she found herself quite advanced in some of the studies, and in a week's time began to feel at home. Two girls were very friendly, Mary Barclay and Annette Beekman.

Perhaps Steve hadn't been quite as disinterested as it seemed. He had met Dolly Beekman at Miss Jane Barclay's party early in the winter. They had taken a mutual fancy. Old Peter Beekman lived at the lower end of Broadway, and had a farm "up the East River," about Ninety-sixth Street. He had five girls, and the two last had been sore disappointments. But Harriet, the eldest, had married her cousin and had four Beekman boys. Two others were married. Dolly had graduated from Rutgers the year before and was now nineteen. Annetje, as the old Dutch name was spelled, was not quite seventeen. Margaret had been put in her class in most branches.

Steve *did* want the Beekmans to think well of his people. He and Dolly were not declared lovers, but they understood each other. Old

Peter made inquiries about the young man, and if they had not been satisfactory Stephen would soon have known it. So he felt quite assured. And though his mother talked of her sons marrying, he knew that just at first it would come a little hard to find she had a rival.

"Well, Peggy," he said, Friday evening of the first week, "how does school go? Seen any girls you like?"

"I've seen two that know you," and Margaret laughed. "Mary Barclay said you had been at their house. And so did Annie Beekman."

"Yes, I was at Miss Beekman's party; quite a fine affair. And I've been there to play whist. They're a jolly crowd. Next winter we must have a few parties. And I'm going to get a piano."

"Oh, you lovely Steve!" She squeezed his arm rapturously.

"You have a very pretty voice, Peggy. Annie Beekman's sister sings beautifully. How do you like Annie?"

"Why, you never can tell whether she is in earnest or quizzing you. But she's ever so much prettier than Mary. Yes, on the whole I like her."

"You ought to see her sister Dolly. She has real flaxen hair and such a complexion!"

"Annie has a lovely complexion, too. There

are a great many pretty girls in the world. I have a curious sort of pity for those who are not a bit pretty," Margaret said sympathetically.

Steve laughed and nodded, as if the idea amused him.

If Margaret and Annie became friends, and if Dolly and Annie came to call—well, he was sure they would all fall in love with Dolly. And then the matter would go on smoothly. People thought more of being friendly with their relations by marriage in those days.

Chapter Four.

ON a Sunday toward the end of April, Stephen took his two sisters down to the Battery for a walk. It was very warm and springlike. The cherry-tree in their yard had come out in bloom. Buds were swelling everywhere, and the gray spots were all green and shining in the soft golden atmosphere. There was the wide, magnificent expanse of the bay, the edge of Brooklyn, the hazy outline of Staten Island, the vague Narrows that seemed to lead to some unknown world. And there was the great round Castle Garden, the Castle Clinton of earlier times, where a few years later the little girl was to hear some of the world's most famous singers. And when she looked out of that weird, narrow waterway and wondered just where Europe was, and how foreign countries must look, she could not by the most vivid stretch of imagination fancy herself sailing out to that unknown country.

The short grass was so lovely and green, and the waves came lapping up with a silvery melody. There were people lounging on the seats, ladies with sunshades in their hands, mothers with some little children, fathers with a son or two, or a little girl like herself in pantalets and white stockings and low shoes. The clothes she thought were beautiful. The hats were full of flowers. She had a new straw gypsy with a wreath of buttercups, and soft yellow strings tied under her chin. Her *challi de laine* had small blue flowers on a white ground, with yellow-brown centres, and there was a blue ribbon tied about her waist, with a bow at the back. She had a white cape of some soft cotton goods with a satiny finish, warranted to wash as good as new. She would have liked a sunshade, but she had so many new things.

She thought quite a good deal about her pretty clothes, and how glad she should be to learn more geography. Stephen was talking about Hudson's expedition up the river to which he gave his name, and a few months later when some hovels were built to shelter the sailors, the beginning of a settlement. And how in 1614 the Dutch erected a rude fort and gave the place the name of New Amsterdam. Then the Dutch West India Company bought Manhattoes Island from the natives for goods of various kinds, amounting to sixty guilders.

"You see the Dutch were thrifty traders even then, more than two hundred years ago," says Stephen with a pleasant laugh.

"How much are sixty guilders?" asks the little girl. It sounds an immense sum to her. And to buy a whole city!

"It was about twenty-four dollars at that time," replies Stephen.

The little girl's face is amusing in its surprise.

"Only twenty-four dollars! And father had three hundred a few days ago. Why, he could have bought"—well, the limitless area takes away her breath.

"I don't believe we should have wanted to live in such a wilderness as it was then."

"But when Walter the Testy came—he was really here?" It is rather chaotic in her mind.

"He was here. Wouter van Twiller was his real name. Then a line of Dutch governers, after which the island was ceded to the British. It became quite a Royalist town until the Revolutionary War. We had a 'scrap' about tea, too," and Stephen laughs. "Old Castle Clinton was a famous spot. And when General Lafayette, who had helped us fight our battles, came over in 1824, he had a magnificent ovation as he sailed up the bay. It's a splendid old place."

Everybody seemed to think so then. The birds were singing in the sunshine, and the rural aspect was dear to the hearts of the older people. They rose and walked about in the fragrant air. Now and then some one bowed gravely to Stephen. There was a Sunday decorum over all.

They rambled up to the Bowling Green. Some quaintly attired elderly people who had the *entrée* of the place were sitting about enjoying the loveliness. One old Frenchman had a ruffled shirt-front and a very high coat-collar that made him look like a picture, and knee-breeches.

Some one sprang up, and coming to the gate said: "Oh, Mr. Underhill, and Miss Margaret! Is this your little sister? Do walk in and chat with us. My sister Jane and I have come down to dine with the Morrises, and it was so lovely out here. Isn't it a charming day?"

There was Miss Jane Barclay very fashionably attired, Miss Morris, and her brother, who was very attentive to Miss Barclay, and a little farther on Mrs. Morris, fat, fair, and matronly. She was reading "The Lady of the Manor," and when the little girl found it afterward in a Sunday-school library, Mrs. Morris seemed curiously mixed up with it. Sunday papers at that period would have horrified most people.

"What a dear little girl!" said Mrs. Morris. "Come here and tell me your name. Why, you look like a lily astray in a bed of buttercups. Is it possible Mr. Stephen Underhill is your brother?"

"The eldest and the youngest," explained Stephen. "And this is my sister, Miss Under-hill."

Mrs. Morris bowed and shook hands. Then she made room on the settee for the child.

"You haven't told me your name, my dear."

Mrs. Morris' voice was so soft, almost pleading. The little girl glanced up and colored, and if the bank could have broken and let her money down in the ocean, or some one could have stolen it and bought a new Manhattan Island in the South Seas,—so that she could have had a new name, she wouldn't have minded a bit. But she said with brave sweetness:

"Hannah Ann. I was named after both grandmothers."

"That's a long name for such a little girl. I believe I should call you Nannie or Nansie. And Mr. Morris would call you Nan at once. I never knew such a man for short names. We've always called our Elizabeth Bess, and half the time her father calls her Bet, to save one letter."

The little girl laughed. The economy of the thing seemed funny.

"What does your father call you?"

" 'Little girl,' most always. Margaret was grown into quite a big girl when I was born, so I was the little girl."

"Well—that's pretty, too. And where are you living?"

"In First Street."

"Why, that's way up-town! And—let me see
—you did live at Yonkers? I've never been
there. Is it a town?"

"We lived on a great big farm. And oh, the
Croton water pipe came right across one corner
of it."

"Ah, you should have seen the celebration!
Such a wonderful, indescribable thing!"

"Margaret came down and most of the boys.
Mother said I would be crushed to death."

"And she couldn't spare her little girl! Well,
I don't blame her. Do you go to school?"

"No, ma'am, not yet." All the children but
the very rough ones said "no, ma'am," and "yes,
ma'am," in those days. "But I did go at Yonkers."

"And what did you learn."

She was quite astonished at the little girl's at-
tainments, and her simplicity she thought charming. When Stephen came for her, Mrs. Morris
said:

"I have really fallen in love with your little
sister. You must bring her down again. *We*
think there's nothing to compare with our Bowling Green and the Battery."

They bade each other a pleasant adieu. It was
time to go home, indeed. The little girl felt very
happy and joyous, and she thought her pretty
clothes had helped. Perhaps they had.

She sat on her father's knee that night telling him about Mrs. Morris. And she suddenly said:

"Father, what was the Reign of Terror?"

"The Reign of Terror? Oh, it was a horrible time of war in France. Where did you pick up that?"

"There was an old man in the Green who had on a queer sort of dress—knee-breeches and buckles on his shoes like those of grandfather's. And ruffles all down his shirt-bosom and long, curly, white hair. And Mrs. Morris said he was in prison in the Reign of Terror, and then came to America with his daughter, and that his mind had something the matter with it. Do you suppose he got awfully frightened?"

"I dare say he did, my dear. When you are a big girl you will learn all about it in history. But you needn't hurry. There are a great many pleasanter things to learn."

She leaned her head down on her father's shoulder and thought how sad it must be to lose one's mind. Was that the part of you always thinking? How curious it was to always think of something! Your feet didn't always walk, your hands didn't always work, but that strange thing inside of you never stopped. Oh, yes, it had to when you were asleep. But then you sometimes dreamed. And the little girl fell fast asleep over psychology that she didn't know a word about.

Early in the next week Mrs. Underhill took the little girl and went up to Yonkers. She said she was homesick to see the boys. And oh, how glad they were to see her! Aunt Crete was laid up with the *tic douloureux*. Retty was full of work and house-cleaning, and her lover had come on. He was a Vermonter by birth, and an uncle in the Mohawk valley had brought him up. Then he had gone West, but not taken especial root anywhere. He was tall and thin, with reddish hair and beard, but the kindliest blue eyes and a pleasant voice. He and George had struck up a friendship already. And Retty confided to Aunt Margaret "that she was going to be married without any fuss, and Bart was goin' to turn in and help run the farm."

Everything wore a different aspect even in this brief while. Mrs. Underhill had some things to pack up, that she was going to leave, a while at least, in the garret. Her sister-in-law was very glad to take anything she wanted to dispose of, since they had sold their furniture at the West.

Oh, how wonderful the world was to the little girl! The trees were coming out in bloom, there were great bunches of yellow daffodils, and the May pinks were full of buds. And then the chickens, the ducks' nests full of eggs, the pretty little dark-eyed calf that the boys had tamed al ready! And the children at school! Everybody was wild over Hanny and glad to get her back.

But it was queer she should miss her father so much when it came night. She went out on the old stoop and felt strangely lonesome. Then the boys came round, having done up their share of the chores.

"Do you *reely* like it, Hanny?" asked Jim.

She knew he meant the city.

"Well—father and Steve and Joe and John are there"—yet her tone was a little uncertain.

"Are there any boys about?"

"I don't know any. I haven't had time to find any girls. But there is a big public school round in Houston Street, and I guess there's a thousand children. You should see them coming out of the gate."

"Hm'n! I don't believe there's a thousand children in all New York. That's ten hundred, Miss Hanny!"

Hanny was sobered by the immensity of her statement, for she was a very truthful little girl.

"What have you been doing all this time?" Jim asked impatiently.

"Well—there was the house to get to rights. And we had to have some new clothes made. A girl laughed at me one day and said I looked queer."

"If I'd been there I'd punched her head. Yes —I see you're mighty fine. Would *I* look queer?"

"Oh, boys always look alike," returned Hanny reflectively. "We had a beautiful walk one Sunday on the Battery, and I think," hesitatingly, "that all the boys had on roundabouts."

"Are you sure they didn't have on overcoats?"

"Don't plague her, Jim. Tell us about the Battery, Hanny."

Hanny could describe that quite vividly. Jim soon became interested. When she paused he said, "What else?" She told them of her ride up to Harlem, and a walk down the Bowery to Chatham Square.

"But there ain't any real bowers in it any more, only stores and such things."

"What a pity," commented Benny Frank.

"Well, I think I'd like to go as soon as mammy can get ready. It isn't as much fun here without you all."

"Oh, Jim, don't say mammy. They don't do it in the city," said the little girl beseechingly.

"If you think I'm going to put on French airs, you're much mistaken, Miss Hanny! I'll say pop and mammy when I like. I'm not going to dress up in Sunday best manners because you wear ruffled pantalets. It makes you look like a feather-legged chicken!"

5

"Don't mind him, Hanny," said Ben tenderly. "I wish I had seen that old man at the Bowling Green——"

"Do they make bowls there?" interrupted teasing Jim.

"Because I've been reading about France and the Reign of Terror," Benny Frank went on, not heeding his brother. "It was in about 1794. Robespierre was at the head of it. And there was a dreadful prison into which they threw everybody they suspected, and only brought them out for execution. It must have been terrible! And the poor old man must have been quite young then. I should think he would have lost his mind."

"Bother about such stuff! You'd rather be in New York, wouldn't you, Hanny? And mother said we might come as soon as she was settled. I'm not going to stay here and be ordered about by this Finch fellow. Retty's soft as mush over him. Say, Ben, you *would* like to go, wouldn't you?"

"Yes, I think I would," answered Ben slowly. "There would be such a splendid chance to learn about everything."

Their mother had been walking around the familiar paths with George, who had developed some ideas of his own in this brief space. And his mother had not realized before how tall and stout he was getting.

"I'd like to see father and Steve and make some plans. I'd like to work part of father's ground on shares or some way. I'm glad Dave Andrews is staying on. I don't altogether like Uncle Faid's ideas, and oh, mother, 'tisn't any such jolly home as you had. Poor Aunt Crete is so miserable. But you see if I really had some interest of my own I'd be learning all the time."

"I'm sure your father will consent." His mother felt so proud, leaning on his arm. And some time *they* would come back. So they talked the matter over with eager interest, and she quite forgot about the little girl's bedtime. Retty had joined them and was rehearsing some of her Western experiences, and the little girl sat with wide-open eyes, looking at Retty in the moonlight, thinking what a great wonderful world it was to have so many places and all so different. Did you have two organs of thought? She was so puzzled about thought, anyhow. For with one side of her that didn't see Retty, she could see her father so plainly in this very corner, and she was in his arms, and with the faculty that wasn't listening to her cousin she could hear her father's voice. You see, she wasn't old enough to know about dual consciousness.

When Hanny went upstairs with her mother the boys went also.

"Say, Ben," and his brother gave him a dig in

the ribs with his elbow; "say, Ben, don't you want to go back to New York with mother? If we just push with all our might and main, together we can."

"Well, don't push me through the side of the house."

"You want to be pushed all the while. You're as slow as 'lasses in winter time. Ben, you take after Uncle Faid. It takes him 'most all day to make up his mind. Now I can look at a thing and tell in a minute."

"You seem ready enough to tell." Ben laughed a little provokingly.

"Well, you can go or not as you like. 'Taint half the fun here that it used to be. I didn't think I cared so much for Hanny."

"Is it Hanny?" in a tone that irritated.

"It's Hanny and mother and John and father and New York, and just a million things rolled into a bundle. And if you don't care I'll fight my way through. There, Benjamin Franklin! You'd sit on a stone in the middle of a field and fly your kite forever!"

Jim was losing his temper.

"Yes, I *think* I'd like to go. There would be so much to see and learn."

"Oh, hang it all! Simply go!"

Ben was thinking of the old man—he must have been quite young then — who was in prison through that awful Reign of Terror. He un-dressed slowly. He was not such a fly-away as Jim. But Jim was asleep before he was ready for bed.

Mrs. Underhill had not really meant to take the boys home with her. She was quite sure the city was a bad place for boys. And the country was so much healthier in the summer. But they coaxed. And somehow, the old home *had* changed already. The air of brisk cheerfulness was gone. Aunt Crete had her face tied up most of the time, or a little shawl over her head. Retty was undeniably careless. Barton Finch played cards with the hired man. Uncle Faid had some queer ideas about farming.

"I'd like wonderful well to have the boys stay," he said. "They're worth their keep. A boy 'round's mighty handy. I'd have to hire one."

Somehow she wasn't quite willing to have her boys put in the place of a hired one, or one bound out from the county house. And Jim had been her baby for so long. The little girl pleaded also. She told them finally they might come down and try. But if they were the least bit bad or diso-bedient they would be sent back at once.

Mrs. Underhill was half-cured of her homesick-ness. She had thought she could never be con-tent in New York; why, she was almost content already.

She and Hanny took a walk the last day of their stay up on the knoll where the new house was to be built.

"When all the children are married and father and I get to be old people, we will come back here. I shall want you, Hanny," and she held the little girl's hand in a tight clasp.

Hanny wondered if she would be stout and have full red cheeks and look like Retty? And oh, she did hope her mother wouldn't have *tic douloureux* and wear shawls over her head. When all the children were married—oh, how lonesome it would be!

But she had been quite a little heroine and gone to school one day to see the girls and boys. And one girl said: "I s'pose it's city fashion to wear pantalets that way, but my! doesn't it look queer!"

She was very glad to get back to her father. The country was beautiful with all its bloom and fragrance, but First Street had such a clean, tidy look with its flagged sidewalks and the dirt all swept up to the middle of the street, leaving the round faces of the cobble-stones fairly shining. It was quite delightful to show the boys all over the house and then go through the yard to the stables and greet Dobbin and Prince. And Battle, the dog, called so because he had been such a fighter, but commonly known as Bat, wagged his whole body with delight at sight of the boys.

Chapter Five.

A WEEK or so after Mrs. Underhill's return, one of the neighbors called one afternoon and brought her two little girls, Josie and Tudie Dean. Tudie stood for Susan. The little girl was summoned, and the three, after the fashion of little girls, sat very stiff on their chairs and looked at each other, then cast their eyes down on the carpet, fidgeted a little with the corners of their white aprons, and then gave another furtive glance.

"Hanny, you might take the little girls out in the yard and gather a nosegay for them." Flower roots and shrubs had been brought down from the "old place," and there was quite a showing of bloom.

The mothers talked meanwhile of the street, and Mrs. Dean spoke of the wonderful strides the city was making up-town. A few objectionable people had come in the old frame houses at the lower end of the street. When Mr. Dean built, some seven years ago, it was all that could be desired, but already immigrants were forcing their way up Houston Street. If something wasn't done to control immigration, we should soon be overrun. The Croton water had been such a great and wonderful blessing. And did her little girl go to school anywhere? Josie and Tudie went up First Avenue by Third Street to a Mrs. Craven, a rather youngish widow lady, who had two daughters of her own to educate, and who was very genteel and accomplished. Little girls needed some one who had gentle and pretty manners. There was a sewing-class, and all through the winter a dancing-class, and Mrs. Craven gave lessons on the piano. Public schools were well enough for boys, but they were too rude and rough for little girls.

Mrs. Underhill assented. "She wouldn't think of sending Hannah Ann to a public school."

"She looks like a very delicate child," commented Mrs. Dean.

"She's always been very well," said the mother, "but she *is* small for her age. And all of my children have grown up so rapidly."

"I couldn't believe those young men belonged to you. And that tall, pretty young girl."

Mrs. Underhill smiled and flushed and betrayed her pride in her eight nice healthy children.

"I envy you some of your sons," Mrs. Dean went on. "I never had but the two little girls."

They came in now, each with the promised

nosegay, and full of delight. They were round and rosy, and looked more like one's idea of a country girl than little lilybud Hannah. But they were all eager now, and even her cheeks were pink. They had talked themselves into friendship. And Josie wanted to know if Hanny couldn't come and see them, and if they couldn't have their dishes out and have tea all by themselves?

Mrs. Dean looked up at Mrs. Underhill, and replied: "Why, yes, if her mother is willing. Saturday would be best, as you are not in school."

That was only two days off. Hanny's eyes entreated so wistfully. And the Deans lived only three doors away.

"Why, yes," answered her mother with a touch of becoming hesitation.

Hanny was telling this eventful interview over to Jim as they sat on the stoop that evening. Ben was reading a book, Jim was trying the toes of his shoes against the iron railing and secretly wishing he could go barefoot.

"And they have a real play-house upstairs in one room. There's two beds in it and two bureaus, and oh, lots of things! Josie has seven dolls and Tudie four. Tudie gave two of hers away, and Josie has a lovely big wax doll that her aunt sent from Paris. And a table, and their mother lets them play tea with bread and cake and real things.   And I'm to go on Saturday."

Hanny uttered this in a rapid breath.

"Sho!" ejaculated Jim rather disdainfully. "They're not much if they play with dolls.   Now *I* know some girls——"

The boys had been at Houston Street public school not quite a week.   Jim knew half the boys at least, already, and all the boys that lived on the block.   He wasn't a bit afraid of girls, either, though he generally called them "gals."

"There's some living down the street, and Jiminy! if they haven't got names!   You'd just die of envy!   Rosabelle May, think of it!   And Lilian Alice Ludlow.   Lily's an awful pretty girl, too.   And they wanted to know all about you and Peggy."

"Did you tell her my name?" asked the little girl timidly.

"Well—don't you know you said you wished it was Anna?" Jim answered slowly.   "I just said it so it sounded like Anna.   And Lily said she'd seen you riding with father.   I wish you'd walk down there," coaxingly.

"I'll see if mother will let me."   Hanny sprang up.

"And put on a nice white apron," said Jim.

"They're too old for Hanny," began Ben, looking up from his book.

"Why, Lily's only eleven. And anyhow——"

Jim didn't know just how to explain it. Lily had begged him that afternoon to bring his little sister down. To tell the truth she was very ambitious to know the Underhills. They must be somebody, for they kept horses and a carriage, and owned their house.

"Do you know," said Belle May as they watched Jim going up the street, "I half believe the little girl who stood on the stoop that day is Jim's sister."

"That little country thing! I never thought of it. But I don't suppose she really heard."

"If she *did*—what will you do?"

"Do?" Lily tossed her head. "Why, I shall act just as if I never said it or had seen her before or anything. You don't suppose I'm a goose in pin-feathers, do you? I want to get acquainted with them. Of course I shall ask both boys to my birthday party. I should only ask the nice people in the street."

Margaret threw her pretty pink fascinator round Hanny's shoulders. She didn't need any hat this warm summer night. Hanny was very proud to walk down the street with her brother, who knew so many girls already. Jim wasn't a bit afraid of being called a "girl boy." Quite a number of people were sitting out on their stoops. It was the fashion then. Some of the ladies were knitting lace on two little needles that had sealing wax on one end, so the stitches could not drop off. There was much pleasant chatting. The country ways of sociability had not all gone out of date.

They walked down to the lower end, where the houses were rather irregular and getting old. Two or three had a small grass door-yard in front. Two girls were walking up and down with their arms around each. Jim knew in a moment who they were, but he loitered behind them until they turned.

"Oh!" exclaimed Lily Ludlow in well-acted surprise. "Are you out taking a walk?"

"Yes," answered Jim, quite as innocently as if the matter had not been arranged a few hours ago. "And this is my sister. And this is Lily Ludlow, and this Belle May."

Alas for Hanny! Lily Ludlow was the girl who had called her "queer" and laughed. The child's face flushed and there was a lump in her throat.

"You don't go to school, do you?" asked Lily with the utmost nonchalance. She was quite ready for anything.

The little girl made an effort, but no words would come. She could never like this girl with the pretty name, she felt very sure.

"No," said Jim. "She's so small for her

size that mother would be afraid of her getting lost."

They all giggled but the little girl, who wanted to run away.

"But you like New York, don't you? Jim thinks he wouldn't go back to the country for anything."

We had not come to "Bet your life," and "There's where your head's level," in those days. But Jim answered for his sister—"You just guess I wouldn't," with a deal of gusto.

They all walked up a short distance. The girls and Jim had all the talk, and they chaffed each other merrily. Hanny was silent. She really was too young for their fun.

Belle May's mother called her presently, and the little girl said in a whisper: "Oh, Jim, we must go home."

Jim wondered if he might ask Lily to walk with them, so he could come back with her. But she settled it with a gay toss of the head.

"Good-night," she said. "Come down again some evening."

"What a little stupid you are, Hanny!" Jim began, vexed enough. "Why didn't you ask them to walk up our way! And you never said a word! I could have given you an awful shake!"

"I—I don't like them."

"You don't know anything about them. Ben and I see them half a dozen times a day, and walk to school with them, and they're nice and pretty and have some manners. You're awful country, Hanny!"

The little girl began to cry.

"Oh, what a baby you are! Well, I s'pose you can't help it! You're only eight, and I'm almost thirteen. And Lily Ludlow's nearly eleven. I suppose you *do* feel strange among girls so much older."

"It isn't that," sobbed the little girl. How could she get courage to tell him?

"Oh, Hanny, dear, don't cry." Jim's voice softened—they were nearing home. "See here, I'll ask father to take us to Tompkins Square on Sunday, and you shall paint out of my new box. There! and don't tell any one—don't say a word to Ben."

He kissed her and wiped her eyes with the end of her starchy apron. Jim was very coaxing and sweet when he tried.

"Joe's here," said Ben. "And he thought the wolves would eat you up if you went too far. He wants to see you."

Jim dropped down on the step. Hanny ran through the hall. They were using the back parlor as a sitting-room, and everybody seemed talking at once. Joe held out his arms and the little girl flew to them.

Then it came out that Joe had taken one of the prizes for a thesis, and he would shortly be a full fledged M. D. He was so jubilant and the rest were so happy that the little girl forgot all about her discomfort.

Jim came rushing in. "Where's the hundred dollars?" he inquired.

Joe laughed. "I have not received the money yet. I thought the announcement was enough for one night."

"You and Hanny'll be so stuck up there'll be no living with you," said Jim.

Hanny glanced up with a smiling face. If she had only looked that way at Lily Ludlow! But even his schoolmate was momentarily distanced by the thought of such a prize. And he remembered later on with much gratification that he could tell her to-morrow.

Miss Chrissy Ludlow had been sitting by the front window in her white gown, half expecting a caller. When Lily entered, she inquired if that little thing was the Underhill girl?

"Oh, that's the baby," and Lily giggled. "There's a young lady who goes to Rutgers—well, I suppose she isn't quite grown up, for she doesn't wear real long dresses. And they have another brother in the country—six brothers!"

Chrissy sighed. If she only knew some way to

get acquainted with the young woman. And all the brothers fairly made one green with envy.

"You keep in with them," she advised her sister. "You might as well look up in the world for your friends."

There were not many people in the street who kept a carriage. Chrissy longed ardently to know them. And she had been almost fighting for a term at Rutgers. Mr. Ludlow was a commonplace man, clerk in a shoe-store round in Houston Street, and capable of doing repairs. They rented out the second floor, as they could not afford to keep the whole house. But since Chrissy had found out that they were distant connections of some Ludlows quite well off and high up in the social scale, she had felt extremely aristocratic. For a year she had been out of school, and now her mother thought she better learn dressmaking, since she was so "handy." She meant to get married at the first good opportunity.

Mr. Thackeray in England was writing about snobs during this period. He thought he found a great many in London. And even among the republican simplicity of New York he could have found some.

Hanny's second attempt at social life was a much greater success. The visit at the Deans' was utterly delightful. The play-house was enchanting. They dressed and undressed the dolls,

they gave Hanny two, and called her Mrs. Hill, because Underhill was such a long name, and they
had an aunt by the name of Hill. They "made
believe" days and nights, and measles and whoop-
ing cough, and earache and sore throat. Josie
put on an old linen coat of her father's and
"made believe" she was the doctor. And oh, the
solicitude when Victoria Arabella lay at the point
of death and they had to go round on tiptoe and
speak in whispers, and the poor mother said: "If
Victoria Arabella dies, my heart will be broken!"
But the lovely child mended and was so weak for
a while that the greatest care had to be taken of
her, for she couldn't sit up a bit. And Hanny
proposed they should take her up to Yonkers,
where she could recruit in the country air.

. Mrs. Dean came up with a basket and said it was
supper time. She arranged a side table to hold
some of the things. There was a nice white table-
cloth and Josie's pretty dishes. There was a pitcher
of hot water to make cambric tea, square lumps
of sugar, dainty slices of bread already spread,
smoked beef, pot-cheese, raspberries, cherry-jam,
and two kinds of cake. Well, it was just splendid.

Then they went out on the sidewalk and
skipped up and down. There was quite an art
in skipping gracefully without breaking step.
When they were warm and tired they came in,
and Mr. Dean played on the piano for them.

At seven o'clock Mr. Underhill walked up for his little girl, whose cheeks were pink and her eyes shining like stars. He sat on the stoop and talked a little while with Mr. Dean, and said most cordially the other girls must come and take tea with Hanny. And if they liked he would take them out driving some day. That was a most delightful proposal.

Jim let the whole school know the next week that his "big brother" had won a prize of one hundred dollars. And when Joseph passed with honor and took his degree, they were all proud enough of him.

"Mother," said the little girl after much consideration, "if any of us get sick will we have to pay Joe like a truly doctor?"

"Well — why not?" asked Mrs. Underhill, "That will be his way of earning his living."

The little girl drew a long breath. "He might come and live with us then. Where will he live, anyway?"

"He is to practise in the hospital awhile."

"Couldn't he doctor us at all?" she asked in surprise?

"Oh, yes, he might if we had faith in him," returned her mother laughingly.

That puzzled the little girl a good deal, and when she had an opportunity she asked her father if he had faith in Joe.

"Well," her father seemed to hesitate, "he might doctor Tabby, but I wouldn't let him experiment on Dobbin or Prince."

Hanny's face was a study in gravity and disappointment. "And if *I* was sick?" she ventured with a very long sigh.

Then her father hugged her up in his arms until she was breathless, and scrubbed her soft little face with his whiskers, and both of them laughed. But Joe promised one day when he was home to doctor her for nothing, so that point was settled.

They had a great time Fourth of July. Lamb and green peas were the regulation dinner. Steve sent a wagon up every morning with the freshest vegetables there were in market, and the meat for the day. Their milk came from the Odells in West Farms, and their butter from Yonkers. To be sure, it wasn't quite like country living, and Mrs. Underhill was positive that no one gave such a flavor to butter as herself.

The Odells and some other relatives were down on Fourth of July. They had the lamb and peas, as I said, and at that date one kind of meat was considered enough. They had green-apple pie. There was a very early pie-apple on the farm and George had brought some down for his mother. He was well and happy as he could be " without the folks," and he shook his head a little ambiguously about Uncle Faid's method, and those of Mr. Finch.

They had some ice-cream and cake afterward. The little girl had never eaten any, and she thought it very queer. It would have been delightful but for the awful coldness of it! It froze the roof of her mouth and made an ache in the middle of her forehead. Steve told her people sometimes warmed it, and she ran out to the stove with her saucer.

"The land alive! What are you going to do with that cream?" almost shrieked Martha, who was washing dishes at the sink.

"Warm it," replied the little girl. "It's so cold."

Martha almost fell into a chair with the dish-cloth in her hand, and laughed as if she would have a fit. There was a suspicious sound from the dining-room as well, and the fair little face grew very red.

Steve came out.

"Here, Nannie, is mine that the weather has warmed, and I'll trade it for your peak of Greenland." He took the chunk out of her saucer, and poured the soft in.

"It is nicer," she said. "And you needn't laugh, Martha. When I am a big woman and make ice-cream I shall just boil it," and she walked back with grave dignity.

She took the Odell girls to Mrs. Dean's, and some other children flocked around the stoop. They had torpedoes and lady-crackers, that two children pulled, when they went off with a loud explosion in the middle and made you jump. There were real fire-crackers that the boys had, and pin-wheels and various simple fireworks. But the great thing would be going down to City Hall in the evening and seeing the fireworks there.

The Odells could not stay, to their sorrow. Mr. Underhill proposed to take the business wagon and put three seats in it, and ask the Deans to go with them. Mrs. Dean was very glad to accept for herself and the children. There was a young lady next door, Miss Weir, that Margaret liked very much, and she accompanied them. John had promised to take charge of the boys. Steve had dressed himself in his new light summer suit and gone off.

The little girl thought the display beyond any words at her command. Such mysterious rockets falling to pieces in stars of every color. There was a great dome of stars, and rays that presently shot up into heaven; there was a ship on fire, which really frightened her. And, oh! the noise and the people, the shouting and hurrahing, the houses trimmed with flags, the brass band that played all the patriotic songs, and the endless confusion! The little girl clung closely to her mother, glad she was not down on the sidewalk, for the people would surely have trodden on her.

They came home very tired. But the little girl had added to her stock of historical knowledge and knew what Fourth of July stood for. It was a very great day, the beginning of the Republic.

The boys were out early the next morning finding "cissers," crackers that had failed to burn out entirely, and still had a little explosive merit when touched by a piece of lighted punk. There was no school that day, and Steve took them up to West Farms to expend the rest of their hilarity. The little girl was pale and languid. Mrs. Underhill was quite troubled at times when friends said:

"Isn't Hanny very small of her age? Is she real strong? She looks so delicate."

This was why she had thought it best not to send her to school this summer. She read aloud to her mother and said one column in a speller and definer, and Margaret taught her a little geography and arithmetic. She could hem very nicely now. She had learned to knit lace, and do some fancy work that was then called lap stitching. You pulled out some threads one way of the cloth, then took three and just lapped them over the next three, drawing your needle and thread through. Now a machine does it beautifully.

There was another fashion, "fads" we should call them nowadays. A school-bag—they didn't call them satchels then—was made of a piece of blue and white bed-ticking, folded at the bottom. Every white stripe you worked with zephyr worsted in briar stitch or herring-bone or feather stitch. You could use one color or several. And now the old work and the bed-ticking has come back again and ladies make the old-fashioned bags with tinsel thread.

Margaret had made one, and the little girl had taken it up. She was quite an expert with her needle. She had found several delightful new books to read. The Deans had some wonderful fairy stories. She was enraptured with the "Lady of the Lake," and some of Mrs. Howitt's stories and poems. She had learned her way about, and could go out to the Bowery to do an errand for her mother. She knew some more little girls, and with her sewing, helping her mother, studying and reading and play, the days seemed too short.

Vacation did not begin until the 1st of August. The boys were to go up to Yonkers and help George and Uncle Faid. They were quite ready for new ventures.

When Margaret came home the last day of school with a really fine report, her mother felt quite proud of her. The little girl, with large eyes and a mysterious expression, begged her to come into the parlor and see something. She smiled and took Hanny's small hand in hers. The furniture had been moved about a little. And oh, what was this? The little girl's eyes were stars of joy.

"It's your piano and mine," she said. "Yours till you get married and go away, and then mine forever and ever. Joe gave fifty dollars of his prize money toward it. Wasn't he lovely? And oh, Margaret, such beautiful music as it makes!"

The little girl with one small finger struck a key. The sound seemed to fascinate her. Margaret caught her in her arms and kissed the enraptured face.

"We shall be too happy, I'm afraid. I shouldn't have had the courage to ask for a piano, but it's the one thing above all others that I have wanted. Oh, it's just too delightful!"

Mrs. Underhill said: "It's a great piece of wastefulness, but the boys would have it. I'm sure I don't see where you're going to get time to learn everything. And you'll never know anything about housekeeping. I should be ashamed to have any one marry you."

People didn't hustle off to the country the day school closed. Indeed, some didn't go at all. The children played on the shady side of the

street.   The little girls had " Ring around a rosy,"
that I think Eve's grandchildren must have invented.   Then there was " London Bridge is falling down," " Open the gates as high as the sky,"
and

> "Here come two lords quite out of Spain
> A-courting for your daughter faire,"

and after a great deal of disputing and beseeching
they obtained "daughter faire," and averted war.
And "Tag" never failed with its "Ana mana
mona mike." You find children playing them
all yet, but I think the wonderful zest has gone
out of them.

In the evening a throng of the First Street children who had pennies to spend used to go up to
the corner of Second Street and Avenue A.   An
old colored woman sat there, with a gay Madras
turban, and a little table before her, that had a
mysterious spring drawer.   On one side she had
an earthen jar, on the other a great pail with a
white cloth over it, that emitted a steamy fragrance.   And she sang in a sort of chanting
tone:

"H-o-t corn, hot corn.   Here's your nice hot
corn, s-m-okin' h-o-t.   B-a-ked pears, baked pears
—Get away, chillen,' get away, 'les you've got a
penny.   Stop crowdin'."

They had enough to eat at home, but the corn
was tempting.   One night one boy would treat

and break the ear of corn in two and divide.   And the baked pears were simply delicious.   The old woman fished them out with a fork and put them on a bit of paper.   Wooden plates had not been invented.   And the high art was to lift up your pear by the stem and eat it.   Sometimes a mischievous companion would joggle your arm and the stem would come out—and oh, the pear would drop in a "mash" on the sidewalk.   You could not divide the pear very well, though children did sometimes pass a "bite" around.   But we lived in happy innocence and safety, for the deadly bacillus had not been invented and ignorance was bliss.

Chapter Six.

It seemed curiously still after the boys went away. Margaret took two music lessons a week and gave the little girl half a one. And one day Stephen came in and said:

"Go dress yourself, Dinah, in gorgeous array,
  And I'll take you a-drivin' so galliant and gay."

"Both of us?" asked the little girl.

"Yes—both of us. I have my new buggy and silver-mounted harness. You must go out and christen it for good luck. Hurry, Peggy, and put on your white dress."

Miss Blackfan had been again and made them two white frocks apiece. The little girl had "wings" over her shoulders and they made her less slim. She wore a pink sash and her hair was tied with pink. Her stockings were as white as "the driven snow," and her slippers looked like dolls' wear. They were bronze and laced across the top several times with narrow ribbon tied in a bow at her instep. She had a new hat, too, a leghorn flat with pale pink roses on it. It cost a good deal, but then it would "do up" every summer and last years and years. Fashions didn't change every three months then. Margaret had a pretty gipsy hat, with a big light-blue satin bow on the top, and the strings tied under her chin, and it made quite a picture of her. Her sleeves came a little below the elbow, and both wore black silk "open-work" mitts that came half-way up the arm.

There had been a shower the night before and the dust was laid. They went over Second Street to the East River, where one or two blocks were quite given over to colored people. There was an African M. E. church, that the little girl was very curious to see. Folks said in revival times they danced for joy. Crowds used to go to hear the singing.

"But do they dance?" asked the little girl wonderingly. She couldn't quite reconcile it with the gravity of worship.

"They simply march up and down the aisles keeping time to the tunes. Well—the Shakers dance in the same fashion." Stephen had been up to Lebanon.

Then a little farther on was another Methodist church, where several notable lights had preached. Nearer the river were some queer old houses, and at almost every corner a store. Saloons were a rarity. Over yonder was Williamsburg, up a lit-

tle farther Astoria, just a place of country greenery.   There were a few boats going up and down,
and the ferry-boats crossing.

The houses were no longer in rows.   There
were some vegetable gardens, and German women
were weeding in them; then tracts of rather
rocky land, wild and unimproved.   After a while
it began to grow more diversified and beautiful
—country residences and well-kept grounds full of
shrubbery at the front and vegetables in the rear,
with barns and stables, betraying a rural aspect.
The air was so sweet and fresh.

"Oh!" exclaimed Margaret, " Annette Beekman
must live somewhere about here.   I promised her
we would come up some day."

Stephen turned into a country road.   There
were many grand old elms, hemlocks, pines, and
fruit-trees as well.   A table stood under one, and
some ladies were sitting there sewing and chatting,
while several children ran about.   And while they
were glancing at them a girl in a pretty blue muslin
sprang up and ran down to the wide-open gate.

"Oh, Margaret!" cried Annette Beekman.
"Why, this is lovely of you, Stephen! Can't you
turn in and stop a while with us?"

" I'm showing Margaret New York," said Steve,
with his pleasant laugh.   "She has begun to think
straight down to Rutgers Institute comprised
every bit there was of it."

"Oh, Stephen!" deprecatingly.

Some one else came out; a fair, tall girl with great braids of flaxen hair and a silver comb in the top to make her look taller still. She smiled very sweetly.

"Oh, Mr. Underhill!" she exclaimed.

"This is my big sister and this is my little one," explained Stephen. "And this," to Margaret, "is Miss Dolly Beekman."

A warm color rose in Margaret's cheeks as a half-suspicion stole over her.

"You must get out and rest a while after this long ride," said Miss Dolly with winsome cordiality. "The rain last evening was delightful, but the day is warm. We are all living out-of-doors, as you see. And this, I suppose, is your little sister? Drive up and help the girls out, and then go round to the barn. You will find some one there."

Stephen wound slowly up the driveway, nodding to the group of ladies. Dolly walked along the grassy path. She wore a white dotted suisse gown with a "baby waist," and had a blue satin sash with ends that fell nearly to the bottom of the skirt. Her sleeves came to the elbow and were composed of three rather deep ruffles edged with lace. Round her pretty white neck she had an inch-wide black velvet, fastened with a tiny diamond that Stephen had brought her a week ago. She looked like a picture, Margaret thought, and later her portrait in costume was exhibited at the Academy of Design.

Stephen lifted his sisters down. Dolly took Margaret's arm and the little girl's hand and introduced them to almost as many sisters and cousins and aunts as there were in "Pinafore." The small person was not quite comfortable. She had a feeling that the back of her nice frock was dreadfully crushed. Margaret was a little confused. Stephen seemed so at home among them all. Annette had spoken so familiarly of him, yet she had not suspected. How blind she had been!

There was young Mrs. Beekman, thirty or so, already getting stout, and with the fifth Beekman boy that she would gladly have changed for a girl; Mrs. Bond, the next sister, with a boy and a girl; Aunt Gitty Beekman, some Vandewater cousins, and some Gessler cousins from Nyack.

They had rush-bottomed and splint chairs, several rockers, some rustic benches, and two or three tables standing about, with work-baskets and piles of sewing or knitting, for people had not outgrown industry in those days, and still taught their children the verses about the busy bee.

Dolly put Margaret in a rocker, untied her bonnet, and took off her soft white mull scarf—

long shawls they were called, and the elder ladies wore them of black silk and handsome black lace. They were held up on the arms and sometimes tied carelessly, and the richer you were, the more handsomely you trimmed them at the ends. Then for cooler weather there were Paisley and India long shawls.

Hanny kept close to her sister and leaned against her knee. She felt strange and timid with the eyes of so many grown people upon her. But they all took up their work and talked, asking Margaret various questions in sociable fashion.

There were three Beekman boys and one little Bond running about. The girl was very shy and would sit on her mother's lap. The Beekmans were fat and chubby, with their hair cut quite close, but not in the modern extreme. They wore long trousers and roundabouts, and low shoes with light gray stockings, though their Sunday best were white. We should say now they looked very queer, and unmistakably Dutch. You sometimes see this attire among the new immigrants. But there were no little Fauntleroy boys at that period with their velvet jackets and knickerbockers, flowing curls and collars.

The boys tried to inveigle Hanny among them. Pety offered her the small wooden bench he was carrying round. Paulus asked her " to come and see Molly who had great big horns and went this way," brandishing his head so fiercely that the little girl shuddered and grasped Margaret's hand.

"Don't tease her, boys," entreated their mother. "She'll get acquainted by and by. I suppose she isn't much used to children, being the youngest?"

"No, ma'am," answered Margaret.

The boys scampered off. Annette knelt down on the short grass, and presently won a smile from the little girl, who was revolving a perplexity as to whether big boys were not a great deal nicer than little boys. Then Stephen came back and Mr. Paulus Beekman, who was stout and dark, and favored his mother's side of the family. The ladies were very jolly, teasing one another, telling bits of fun, comparing work, and exchanging cooking recipes. Miss Gitty asked Margaret about her mother's family, the Vermilyeas. A Miss Vermilye, sixty or seventy years ago, had married a Conklin and come over to Closter. She seemed to have all her family genealogy at her tongue's end, and knew all the relations to the third and fourth generation. But she had a rather sweet face with fine wrinkles and blue veins, and wore her hair in long ringlets at the sides, fastened with shell combs that had been her mother's, and were very dear to her. She wore a light change-able silk, and it still had big sleeves, such as we are wearing to-day. But they had mostly gone out. And the elder ladies were combing their hair down over their ears. There were no crimp-ing-pins, so they had to braid it up at night in "tails" to make it wave, unless one had curly hair. Most of the young girls brushed it straight above their ears for ordinary wear, and braided or twisted it in a great coil at the back, though it was often elaborately dressed for parties.

Aunt Gitty was netting a shawl out of white zephyr. It was tied in the same manner that one makes fish-nets, and you used a little shuttle on which your thread was wound. It was very light and fleecy. Aunt Gitty had made one of silk for a cousin who was going abroad, and it had been very much admired. The little girl was greatly interested in this, and ventured on an attempt at friendliness.

Dolly took them away presently to show them the flower-beds. Mr. Beekman had ten acres of ground. There were vegetables, corn and potato fields and a pasture lot, beside the great lawn and flower-garden. Old Mr. Beekman was out there. He was past seventy now, hale and hearty to be sure, with a round, wrinkled face, and thick white hair, and he was passionately fond of his grand-children. He had not married until he was forty and his wife was much younger.

There were long walks of dahlias of every color and kind. They were a favorite autumn flower. A great round bed of "Robin-run-away," bergamot, that scented the air and attracted the humming-birds. All manner of old-fashioned flowers that are coming around again, and you could see where there had been magnificent beds of peonies. In the early season people drove out here to see Peter Beekman's tulip-beds.

There were borders of artemisias, as they were called, that diffused a pungent fragrance. We had not shaken hands so neighborly with Japan then, nor learned how she evolved her wonderful chrysanthemums.

The little girl grew quite talkative with Mr. Beekman. You see, in those days there was a theory about children being seen and not heard, and no one expected a little six-year-old to entertain or disturb a room full of company. The repression made them rather diffident, to be sure. But Mr. Beekman gathered her a nosegay of spice pinks, carnations now, and took her to see his beautiful ducks, snowy white, in a little pond, and another pair of Muscovy ducks, then some rare Mandarin ducks from China. She told him about the ducks and chickens at Yonkers and how sorry she was to leave them.

And then came the handsome white Angora cat with its long fur and curious eyes that were almost blue, and when she said " mie-e-o-u" in a rather delighted tone, it seemed as if she meant " O master, where have you been? I'm so glad to see you!"

He stood and patted her and they held quite a conversation as she arched her neck, rubbed against his leg, and turned back and forth. Then she stretched way up on him and gave him her paw, which was very cunningly done.

"This is a nice little girl who has come to see me," he said, as she seemed to look inquiringly at Hanny. "She's fond of everything, kitties especially."

Kitty looked rather uncertain. Hanny was a little afraid of such a curious creature. But presently she came and rubbed against her with a soft little mew, and Hanny ventured to touch her.

"She likes you," declared old Mr. Beekman, much pleased. "She doesn't often take fancies. She loves Dolly, and she won't have anything to do with Annette, though I think the girl teases her. Nice Katschina," said her master, patting her. "Shall we buy this little girl?"

Perhaps you won't believe it, but Katschina really said "yes," and smiled. It was very different from the grin of the "Chessy cat" that Alice saw in Wonderland.

Some one came flying down the path.

"Father," exclaimed Dolly," come and have a cup of tea or a glass of beer. Stephen and his sister think they can't stay to supper. But may be they'll leave the little girl—you seem to have taken such a notion to her."

Hanny didn't want to be impolite and she really *did* like Mr. Beekman, but as for staying—her heart was up in her throat.

Dolly picked up Katschina and carried her in triumph. Two white paws lay over Dolly's shoulder.

There was a table with a shining copper tea-kettle, a pewter tankard of home-brewed ale, bread and butter, cold chicken and ham, a great dish of curd cheese, pound cake, soft and yellow, fruit cake, a heaping dish of doughnuts and various cookies and seed cakes. Scipio, a young colored lad, passed the eatables. Young Mrs. Beekman poured the tea. The mother sat near her. She was short and fat and wore her hair in a high Pompadour roll, and she laughed a good deal, showing her fine white teeth of which she was very proud.

Katschina sat in her master's lap, and the little girl was beside him. The boys were given their hands full and sent away. It was a very pretty picture and the little girl felt as if she was reading an entertaining story. One of the Gessler cousins had been knitting lace, double oak-leaf with a heading of insertion. It looked marvellous to the little girl. She said she was making it to trim a visite. This was a Frenchy sort of garment lately come into vogue, though the little girl did not know what it was, and was too well trained to ask questions.   But the lace might be the de-sire of one's heart.

They sipped their tea or raspberry shrub, or enjoyed a glass of ale.   They were all very merry. The little girl wondered how Dolly dared to be so saucy with Stephen when she only knew him such a little.   Mrs. Beekman could hardly accept the fact that they would not stay to supper, and said they must come soon and spend the day, and have Stephen drive up for them, and that she hoped soon to see Mrs. Underhill.   "It is quite delight-ful and we are all well satisfied," she added, nod-ding rather mysteriously.

Dolly put on the little girl's hat and kissed her, giving her a breathless squeeze.   Miss Gitty kissed her as well and told her she was a "very pretty behaved child."   The buggy came round and Stephen put them in amid a chorus of good-bys.

"The little one looks delicate," commented the younger Mrs. Beekman when they had driven away.   "I'm afraid she doesn't run and play enough.   But she's beautifully behaved.   And what a fancy father took to her!"

"Miss Underhill doesn't seem like a real coun-try girl," said another.

"The Underhills are a good family all through. English descent from some Lord Underhill. They were staunch Royalists at one time."

"And the Vermilyeas are good stock," said Aunt Gitty. "There's nothing like being particular as to family. It tells in the long run."

"Well, Dolly, we think he will do," said Mrs. Beekman laughingly, as Dolly, having said her good-bys, sauntered back to the circle. "He might be richer, of course. There's a large family and they can't have much apiece."

"Stephen Underhill's got the making of a good substantial man in him," grunted father Beekman. "If he'd been a poor shoat he wouldn't have hung around here very long, would he, Katschina? We'd 'a put a flea in his ear, wouldn't we."

Katschina arched her back. Dolly laughed and blushed. Stephen was her own true-love anyway, but she was glad to have them all like him. With the insistence of youth she felt she never could have loved any other man.

Stephen clicked to Prince, who was rested and full of spirits. They drove almost straight across the city, about at the end of our first hundred numbered streets. But the road wound around to get out of a low marshy place, a pond in the rainy season, and some rocks that seemed tumbled up on end. They struck a bit of the old Boston Post Road, and that caused the little girl to stop her prattle and think of the old ladies they had never visited. She must "jog" her father's memory. That was what her mother always said when she recalled half-forgotten things.

Stephen and Margaret had only spoken in answer to the little girl. He had a young man's awkwardness concerning a subject so dear to his heart. Margaret was awed by the mystery of love, captivated by Dolly's friendliness, and puzzled to decide what her mother would think of it. Stephen married! Any of them married for that matter. How strange it would seem! And yet she had sometimes said, "When I am married."

The place was wild enough. You would hardly think so now when hollows have been filled and hills levelled, and rocks blasted away. After they turned a little stream wound in and out through the trees and bushes. Amid a tangled mass the little girl espied some wild roses.

"Oh, Steve!" she cried, "may I get out and pick some?"

"I will." He handed the reins over to Margaret and sprang down, running across a little bridge, and soon gathered a great handful.

"Oh, thank you," and her eyes shone. "What a funny little bridge."

"That's Kissing Bridge."

"Who do you have to kiss?" asked the little girl mirthfully.

"Well, a long while ago, in Van Twiller's time, I guess," with a twinkle in his eye, "there wasn't any bridge. The lovers used to carry their sweethearts over, and the charge was a kiss."

"But there wasn't any kissing *bridge* then," she said shrewdly.

"When the bridge was built they stopped and kissed out of remembrance."

"Was it really so, Margaret?"

"It has been called that ever since I can re-member."

"You unkind girl, not to believe me!" exclaimed Stephen, with an air of offended dignity. "And I am ever so much older than Margaret."

"You didn't carry *me* over, but you carried the roses, so you shall have the kiss all the same," and as she reached up to his cheek they both smiled.

Then they came down Broadway to Bleecker Street, and over home. Father Underhill was sitting on the stoop reading his paper. Jim begged to take the horse round to the stable. Margaret went up-stairs to pull off her best dress and put on her pink gingham. She had just finished and was calling for Hanny, when Stephen caught her in his arms.

"Dear Peggy—you must have guessed."

"Oh, Stephen! It seems so strange. Is it really so? I never dreamed——"

"I fell in love with Dolly months ago. There were so many caring for her that I hardly hoped myself. But there's some mysterious sense about it, and I began to see presently that she preferred me. Though I didn't really ask her until Sunday night. And they all consented. We are regularly engaged now."

"Oh, Stephen! To lose you!"

That is the first natural thought of the household.

"You are not going to lose me. We shall be engaged a long while; a year surely."

"But, father—and our coming here."

"That is all right. It can't make any difference. Only you will have a new sister. Oh, Peggy, try to love her," persuasively, yet knowing she could not resist her.

"She is very sweet."

"Sweet! She's just cream and roses and all the sweetest things of life put together! I tell you, Peggy, I'm a lucky fellow. Of course it will seem a little strange at first. But some day you'll have your romance, only I don't believe you can ever understand how glad the other fellow will be to get you. Girls can't. And you'll try to make things smooth with mother if she feels a little put out at first? Dolly wants to love you all. She's admired Joe so much, and they are all proud of him."

The supper bell rang impatiently. Stephen kissed his sister and gave her a rapturous hug.

Hanny came up-stairs and Margaret hurried through her change of attire.

"I thought you never were coming," began their mother tartly. "'Milyer, you're the worst of the lot when you get your nose buried in a newspaper. Boys, do keep still, though I suppose you're half starved," with a reproachful look at those who had delayed the meal.

The little girl had eaten so many of the delicious cookies that she wasn't a bit hungry. So she entertained her father with the miles of dahlias and the wonderful cat, so soft and furry and different from theirs, and with truly blue eyes, and who could understand everything you said to her. And Mr. Beekman was very nice, but not as nice as father. The little boys were so short and so funny. "And I don't believe I like *little* boys. Jim and Benny, Frank and all of you are nicer. Perhaps it *is* the bigness."

They all laughed at that.

She sat in her father's lap afterward and went on with her quaint story, until her mother came and routed her out and said, "I do believe, 'Milyer, you'd keep that child up all night."

Afterward Mr. Underhill went out on the front stoop, where he and Stephen had a long talk, while Margaret sat at the piano making up for her afternoon's dissipation, but in the soft, vague ight she could see Dolly Beekman with her laughing eyes and crown of shining hair, and was sure she would make a delightful sister. Mrs. Underhill sat and darned stockings and sighed a little. Yet she was secretly proud of Margaret, even if she did study French and music. Whether they would ever help her to keep house was a question. Where would she have found time for such things?

Chapter Seven

MISS LOIS AND SIXTY YEARS AGO.

"Yes; come get out once in a while."

"I've no time to spare," said Mrs. Underhill. "Some one has to work or you'd all be in a fine case. Here's Margaret spending her time drumming on the piano and studying French and what not. I dare say you'll be called upon some time to take your daughter to Paris to show off her accomplishments."

"I hope we'll do credit to each other," he returned with a dry, humorous laugh, as if amused.

"The world goes round so fast one can't keep up with it. If the work only rushed on that way! Why don't some of you smart men who have plenty of time to sit round, invent a machine to cook and sew and sweep the house?"

"Martha's a pretty good housekeeping machine, I think. And you might find another to sew."

She had no idea that Elias Howe was hard at work on a tireless iron and steel sewing-woman and was puzzling his brains day and night to put an eye in the needle that would be satisfactory.

"You'd need to be made of money to hire all these folks! Margaret ought to be sewing this very minute, but she's fussing over those drawings of John's. I've such a smart family I think they'll set me crazy. And what you will do when I am gone——"

"We're not going to let you get away so easy. And if you would just go out a bit now and then. Come, mother," with entreaty in his voice.

"Oh, 'Milyer," she said, touched by something in the tone, "I really can't go to-day. I've all those shirts to cut out, and Miss Weir told me of a girl who would be glad to come and sew for fifty cents a day. I think I'll have her a few days. And you look up the poor old creatures and see if they are in any want. Then if I really *can* do them any good I'll go."

She always softened in the end. She felt a little sore and touchy about Steve's engagement, and proud, too, that Miss Beekman had accepted him. Stephen had insisted some one must come in and help sew, and that his mother must have a little time for herself. Seven men and boys to make shirts for was no light matter. The little girl was learning to darn stockings very nicely and helped her mother with those.

So father Underhill took the little girl and Dobbin and the ordinary harness, for Steve had Prince and the silver-mounted trappings, and the elders could guess where he had gone. Business was dull along in August, so the men had some time for diversion, and the father always enjoyed his little daughter. Her limited knowledge and quaint comments amused him, and her sweet, innocent love touched the depths of his soul.

It was quite in the afternoon when they started. Dobbin was not as young and frisky as Prince, so they jogged along, looking at the gardens, the trees, the wild masses of vines and sumac, and then stretches of rocky space interspersed with squatters' cabins and the goats, pigs, geese, and chickens. Sometimes in after years when she rode through Central Park, she wondered if she had not dreamed all this, instead of seeing it with her own eyes.

They went over to Mr. Brockner's to inquire.

"Oh," he exclaimed, " Mrs. Brockner will be so sorry to miss you. She has talked so much about your little girl, and threatened to hunt her up. And now she's gone to Saratoga for a fortnight, to see the fashions. But you must come up again."

Then he directed them, and they drove over in a westerly course and soon came to the little stone house that bore evident marks of decay from neglect as well as age. The first story was rough stone, the half-story of shingles, that had once been painted red. There were two small windows in the gable ends, but in front the eaves overhung the doorway and the windows and were broken and moss-grown. There was a big flat stone for the doorstep, a room on one side with two windows, and on the other only one. The hall door was divided in the middle, the upper part open. There was a queer brass knocker on this, and the lower part fastened with an old-fashioned latch. The little courtyard looked tidy, and there was a great row of sweet clover along the fence, but now and then the goats would nibble it off.

When they stepped up on the stoop they saw an old lady sitting in a rocking-chair, with a little table beside her, and some knitting in her lap. She had evidently fallen into a doze. Hanny stretched up on tiptoe. A great gray cat lay asleep also. There were some mats laid about the floor, two very old arm-chairs with fine rush bottoms painted yellow, a door open on either side of the hall, and a well-worn winding stairs going up at the back.

Mr. Underhill reached over and gave a light knock. The cat lifted its head and made a queer sound like a gentle call, then went to the old lady and stretched up to her knees. She started and glanced toward the door, then rose in a little confusion.

"I am looking for a Miss Underhill," began the visitor.

"Oh, pardon me." She unbolted the lower door. "I believe I had fallen asleep. Miss Underhill?" in a sort of surprised inquiry. "I am —one of the sisters. Walk in."

She pushed out one of the arm-chairs and gave her footstool to the little girl.

"I am an Underhill myself, a sort of connection, I dare say. We heard of you some time ago, but I have been much occupied with business, yet I have intended all the time to call on you."

"You are very good, I am sure. We had some relations on Long Island, and I think some hereabout, but we lost sight of them long ago. We really have no one now. My sister Jane is past eighty, and I am only three years younger."

She was a slim, shrunken body and her hands were almost transparent, so white was her skin. Her gown was gray, and she wore a white kerchief crossed on her bosom like a Quakeress. Her fine muslin cap had the narrow plain border of that denomination.

Mr. Underhill made a brief explanation of his antecedents, and his removal to the city,—then mentioned hearing of them from Mr. Brockner.

"You are very good to hunt us up," she said, with a touching tremble in her voice. "I don't think now I could tell anything about my father's relatives. He was killed at the battle of Harlem Heights, and my only brother was taken prisoner. The Ferrises, my mother's people, owned a great farm hereabout. But much of it was laid waste, and a little later the old homestead burned down. This house was built for us before the British evacuated the city. My brother had died in prison of a fever, and there were only my mother and us two girls."

Hanny was sitting quite close by her. She reached over and took the wrinkled hand gently.

"Do you mean you were alive then—a little girl in the Revolutionary War?" she exclaimed in breathless surprise.

"Why, I was nine years old," and she gave a faded little smile. "I doubt if you're more than that."

"I am a little past eight," said Hanny.

"And the battle was just over yonder," nodding her head. "We all hoped so that General Washington would win. My father was very patriotic and very much in earnest for the independence of the country. The armies were separated by Harlem Plains, and General Howe pushed forward through McGowan's Pass, the rocky gorge over yonder. But our men forced them into the cleared field, and if it had not been for a troop of Hessians they would have driven the British off the field. But I believe Washington thought it best to retreat. I've heard it was almost a victory, still it wasn't quite. But we were wild with apprehension, for we could hear the noise and the firing. And then the awful word came that father was killed."

"Oh!" cried the little girl, and she laid her soft cheek on the wrinkled hand. What if she had been alive then!—and she looked over at *her* father with tears in her eyes.

"It was a sad, sad time. Some of the Ferrises were on the King's side. You know a great many people believed the rebels all wrong and said they never could win. My Uncle Ferris was bitterly opposed to father's espousing the Federalists' cause."

"But you didn't want England to win, did you?" inquired the little girl, wide-eyed.

"We were so full of trouble. Mother was very bitter, I remember, and folks called her a Tory. Then brother, who was only seventeen, was taken prisoner. Uncle Ferris said it would be a good lesson for a hot-headed young fellow, and that two or three months in prison would cool his ardor. But he was taken sick and died before we knew he was really ill. Then our house burned down. Mother thought it was set on fire. Oh, my child, such quantities of things as were in it!

My mother had never gone away from the old house because grandmother was a widow. Then the land was divided, and this smaller house built for mother and us. The British took possession of the city, and it was said uncle made money right along. But the English were very good to us, and no one ever molested us after that. Dear, we used to think it almost a day's journey to go down to the Bowling Green."

The little girl was listening wide-eyed, and drew a long breath.

"There have been many changes. But somehow we seem to have gone on until most everybody has forgotten us. You might like to see sister Jane, though she's quite deaf and hasn't her mind very clear. I don't know,"—hesitatingly.

"Do you live all alone here?" Mr. Underhill asked.

"Not exactly alone; no. We sold the next-door lot four years ago to some Germans, very nice people. The mother comes in and helps with our little work and looks after our garden, and sleeps here at night. The doctor thought it wasn't safe to be left here alone with sister Jane. It made it easy for them to pay for the place. It's nearly all gone now. But there'll be enough to last our time out," she commented with a soft sigh of self-abnegation.

"And you have no relatives, that is, no one to look after you a bit?"

"Well, you see grandmother made hard feelings with the relatives. She didn't think the colonies had any right to go to war. And after father's death mother felt a good deal that way. They dropped us out, and we never took any pains to hunt them up. We never knew much about the Underhills. I must say you are very kind to come," and her voice trembled.

Just then the door opened and Miss Underhill sprang up to take her sister's arm and lead her to a chair. She was taller and stouter, and the little girl thought her the oldest-looking person she had ever seen. Her cap was all awry, her shawl was slipping off of one shoulder, and she had a sort of dishevelled appearance, as she looked curiously around.

Lois straightened her up, seated her, and introduced her to the visitors.

"I'm hungry. I want something to eat, Lois," she exclaimed in a whining, tremulous tone, regardless of the strangers.

Miss Underhill begged to be excused, and went for a plate of bread and butter and a cup of milk.

"Perhaps you'd like to see our old parlor," she said to her guests, and opened the door.

There were two rooms on this side of the

house. The back one was used for a sleeping chamber. She threw the shutters wide open, and a little late sunshine stole over the faded carpet that had once been such a matter of pride with the two young women. There were some family portraits, a man with a queue and a ruffled shirt-front, another with a big curly white wig coming down over his shoulders, and several ladies whose attire seemed very queer indeed. There was a black sofa studded with brass nails that shone as if they had been lately polished, a tall desk and bookcase going up to the ceiling, brass and silver candlesticks and snuffers' tray, as well as a bright steel "tinder box" on the high, narrow mantel. A big mahogany table stood in the centre of the room, polished until you could see your face in it. But there was an odd tall article in the corner, much tarnished now, but ornamented with gilt and white vines that drooped and twisted about. Long wiry strings went from top to bottom.

"I suppose you don't know what that is!" said Miss Lois, when she saw the little girl inspecting it. "That's a harp. Young ladies played on it when we were young ourselves. And they had a spinet. I believe it's altered now and called a piano."

"A harp!" said the little girl in amaze. Her ideas of a harp were very vague, but she

thought it was something you carried around with
you.   She had heard the children sing:

> "I want to be an angel
> And with the angels stand;
> A crown upon my forehead,
> A harp within my hand,"

and the size of this confused her.

"But how could you play on it?" she asked.

"You stood this way.   You could sit down, but
it was considered more graceful to stand.   And
you played in this manner."

She fingered the rusted strings.   A few emitted a doleful sort of sound almost like a cry.

"We've all grown old together," she said sor-
rowfully.   "It was considered a great accomplishment in my time.   I believe people still play on
the harp.   We had a great many curious things,
but several years ago a committee of some kind
came and bought them.   We needed the money
sadly, and we had no one to leave them to when
we died.   There was some beautiful old china,
and a lady bought the fan and handkerchief that
my grandmother carried at her wedding.   The
handkerchief was worked at some convent in Italy
and was fine as a cobweb.   My mother used it,
and then it was laid by for us.   But we never
needed it," and she gave a soft sigh.

She had glided out now and then to look after

Jane, who was eating as if she was starved. And in the broken bits of talk Mr. Underhill had learned by indirect questioning that they had parted with their land by degrees, and with some family valuables, until there was only this old house and a small space of ground left.

Miss Jane was anxious now to see the visitors. But she was so deaf Lois had to repeat everything, and she seemed to forget the moment a thing was said. Dobbin whinnied as if he thought the call had been long enough.

Mr. Underhill squeezed a bank-note into the hand of Miss Lois as he said good-by. "Get some little luxury for your sister," he added.

"Thank you for all your friendliness," and the tears stood in her eyes. "Come again and bring your sister Margaret," she said to the little girl.

They drove over westward a short distance. The rocky gorge was still there, and at its foot was one of the first battle-fields of this vicinity. Hanny looked at it wonderingly.

"Then Washington retreated up to Kingsbridge," began her father. "They found they could not hold that, and so went on to White Plains, followed by some Hessian troops. They didn't seem very fortunate at first, for they were beaten again. Grandmother can tell you a good deal about that. And a great-uncle had his house burned down and they were forced to fly to a

little old house on top of a hill. My father was
a little boy then."

The little girl looked amazed. Did he know
about the war?

"It seems such a long, long time ago—like the
flood and the selling of Joseph. And was grandmother really alive?"

"Grandmother is about as old as Miss Lois."

"Miss Lois doesn't look so awful old, but the
other lady does. I felt afraid of her."

"Don't think of her, pussy. It's very sad to
lose your senses and be a trouble."

"You couldn't," was the confident reply after
much consideration. She didn't see how such a
thing could happen to him.

"I hope I never shall," he returned, with an
earnest prayer just under his breath.

Dobbin insisted upon going home briskly. He
was thinking of his supper. The little girl was
so sorry not to have Benny Frank to talk over her
adventures with. Margaret and her mother were
basting shirts; John was drawing plans on the
dining-room table. He had found a place to work
at house-building and was studying architecture
and draughting. A man had come in to see her
father, so she was left quite alone. The Deans
and several of the little girls on the block had
gone visiting. She walked up and down a while,
thinking how strange the world was, and what

wonderful things had happened, vaguely feeling that there couldn't be any to come in the future.

At the end of the week she and Margaret went up to White Plains, as grandmother was anxious to see them.

Her grandmother was invested with a curious new interest in her eyes. That any one belonging to her should have lived in the Revolutionary War seemed a real stretch of the imagination for a little girl eight years old. Grandmother considered *her* wonderful also. She wasn't so much in favor of short frocks and pantalets that came down to your ankles, but the little girl did look pretty in them. And when she found how neatly she could hemstitch and do such beautiful featherstitch, and darn, and read so plainly that it was a pleasure to listen to her, she had to admit that Hannah Ann was a real credit, and, she confessed in her secret heart, a very sweet little girl.

"I've begun your new Irish chain patchwork," she said. "I've made one block for a pattern, and cut out quite a pile. Aunt Eunice lighted upon some beautiful green calico. I was upon a stand whether to have green or red, but an Irish chain generally is pieced of green. It seems more appropriate."

And yet people had not begun to sing "The Wearing of the Green."

"I declare," said Cousin Ann, "you're such an old-fashioned little thing one can hardly tell which is the oldest, you or grandmother."

"Is it anything"—what should she say?—wrong or bad seemed too forcible—"queer to be old-fashioned?"

"Well, yes, *queer*. But you're awful sweet and cunning, Hannah Ann, and we'd just like to keep you forever."

"With that she almost squeezed the breath out of the little girl and kissed her a dozen times.

Grandmother could tell such wonderful stories as they sat and sewed. All the glories of the old Underhill house, and the silver and plate that had come over from England, and the set of real china that a sea captain, one of the Underhills, had brought from China and how it had taken three years to go there and come back. And the beautiful India shawl it had taken seven years to make, and the Persian silk gown that had been bought of some great chief or Mogul—grandmother wasn't quite sure, but she thought they had a king or emperor in those countries. She had a little piece of the silk that she showed Hanny, and a waist ribbon that came from Paris, "For you see," said she, "we were so angry with England that we wouldn't buy anything of her if we could help it. And the French people came over and helped us."

"What did they fight about?" grandmother.

"Oh, child, a great many things. You can't understand them all now, but you'll learn about them presently. The people who came here and settled the country wanted the right to govern themselves. They thought a king, thousands of miles away, couldn't know what was best for them. And England sent over things and we had to pay for them whether we wanted them or not. And it was a long struggle, but we won, and the British had to go back to their own country. Why, if we hadn't fought, we wouldn't have had any country," and grandmother's old face flushed.

The little girl thinks it would be dreadful not to have a country, but her mind is quite chaotic on the subject. She is glad, however, to have been on the winning side.

Nearly every day Uncle David took her out driving. They saw the old house on the hill in a half-hidden, woody section where the family had to live until the new house was built. They went round the battlefield, but sixty years of peace had made great changes, and the next fifty years was to see a beautiful town and many-storied palaces all about. She dipped into the history of New Amsterdam again and began to understand it better, though she did mistrust that Mr. Dederich Knickerbocker now and then "made fun," not un-like her father.

The visit came to an end quite too soon, grandmother thought, and she was very sorry to part with the little girl. She thought she would try and come down when the fall work was done, and she gave Hanny only four blocks of patchwork, for if she went to school there wouldn't be much time to sew.

They stopped at Yonkers two days and picked up the boys, who were brown and rosy. Aunt Crete was much better and did not have to go about with her face tied up. She said there was no place like Yonkers, after all. Retty seemed happy and jolly, but there was a new girl in the kitchen, for Aunt Mary had gone to live with her children. George said he should come down a while when the crops were in.

School commenced the 1st of September sharp. It was hot, of course. Summer generally does lap over. The boys who had shouted themselves hoarse with joy when school closed, made the street and the playground ring with delight again. If they were not so fond of studying they liked the fun and good-fellowship. And when they marched up and down the long aisles singing:

> "Hail Columbia, happy land;
> Hail ye heroes, heaven-born band,
> Who fought and bled in freedom's cause!"

you could feel assured another generation of patriots was being raised for some future emergency. Oh, what throats and lungs they had!

Mrs. Underhill had been around to see Mrs. Craven, and liked her very well indeed. So the little girl was to go to school with Josie and Tudie Dean.

Some new people had come in the street two doors below. Among the members was a little girl of seven, the child of the oldest son, and a large girl of fourteen or so, two young ladies, one of whom was teaching school, and the other making artificial flowers in a factory down-town, and two sons. The eldest one was connected with a newspaper, and was in quite poor health. His wife, the little girl's mother, had been dead some years. The child was rather pale and thin, with large, dark eyes, and a face too old for her years and rather pathetic. And when Mrs. Whitney came in a few days later to inquire where Mrs. Underhill sent her little girl to school, she decided to let her grandchild go to Mrs. Craven's also.

"She's quite a delicate little thing and takes after her mother. I tell my son, she wants to company with other children and not sit around nursing the cat. But Ophelia, that's my daughter who teaches down-town, where we used to live, says the public school is no place for her. And your little girl seems so nice and quiet like."

Nora, as they called her, was very shy at first.

Hanny went after her, and found the Deans waiting on their stoop.   Nora never uttered a word,
but looked as if she would cry the next moment.
Mrs. Craven took her in charge in a motherly
fashion, but it seemed very hard for her to frater-
nize with the children.

Mrs. Craven lived in a corner house.   The en-
trance to the school was on Third Street, and the
school-room was built off the back parlor, which
was used as a recitation-room for the older class.
There were about twenty little girls, none of
them older than twelve.   At the end of the yard
was a vacant lot, fenced in, which made a beautiful playground.

There were numbers of such schools at that
period, but they were mostly for little girls.
Hanny liked it very much.   On Wednesday afternoon they had drawing, and reading aloud, when
the girls could make their own selections, which
were sometimes very amusing.   On Friday afternoon they sewed and embroidered and did worsted
work.   There was quite a rage about this.   One
girl had a large piece in a frame—" Joseph Sold by
his Brethren. "   Hanny never tired of the beautiful
blue and red and orange costumes.   Another girl
was working a chair seat.   And still another had
begun to embroider a black silk apron with a soft
shade of red.   Then they hemstitched handkerchiefs, they marked towels and napkins with or-

nate letters, and really were a busy lot. Little Eleanora Whitney couldn't sew a stitch, and some of the girls thought it " just dreadful."

Friday from half-past three until five Miss Helen Craven gave the children, whose parents desired it, a dancing lesson. If Nora couldn't sew, she could dance like a fairy. Her education was a curious conglomeration. She could read and declaim, but spelling was quite beyond her, and her attempts at it made a titter through the room. She could talk a little French, and she had crossed the ocean to England with her papa So she wasn't to be despised altogether.

Chapter Eight

THE END OF THE WORLD.

'TAINT no such thing! The world couldn't come to an end!" Janey Day quite forgot Mrs. Craven's strictures on speech. "It's too strong. And—and——"

"And it's round," said the wit of the school. "Round as a ring and has no end. There now."

"But the world ain't like a ring."

"So is*n't* my love for you, my friend."

There was quite a little shout of laughter.

One of the larger girls, Hester Brown, stood with upraised head and earnest countenance.

"It *is* coming to an end in October. It is only two or three weeks off. My father has read it all in the Bible. And we are getting ready."

Her demeanor silenced the little group.

"But how *do* you get ready?"

"We must repent of our sins. And that's why mother wouldn't let me come to the dancing-class. She thinks it wrong, any way. And mother and Auntie are making their ascension robes. We go to church every night."

The girls stood awestruck.

"What's going to happen?" asked one.

"Why, the world will be burned up. All those who love God are to be caught up to heaven. Then the dead people who have been good will rise out of their graves. And all the rest—everything will be burned."

The solemnity of the girl's voice impressed so that they looked at each other in silent fear.

"I just don't believe a word of it," declared Janey Day, drawing a long breath. "My father's a good man and goes to church and reads the Bible every night. He's read it through more than fifty times, and he's never said a word about the world coming to an end. And he's building a new house for us to move into next spring."

"Fifty times, Janey Day! It takes a long, long while to read the Bible through. My grandmother's read it all through twice, and she's awful old."

"Well—twenty times at least. And don't you 'spose he'd found something about it?"

"Everybody can't tell. It's in Daniel. There's days and times to be added up."

"Five of *you*, Janey," said the wit with a child's irreverence.

"Just *when* is it coming to an end? Girls, there's no use to study any more lessons."

"It will be next week," said Hester with almost

tragic solemnity. "But you must all go on doing your work just the same."

"I don't see the sense. I've just begun fractions, and I hate them. I won't do another sum."

The bell rang and recess was at an end. The girls straggled until they reached the doorway, then suddenly straightened themselves into an orderly line and took their seats quietly. There was a sound of rapidly moving pencils—slates and pencils were in full swing then. No one had invented "pads."

One after another read out answers. A few went up to Mrs. Craven for assistance.

"Lottie Brower," the lady said presently.

Lottie colored. She had a kind of school-girl grudge against Hester.

"I—I haven't done my sums," she replied slowly.

"Why not?"

"Because the world is coming to an end. They're so hard, and what is the use if we're not going to live longer than next week?"

Every girl stopped her work and stared at Hester, amazed, yet rather enjoying Lottie's audacity.

"How did you come by such an idea?" asked Mrs. Craven quietly.

"But *is* there any use of studying or anything?"

Lottie's voice had a little tremble in it. "I'm sure I don't want the world to come to an end, but——"

"Do your people believe this?"

"No, ma'am," replied Lottie.

"Where, then, did you get the idea?"

"Hester Brown is sure——"

Hester's face was scarlet. She felt that she was called upon to bear witness.

"My father and mother believe it, and we are all getting ready. My uncle means to give away all his things next week."

The girl was in such earnest that Mrs. Craven was puzzled for a moment.

"I do not think we shall know the day or the hour," was the reply. "We are all exhorted to go on diligently with whatever we are doing. And Lottie, Hester has certainly set you an example. She did her sums correctly. She has added works to her faith as the Bible commands. I am aware many people think the end of the world is near, but that is no reason for our being careless and indolent. I doubt if that excuse would be accepted; at all events, I cannot accept yours."

"But I hate fractions! The divisors and the multiples get all mixed up and go racing round in my head until I can't tell one from the other."

"Bring your slate here." Mrs. Craven made

room for her by the table. "Now, what is the trouble?"

Twelve o'clock struck before Lottie was through, but she had to admit that it wasn't so "awful" when Mrs. Craven explained the sums in her quiet, lucid manner. The girls rose and went to the closet for their hats and capes.

"Girls," began Mrs. Craven, "I want to say a word. I hope each one of you will respect the other's religious belief. Our country has been founded on the corner-stone of liberty in this matter, and one ought to be noble enough not to ridicule or sneer at any honest, sincere faith, remembering that we cannot all believe alike."

Hester went out with two or three of the larger girls.

"I do not think you were quite kind, Lottie," said her teacher, in a soft tone.

"But what would be the use of fractions if the world came to an end?"

"Oh, Mrs. Craven! *do* you believe it? I should feel just dreadful. The world has so many splendid things in it—and to be burned up."

"I should just be frightened to death," and one little girl shuddered.

"Children, I am sorry anything has been said about this. There are a good many people who believe and who have preached for the last three years that the end of the world is near. The time has been set for next week. Yet the Bible *does* say that *no* man knoweth the day nor the hour. I do not believe in these predictions," and she smiled reassuringly. "I think we can all count on Thanksgiving and a merry Christmas as well as a happy New Year. I want you all to be kind to each other, and when Hester is disappointed next week, to refrain from teasing her. If you think for a moment, you will find it very easy to believe just as your parents do, for you love them the best of any one in this world. And the more you respect and obey them, the more ready you are to be kind and gentle and truthful to all about you, the better you are serving God. You must leave this matter in His hands, and remember that He loves you all, and will do whatever is best. Don't feel troubled about the world coming to an end. I am afraid Lottie here will have a great deal more trouble about fractions. I doubt if she gets through by Christmas. Now run home or you will be late for dinner."

The little girl sat very quiet at the table. There was only her mother, John, and the boys. She wished that her father or Steve were here so she could ask them. A strange awe was creeping over her. It seemed so dreadful to have all the world burned up. There might be some people left behind in the hurry. It hurt terribly to be burned even a little.

'There was a very sober lot of girls at school that afternoon. The jest was all taken out of recess. Hester sat on the steps reading a little pocket Testament. The others huddled together and shook their heads mysteriously, saying just above a whisper, "I don't believe it." "My mother says it isn't so." But somehow they did not seem to fortify themselves much with these protestations.

Some of the elder cousins had come to visit and take tea. People went visiting by three in the afternoon and carried their work along. There was an atmosphere of relationship and real living that gave a certain satisfaction. You enjoyed it. It was not paying a social debt reluctantly, relieved to have it over, but a solid, substantial pleasure.

Martha took the little girl upstairs and put on a blue delaine frock and white apron, and polished her "buskins," as the low shoes were called. Then she went into the parlor and spoke to all the ladies. She had her lace in a little bag, and presently she sat down on an ottoman and took out her work.

"You don't mean to say that child can knit lace? And oak-leaf, too, I do declare! What a smart little girl!"

"Oh, she embroiders quite nicely, also. Hannah Ann, get your apron and show Cousin Dorcas."

The apron was praised and the handkerchiefs she had marked for her father were brought out. Then she was asked what she was studying at school.

Cousin Dorcas was knitting "shells" for a counterpane. There was one of white and one of red, and they were put together in a rather long diamond shape with a row of openwork between every block. It was for her daughter, who was going to be married in the spring, and it interested the little girl wonderfully.

Then they talked about Steve and Dolly Beekman. While the girls were at White Plains, Steve had coaxed his father and mother up to the Beekmans', and the engagement had been settled with all due formality. Dolly and her mother had been down and taken tea. And now Steve went up every Sunday afternoon and stayed to supper, and once or twice through the week, and took Dolly out driving and escorted her to parties.

The Beekmans were good, solid people, and Peggy ought to be satisfied that Stephen had chosen so wisely. "Was it true that Steve had been buying some land way out of town? Did he mean to build there?"

"Oh, dear, no!" answered his mother. "It was a crazy thing, but John had really persuaded him, and John was too young to have any judgment.

But he said the Astors were buying up there, and land was almost given away."

"I don't know what it's good for," declared Aunt Frasie. "Why it'll be forty years before the city'll go out there. Well, it may be good for his grandchildren."

They all gave a little laugh.

Presently another of the cousins sat down at the piano and played the " Battle of Prague."

Then Aunt Frasie said, "Do sing something. It doesn't seem half like music without the singing."

Maria Jane ran her fingers over the keys, and began a plaintive air very much in vogue:

"Shed not a tear o'er your friend's early bier,
     When I am gone, I am gone."

Aunt Frasie heard her through the first verse, and then said impatiently:

"You've sung that at so many funerals, Maria Jane, that it makes me feel creepy. You used to sing 'Banks and Braes.' Do try that."

It had been said of Maria Jane in her earlier years that she had sung "Bonnie Doon" so pathetically she had moved the roomful to tears. Her voice was rather thin now, with a touch of shrillness on the high notes, but the little girl listened entranced. Then she sang "Scots wha' hae" and "Roy's wife of Aldivaloch." Margaret had come home, the supper-table was spread, the men came in, and they sat down to the feast. They teased Steve a little, and bade John beware, and were so merry all the evening that when it came her bedtime the little girl had forgotten all about the world coming to an end.

The girls discussed it the next day. Most of their mothers and fathers had scouted the idea. Josie Dean was very positive it couldn't be—her father had been going over the Bible and the Millerites had made a big mistake.

"And girls," said Josie earnestly, "St. John, one of the disciples of our Saviour, lived to be a hundred years old. Some people taught that the world would come to an end before he died. And now it's 1843, and it's stood all this while, though every now and then there's been an excitement about it. And I ain't going to be afraid at all, there now!"

The little girl wondered whether she would be afraid. But Friday evening the boys were full of it, and Steve said it was nonsense. She crept up into her father's lap and asked him in a tremulous whisper if he was afraid.

"No, dear," he answered, pressing her to his heart.

"But if it *should* come."

"Well—I'd take my little girl and mother and Margaret.——"

"And what would you do?" as he made a long pause.

"I'd beg to be taken into heaven. And we would all be together. I think God would be good to us."

"And the boys."

"Yes, the boys." He wondered within himself if they were all fit for heaven. But he was quite sure the little girl was.

There was a very great excitement. For months there had been meetings of exhortation and prophesying, and appeals to conscience, to terror, to the desire of being saved from impending destruction. Last winter there had been revivals everywhere, yet during the summer thoughtful people had questioned whether the moral tone of the community had been any higher. There were heroic souls, that always rise to the surface in times of spiritual agitation. There were others moved by any excitement, who seized on this with a kind of ungovernable rapture.

No one spoke of it in Sunday-school. Hanny brought home "Little Blind Lucy," and was so lost in its perusal that she hardly wanted to leave off for half an hour with Joe. But her mother let her look over to see whether Lucy really did have her eyesight restored. She was so sleepy that when she had said her little prayer she felt quite sure that God would take care of her and the beautiful world He had made.   It would be cruel to burn it all up.

But the children went to school on Monday. Martha washed as usual.   She did think it would be a waste of labor and strength if the world came to an end, though she was sure clean clothes would burn up quicker, and if it had to be, one might as well have it over as soon as possible.

All things went on, the buying and selling, the business of the day, and in some houses there were weary pain-racked bodies that slipped out of life gently without waiting for the general conflagration.

Still a strange awe did pervade the city.   Some of the churches were open, and people were on their knees weeping and sobbing to be made ready; others were full of faith and expectations, singing hymns, and impatiently waiting the moment when the trump would sound and they be caught up to glory.   Down on Grand Street Hester Brown's uncle was giving away shoes, and wondering at the fatal unbelief of those who were so ready to accept.   Here and there another of abounding faith was doing the same thing, or perhaps giving away things they did not need, hoping it would be accounted to them for good works.

Hester was not in school.   Neither did she come

on Tuesday, and that night was to be the fatal end of all things. A great many people went to church that day. The children did suffer from dread, though Lottie Brower kept up a sort of cheery bravado, as one whistles or sings in the dark.

"And I don't think Hester's been such an awful sight better than the rest of us. She answered correct one day when she had talked, and pretended she had forgotten all about it. And she was just mean enough about that clover-leaf pattern and wouldn't show a single girl. And she gets mad just as easy as the rest of us."

"I think we oughtn't get mad any more. And, girls, I'll lend you my knife to sharpen your pencils. We ought to *try* to be just as good as we could, for my Sunday-school teacher said if we died the world came to an end for us."

They made many resolves. Mrs. Craven thought they had never been so angelic in their lives.

But the little girl was very much "stirred up."

People didn't say nervous so much in those days. In fact nervousness was rather associated with whims and tempers. Joe came over to supper—he could get off from the hospital now and then. They were all talking about going to Delancey Street Church, where it was said people would be dressed in their ascension robes, and remain to the final change.

Margaret begged to go, and said she knew all her lessons. The boys had theirs to study. Jim scouted the idea of the world's coming to an end. Benny adduced several remarkable reasons why it couldn't come just yet. The Millerites had made a mistake in the true meaning of the "days" in Daniel.

"Are you quite sure?" asked the little girl timidly.

"Well—you'll see the same old world next week this time. Don't you get frightened, Hanny dear," and Ben kissed her reassuringly.

She sat by the boys and knit on her lace a while. Then her mother looked up from the stockings she was darning. She said "she always took Time by the forelock," and the little girl had a fancy some time she would drag him out. She wondered if she would really like to see Time with his hour-glass and scythe, and all his bones showing.

Mrs. Underhill looked up at the clock.

"My goodness, Hanny!" she exclaimed, "it's time you were in bed half an hour ago. Put up your lace. You'll be sleepy enough in the morning."

The little girl wound it round her needles and then stuck the ends in the stem of the spool and put it away in her basket. She kissed Ben and Jim good-night, and followed her mother. Her eyes had a half-frightened look and the pupils were very large. Mrs. Underhill felt out of patience that there should be so much talk about the world coming to an end before children. She knew Hanny was "just alive with terror." She couldn't pretend to explain anything to her; she was of the opinion that as you grew older "you found out things for yourself." And I am really afraid she didn't believe in total depravity for sweet little girls like Hanny. It was well enough for boys. So much of her life had been spent in doing, that she might have neglected some of the "mint, anise, and cummin." She undressed the little girl. Oh, how fair and pretty her shoulders were, and her round white arms that had a dimple at the top of the elbow. She was small for her age, but nice and plump, and her mother felt just this minute as if she would like to cuddle her up in her arms and kiss her as she had in babyhood. If she had, all the fear would have gone out of the little girl's heart.

Hanny said her prayer, and added to it, "Oh, Lord Jesus, please don't let the world come to an end to-night." Then her mother patted down the bed, took off one pillow and the pretty top quilt, and put her in, kissing her tenderly, the little trembling thing.

Then she stood still awhile.

"I do wonder what I did with your red coat," she began. "Cousin Cynthia said it might be let down and do for this winter. There's no little girl to grow into your clothes. Let me see—I put a lot of things in this closet. I remember pinning them up in linen pillow-cases, but I meant to store them in the cedar chest. I wonder if I have been that careless."

She stood up on a chair and threw down some bundles with unnecessary force. Then she stepped down and began to look them over, keeping up a running comment She would not have admitted that she was talking against time, secretly hoping the little girl would drop off to sleep. But the coat was not in any of the bundles.

"I think it must be in the chest. While I'm about it I may as well go and see. If you have outgrown it, it could be made over into a dress; it's nice, fine merino, a little thicker than I'd buy for a dress, but your father would have just that piece. I'll get a candle and go up-stairs—I wouldn't trust a glass lamp with this horrid burning-fluid in *my* storeroom. Hanny, be sure you don't get up and touch it," as if there was the slightest possibility. "I'll be down again in five minutes."

That was a shrewd motherly excuse not to

leave the little girl alone in the dark, though she was never afraid.

She lay there very still, with a feeling of safety since her mother was up-stairs. Of course she was old enough to know a great many things and to have ideas on religious subjects. But I think the Underhills were more intelligent than intellectual, and people were still living rather simple lives, not yet impregnated with ideas. They had not had the old Puritan training, and the ferment of science and philosophy and transcendentalism had not invaded the country places. To-night in the city there were wise heads proving and disproving the times and half times, and days and signs, but they really had no interest for Mrs. Underhill, who was training her family the best she knew how, making good men and women.

And the little girl's ideas were extremely vague. She thought her soul was that part of her heart that beat. When it ceased beating you died and the body was left behind; so of course that was what went to heaven. And when she had been naughty or when she had left something undone and was hurrying with all her might to do it, this thing beat and throbbed. If she wanted something very much and was almost tempted to take it, the feeling came up in her throat, and she knew that was conscience. She was trying now to recall and repent of her sins, and oh, she did so wish her father was here. Would he be back before the end came, and take them all in his strong arms? and they would run—Oh, no! they were to be caught up in the clouds. But she would be safe where he was.

Years afterward, she was to understand how human and finite love foreshadowed the eternal. But then she could only believe, and her faith in her human father was the rock of her salvation.

And when her mother came down she *had* fallen asleep, but she thought it would be just as well to leave the lamp burning until Margaret's return. She would look in now and then to see that it didn't explode. Burning-fluid was considered rather dangerous stuff.

Hanny was so tired that she slept soundly. It was almost midnight when the folks came home, and Mrs. Underhill begged Margaret to go to bed quietly and not disturb her. And it was all light with the sun rising in the eastern sky and shining in one window when she opened her eyes. Margaret stood before the glass plaiting her pretty, long hair.

The little girl sat up. Something had happened. There was a great weight—a great fear. What was it? Oh, yes, this was their room; they were all alive, for she heard Jim's breezy voice, and Joe, who had stayed all night, said impatiently:

"Peggy, are you never coming down?"

Hanny sprang out of bed and clasped her little arms about her sister.

"Oh!" with a great exultation in her sweet child's voice—"the world didn't come to an end, did it? Oh, you beautiful world! I am so glad you are left. And everybody—only—Margaret, were the people at the church dreadfully disappointed? What a pity God couldn't have taken those who wanted to go; but I'm so glad we are left. Oh, you lovely world, you are too nice to burn up!"

I think there were a great many people in the city just as glad as Hanny, if they did not put it in the same joyful words.

Margaret smiled. "Hurry, dear," she said, "Joe will have to go, and I know he wants to see you."

Hanny put on her shoes and stockings, and Margaret helped her with the rest, washed her and just tied up her hair with a second-best ribbon. Joseph had eaten his breakfast and was impatiently waiting to say good-by. John was off already.

Nothing had happened. The world was going on as usual. True there had been the comet and falling stars and wars and rumors of wars, but the old world had sailed triumphantly through them all. The dear, old, splendid world, that was to grow more splendid with the years.

Perhaps it did rouse people to better and kind-lier living and more serious thought. Before Mr. Underhill went away his wife said:

"'Milyer, hadn't you better look after those old people up at Harlem. I suppose they had some garden truck, but there's flour and meat and little things that take off the money when you haven't much. And fuel. I'll try to go up some day with you and see what they need to keep them comfortable in cold weather."

The girls could hardly study at school, there was so much excitement. Did people really have on their ascension robes? What *would* Hester say?

Hester did not come to school all the week. Of course they had made a mistake in computing the time, but a few weeks couldn't make much difference. Still, the worst scare was over, and if one mistake could be made, why not another? Were they so sure all the signs were fulfilled?

Chapter Nine.

A WONDERFUL SCHEME.

THE Whitneys and the Underhills became very neighborly. Mr. Theodore Whitney often stopped for a little chat, and he was very fond of a good game of checkers with Steve or John. He was on the other side in politics and they had some warm discussions. Ophelia, the oldest girl, was engaged and deeply absorbed with her lover. Frances went away early in the morning and did not get back until after six. Mrs. Whitney, a Southern woman by birth, was one of the easy-going kind and very fond of novels. Mr. Whitney brought them home by the dozen. The house seemed somehow to run itself, with the aid of Dele, as she was commonly called.

Dele proved a powerful rival to Miss Lily Ludlow. Lily was much prettier and more delicate looking. Dele had brown-red hair, dry and curly. She was a little freckled, even in the fall. Her mouth *was* wide, but she was always laughing, and she had such splendid teeth. Then her eyes were so full of fun, and her voice had a sort of rollicking sound. She knew all kinds of boys' play, and was great at marbles. Then she had so many odd, entertaining things, and their parlor wasn't too good for use when 'Phelia's beau was not there. But the children lived mostly on the stoop and the sidewalk.

Delia went to Houston Street school. She could walk farther up the street with the boys, and watch out for them when they went. Ben liked her better than he did Lily or Rosa, but Jim was quite divided. He, like the other poor man with two charmers, sometimes wished there was only one of them. But Lily was a born coquette, and jealous at that. She had a way of calling back her admirers, while Dele didn't care a bit for admiration, but just wanted a good time.

Benny Frank was something of a bookworm and student. Jim, who was growing very fast, was a regular boy, and, I am sorry to say, did not always have perfect lessons. He was so very quick and correct in figures that he managed to slip through other things. Moreover he carried authority. The boys had called him "country" at first and teased him in different ways until small skirmishes had begun. And one day there was a stand-up fight at recess. Jim thrashed the bully of his class. It was a forbidden thing to fight in the school-yard, or in school hours, and so Jim was thrashed again for his victory. But

Mr. Hazeltine shook hands with him afterward and said "it wasn't because he thrashed Upton, but because he had broken the rules, and he liked to see a boy have courage enough to stand up for himself." So Jim did not mind it very much, though he had a black eye for two or three days.

After that he was a sort of hero to the boys, and Upton did not bully as much. But some of the boys delighted to "pick" at Benny Frank, who would have made a good Quaker. Jim sometimes felt quite "mad" with him.

Lily did not seem to get along very rapidly with her intimacy. Hanny was too young, and now that she had the Deans on one side and little Nora Whitney on the other, was quite out of Lily's reach. And she did enjoy Delia immensely, though she was past thirteen and such a tall girl. So Lily tried all her arts on Jim, and succeeded very well, it must be confessed.

It was Saturday, and the world had not come to an end yet. Benny had gone down-town with Steve in the morning, but he would not have both boys together, for Jim was so full of "capers." So he had done errands for his mother, blackened the boots and shoes — the bootblack brigade had not then come in fashion, and you hardly ever saw an Italian boy. He had cleared up the yard and earned his five cents

He was wondering a little what he would do all the afternoon.

Dele came flying in, eager and impetuous.

"Oh, Mrs. Underhill!" she cried, "can't Hanny go to the Museum this afternoon? The"—it seemed so odd, Hanny thought, to call grave-looking Mr. Whitney that, but she said Steve to her big brother. "The brought home four tickets. My cousin, Walter Hay, is here, and he will go with us and then go down home. And Nora does so want Hanny to go. Oh, won't you please let her? I'll take the best of care of her. I've taken Nora and my little Cousin Julia ever so many times. Oh, Jim, what a pity! If I had one more ticket!"

"Sho!" and Jim straightened himself up. "I have twenty-eight cents, and I wouldn't want to go sponging on a girl anyhow! Oh, mother, do let us go? Hanny, come quick! Oh, do you want to go to the Museum?"

"To the Museum?" Hanny drew a breath of remembered delight and thrilling anticipation.

Dele and Jim talked together. They were so earnest, so full of entreaty. Jim might have gone in welcome, but Hanny——

"Why, we shall just take the stage and ride to the door, and we'll be so careful getting out. They drive clear up to the sidewalk, you know. Walter is fourteen and he takes his little sisters out, and knows how to care for girls. And there's such a pretty play; just the thing for children, The said."

"Oh, mother, please do," and the little girl's voice was so persuasive, so pleading.

"Oh, please, mother! I'll see that nothing happens to Hanny."

"Oh, Mrs. Underhill, Nora would be so disappointed. And we all want Hanny."

Mrs. Underhill had told her husband if he would come up about three she would take the drive to Harlem with him. Of course she meant to take the little girl. Which would Hanny rather do?

The fascinations of the Museum outweighed the drive. Margaret was up to the Beekmans' spending the day, their last week on the farm. Of course Jim could go—and when she looked at all the eager faces she gave in, and Hanny danced with delight.

It was almost three before they could get off, and the play began at that hour. However they caught a stage out on the Bowery and were soon whirled down to the corner of Broadway and Ann Street.

People were crowding in, it was such a beautiful day, and this was considered the place pre-eminently for children. People who would have been horrified at the thought of a theatre did not have a scruple about the lecture-room.

"We better not stop to look at things," advised

Delia. "We can do that afterward. Let's go in and get our seats."

They had to go way up front, but they didn't mind that so long as they were all together. They studied the wonderful Venetian scene on the drop-curtain, and the young lad in a supposedly green satin costume, with a long white feather in his hat, who was just stepping into a gondola where a very lovely lady was playing on a guitar. Then the orchestra gave a clash of drums, cymbals, French horns, and a big bass viol, and up went the curtain.

A musical family came out and sang. Then there were some acrobatic performances. After that the pantomime.

Grandpapa Jerome, in a very foreign costume and a bald head which he tried to keep covered with a black velvet cap, had two extremely tricksy sprites for grandchildren. They were very pretty, the girl with long, light curls, the boy with dark ones. But of all mischief, of all tormenting deeds and antics with which they nearly set grandpapa crazy and threw the audience into convulsions! They took the nice fat boiled ham off the table and greased the doorstep so thoroughly you would have thought every bone in the old man's body would have been broken by the repeated falls. They cut the seat out of the chair, and when he went to sit down he doubled up equal to any modern folding-bed, and he kicked and turned summersaults until the maid came out and rescued him. Then he spied the author of the mischief asleep on a grassy bank, and he found a big strap and went creeping up cautiously, when—whack! and the little boy flew all to pieces, and the old man was so amazed at his cruelty that he sat down and began to weep and bewail when the little lad peeped from behind a tree and, seeing poor grandfather's grief, ran out, hugged him and kissed him and wiped his eyes, and you could see he was promising never to do anything naughty again. But that didn't hinder him from cutting out the bottom of the basket into which the old man was cutting some very splendid grapes. There were not more than half a dozen bunches, and the children ran away with them. The old man descended so carefully, put his hand in the basket, his whole arm, and not a grape. There was none on the ground. Where had they gone! Oh, there was the cat. But pussy was much spryer than the old man, and the audience knew she had not touched a grape.

After that some Indians came on the scene of action, fierce red men of the forest, and their language was decidedly Jabberwocky. The little girl was quite frightened at the fierce brandishing of tomahawks. Then they had a war dance.

And oh, then came the marvel of all! Four beautiful Shetland ponies with the daintiest carriage and six lads in livery. There sat General Tom Thumb, the curiosity of the time, the smallest dwarf known. He was not much bigger than a year-old baby, but he dismounted from his carriage, gave orders to his servants; a bright-eyed little fellow with rosy cheeks, graceful and with a variety of pretty tricks. He sang a song or two, then sprang into his carriage and the ponies trotted off the stage. The curtain came down.

The children were breathless at first. The crowd was surging out and the place nearly empty before they found their tongues. And then there was so much else to see. The various stuffed animals, the giraffe with his three-story neck, the mermaid, the wax figures, the birds and beasts and serpents, and a model of Paris, of London, and of Jerusalem. The place looked quite gorgeous all lighted up.

The people were beginning to thin out. They had not seen half, Jim thought.

"Oh, we haven't been up-stairs!" exclaimed Walter. "There's a great roof-garden. And you can see all the city."

They trudged up-stairs. Dele kept tight hold of the little girl's hand. It was quite light up here. What a great space it was! One large flag was flying, and around the edge of the roof numberless smaller ones. Some evergreen shrubs in boxes stood around, and there were wooden arm-chairs, beside some settees. It was rather chilly, though the day had been very pleasant. And oh, how splendid the lights of Broadway looked to them, two long rows stretching up and up until lost in indistinctness The stores were all open and lighted as brilliantly as one could with gas. No one thought of Saturday half-holidays then. It was very grand. But what would they have said to the Columbian nights and electric lights?

"I don't feel as if I had seen it half," said Jim. He was not grudging his quarter. "If we had come about one o'clock."

"We'll have to piece it on this end," and Walter laughed. "We must get our money's worth."

"We might stay over," suggested Dele mirthfully.

"Just the thing," returned Jim, "and all for the same money."

The children glanced at each other in sudden surprise. The glory of a grand conspiracy shone in their eyes.

"Well, that's too good!" declared Walter. "Won't I just brag of that at school on Monday. Oh, yes, let's stay."

"We had better go down, for it is getting cool up here. If we only had something to eat.

Hanny, are you hungry? I don't believe Nora ever knows whether she has eaten or not. Mother says she's just the worst. I don't mind a bit, but you all——"

"I wouldn't give a copper for supper. It's ever so much more fun staying," rejoined Walter.

"I'm always nungry as a bear, but I'd a hundred times rather stay," Jim replied. "Hanny, will you mind?"

"I'm not a bit hungry," answered Hanny. "It's all so beautiful. Oh, do let's stay!"

"That settles it. Dele, you are a trump."

They picked their way carefully down-stairs. The room was not very brilliantly lighted, but they found many curiosities that had escaped their attention before. They espied the diorama and it interested them very much. Half a dozen people straggled in. The janitor turned on more light, and began to arrange a platform in a recess.

How any one would feel at home Jim never thought. The rest were in the habit of doing quite as they liked, and Delia often stayed at her aunt's until nine o'clock.

At seven the main hall was quite full. The people were crowding up around the platform. The children went too. The curtain was swung aside and out stepped Tom Thumb, to be received with cheers. He sang a song and went through with some military evolutions. There was a railing around and no one could crowd upon him, but a number spoke to him and shook hands.

"My little girl," said a tall gentleman who had watched Hanny's ineffectual efforts to make herself taller, "will you let me hold you up? Wouldn't you like to shake hands? You're not much bigger yourself."

"Oh, please do," entreated Dele in her eager young voice. "She is so small."

Hanny was a little startled, but the man held her in his arms and she smiled hesitatingly. As she met the kindly eyes she said, "Oh, thank you. It's so nice."

The general came down that end.

"Here is a little lady wants to shake hands with you," the gentleman said, who was quite a friend of Tom Thumb's.

The small hand was proffered. Hanny was almost afraid, but she put hers in it and the gallant little general hoped she was well. Then he made a bow and retired behind the curtain, and it was announced that he would appear again after the lecture-room performance.

They went in and took their seats. Nora was tired, and leaning her head on Dele's shoulder went sound asleep. Hanny was getting tired; perhaps, too, she missed her supper.

It wasn't quite so much fun, for the play was just the same. The audience enjoyed it greatly. The Indians were more obstreperous, and sang a hideous song. The vocalists sang many popular songs of the day, "Old Dan Tucker," "Lucy Long," "Zip Coon," and several patriotic songs. There was more dancing than in the afternoon, and the boys enjoyed the Juba in song and dance by a "real slave darkey" who had been made so by a liberal application of burnt cork, and who could clap and pat the tune on his knee.

They did not stop to see Tom Thumb again, but went straight down-stairs. Walter said good-night and declared he had had a splendid time, and Dele must thank Cousin The again. The four others bundled into the stage, which was crowded, but some kindly disposed people held both Nora and Hanny. They had quite a habit of doing it then.

Jim had been wondering what they would say at home. Of course he knew now he ought not have stayed. But nothing *had* happened, and Hanny was all right, and—well, he would face the music whatever it was. If Dele could be trusted, why not he?

There had been a good deal of anxiety. Mrs. Underhill had expected them home by six, but their father said: "Oh, give them a little grace." But when seven o'clock came she went down to

Whitney's to inquire. The table was still standing. Mrs. Whitney sat at the head with a book
in her hand; Dave, the second son, was smoking
and reading his paper. Both girls had gone out.

"Oh, Mrs. Underhill, don't feel a bit worried!
They'll come home all safe. I shouldn't wonder
if Dele had taken them over to her aunt's, and
she'll never let them come home without their
supper. She's the greatest hand for children I
ever saw. And Dele's so used to going about.
Then everybody's out on Saturday night.
Dear me! I haven't given it an anxious thought,"
declared Mrs. Whitney.

But Mrs. Underhill could not take it so comfortably.

"There's so many of them we should hear if
anything had happened," said John. "And there
is no use looking, for we shouldn't know where
they are; Jim's pretty good stuff too, for a country boy. Now, mother, don't be foolish."

But she grew more and more uneasy. If she
had not let Hanny go! What could she have been
thinking of to do such a thing?

After nine Mr. Underhill walked out to the
Bowery, and watched every stage that halted at
the corner. Men, women, and children alighted,
but no little girl. Oh, where could she be? He
felt almost as if the world was coming to an end.

Then a familiar group all talking at the same

time stepped out on the sidewalk. A big girl and two little ones.

"O father, father!" cried Hanny.

He wanted to hug her there in the street. It seemed to him he had never been so glad and relieved in all his life, or loved her half so well.

"Where *have* you stayed so long?"

"We went to two museums," said Hanny, before the elders could find their tongues. "And oh, father, we saw Tom Thumb and he's just as little and cunning as a baby! And he shook hands with me. A gentleman held me up. It was beautiful, but I'm awful tired."

"Oh, *were* you troubled?" cried Delia. "Why didn't you just go in to ma and she would have told you that I always come up right, and that nothing ever happens to me, I'm so used to taking care of children. Why, when we lived down town I used to take out the neighbors' children— over to Staten Island and to Williamsburg, and always brought them home safely. Then we hadn't half seen the curiosities, and we should have missed the nice time with that lovely little Tom Thumb. And we thought it such capital fun!"

Mr. Underhill really could not say a word. Tired as she was, the little girl was full of delight. Jim tried to make some explanations and take part of the blame, but Delia talked them all down and was so fresh and merry that you couldn't imagine she had gone without her supper.

Mrs. Underhill stood at the area gate with a shawl about her shoulders. The little girl let go of her father's hand and ran to her.

"Dear Mrs. Underhill," began Dele, "I expect you'll almost want to kill me, but I never thought about your being worried, for no one ever worries about me. I suppose it is because I never do get into any danger. And you must not scold any one, for I was the eldest, except Cousin Walter, and it was my place to think, but I didn't one bit. It seemed awful funny, you know, to have it all over for the same money, and we not paying anything at all! And I did take good care of Hanny. She's had a lovely time—we all have. And please don't scold Jim. He's been a perfect gentleman. We didn't do anything rude nor coarse, and everybody was as polite to us as if we'd been Queen Victoria's children. And so good-night."

"Jim, your father ought to give you a good thrashing. The idea! I wouldn't have believed any child of mine could have had such a little sense." his mother declared.

I don't know what might have happened, but just then Steve and Margaret returned. And when Steve caught sight of Jim's sober face and heard the story, he thought it very boylike and rather amusing. Besides, it seemed a pity to

spoil the good time.   So he laughed, and told Jim
he had cheated Mr. Barnum out of a quarter, and
that he would have to save up his money to make
it good.

"And he owes me nine cents toward the omnibus ride.   He must pay me that first," said his
mother sharply.

"I wasn't admitted *twice*," rejoined Jim.   "It
is the admittance.   I didn't see any notice about
not staying, and I don't believe I really owe Mr.
Barnum another quarter."

"Jim, I think I'll educate you for a lawyer.
You have such a way of squirming out of tight
places."

They all laughed.

"Mother, do give the children some supper,"
said their father.

"Here, Jim, pay your mother."   Steve laid him
down sixpence and three pennies.   We had Mexi-
can sixpences and shillings in those days.
"You'll have enough on your mind without that
debt.   And next time think of the folks at
home."

"Why didn't the Whitneys feel worried?   Oh,
thank you, Steve."

"It did beat all," said Mrs. Underhill.   "There
Mrs. Whitney sat reading a novel——"

"Perhaps it was her French exercise," interrupted Steve, with a twinkle in his eye.

" It was no such thing!   It was a yellow-covered novel!"   I don't know why they persisted in putting novels in pronounced yellow covers to betray people, unless it was that publishers wouldn't use false pretences.   And to put a story in the fatal color made it as reprehensible to most people as a yellow aster.   "And such a table!" Mrs. Underhill caught her breath.   "Everything at sixes and sevens, and the cloth looking as if it had been used a month, and Mrs. Whitney as unconcerned as if the children had only gone down to the corner.   I declare I couldn't be so—so——"

" But they're a jolly lot.   They save a great deal of strength in not worrying.   And they know Dele is trusty.   She's a smart girl, too."

"Well, I wouldn't want any of my sons to marry girls brought up as those Whitneys."

" Hear that, Jim.   You are fairly warned."

Jim turned scarlet.

" Jim will have to be in better business many a year than thinking of girls," subjoined his mother decisively.

The little girl didn't seem very hungry.   She ate her bread-and-milk and talked over the delights of the afternoon, and her enjoyment mollified her mother a good deal.   Jim considered at first whether it wouldn't rather even up things if he went without his supper, but the biscuits and the boiled beef were so tempting, and in those days boys could eat the twenty-four hours round. People were wont to say they had the digestion of an ostrich. But I think if you had tried them on nails and old shoes the ostrich would have gone up head.

"Oh, do you see how late it is? I know Hanny will be sick to-morrow! And Jim, you'll have the doctor's bill to pay."

"Oh, no," said Hanny with a smile, "Joe has promised to doctor me for nothing."

Mrs. Underhill lost her point. Jim wanted a good laugh, but he thought it would hardly be prudent.

Of course something ought to have happened to impress their wrong-doing on the children. But it didn't. They were all well and bright the next morning. Mr. Theodore Whitney took occasion to say that he hoped the Underhills wouldn't feel offended. It was just a young people's caper, and he thought it rather amusing.

Mrs. Whitney said in the bosom of her household: "Well, I wonder that Mrs. Underhill has an ounce of fat on her bones if she's worried that way about her eight children! I always felt to trust mine to Providence."

Jim "gave away" the thing at school, and was quite a hero. But some of the boys had crawled under a circus tent. And a circus was simply immense!

Lily Ludlow said, out of her bitterest envy, "I shouldn't have thought you would let a girl take you out, Jim Underhill!"

"She didn't take me! I bought my own ticket. And there was her cousin——"

"Well—if you like *that* style of people—and red hair—and Dele Whitney has no more figure than a post! I wouldn't be such a fat chunk for anything! And her clothes are just wild."

"Of course you're ever so much the prettiest. And I wish *we* could go to the Museum together, just us two." Jim thought it would be fine to take out *one* girl.

That mollified Lily a little.

"And I just wish you lived up by our house. It seems so easy then to come in. And when you once get real well acquainted—intimate like— well, you know I like you better than any girl in school;" though Jim wondered a little if it was absolutely true.

"Do you, really?" The eyes and the smile always conquered him. She made good use of both.

"Oh, you know I do."

Chris didn't see why she couldn't get acquainted with Margaret. She wanted her mother to call, but Mrs. Ludlow said, "I've more friends now than I can attend to." And Miss Margaret seemed to hold up her head so high. Then Mr. Stephen was going to marry in the Beekman

family.   And Chris wondered why Mr. John
didn't go in some store business instead of learning a carpenter's trade.

Hester Brown was out of school a week.   Mrs.
Craven had begged the girls not to tease her, but
after a few days she announced that a mistake
had been made in the calculation—some people
thought three years — but the end was sure.
However three years seems a lifetime to children.

Chapter Ten.

A MERRY CHRISTMAS.

GEORGE UNDERHILL came down and made a nice long visit. He felt he liked his own home people a little the best, but his heart was still set on farming. Thanksgiving came after a lovely Indian summer, such as one rarely sees now. Then each State appointed its own Thanksgiving, and there were people who boasted of partaking of three separate dinners.

After that it was cold. The little girl had a good warm cloak and hood and mittens, and it was nothing to run to school. She studied and played, and knew two pretty exercises on the piano. Jim and Benny Frank grew like weeds. But Benny somehow " gave in" to the boys, and two or three of the school bullies did torment him.

" I'd just give it to them!" declared Jim. " I wouldn't be put upon and called baby and a molly-coddle and have that Perkins crowding me off the line and losing marks. I'd give him such a right-hander his head would hum like a swarm of bees."

It was not because Benny was afraid. But he

was a peace-loving boy and he thought fighting brutal and vulgar. His books were such a delight. He liked to go in and talk to Mr. Theodore, as they all called the eldest Whitney son. Mr. Theodore in his newspaper capacity had found out so many queer things about old New York, they really called New York that in early 1800. He had such wonderful portfolios of pictures, and nothing in the Whitney house was too good to use.

Hanny often went in as well. And though Dele was such a harum-scarum sort of girl, she was good to the children and found no end of diversions for them. Nora was a curious, grave little thing, and her large dark eyes in her small, sallow face looked almost uncanny. She devoured fairy stories and knew many of the mythological gods and goddesses. They had a beautiful big cat called Old Gray. It really belonged to Mr. Theodore, but Nora played with it and tended it, and dressed it up in caps and gowns and shawls and carried it around. It certainly was a lovely tempered cat. Hanny was divided in her affection between the Deans' dolls and Nora's cat. The play-house was too cold to use now, and Mrs. Dean objected to having it all moved down to her sewing-room. But Mr. Theodore's room had a delightful grate, a big old lounge, a generous centre-table where the girls used to play house

under the cover, and such piles of books everywhere, so many pictures on the wall, such curious
pipes and swords and trophies from different
lands. You really never knew whether it was
cleared up or not, and the very lawlessness was
attractive.

Sometimes they sat in the big rocker, that would
hold both, and they would divide the cat between
them and sing to her. Occasionally kitty would
tire of such unceasing attention, and emit a long,
appealing m-i-e-u. If Mr. Theodore was there—
and he never seemed to mind the little girls playing about—he would say, " Children, what are you
doing to that cat?" and they would no longer try
to divide her, but let her curl up in her own
fashion.

"Oh, mother!" said the little girl, one rainy afternoon when she had to stay in, " couldn't we have
a Sunday cat that didn't have to stay out in the
stable and catch mice for a living? Nora's is so
nice and cunning and you can talk to it just as if
it was folks. And you can't quite make dolls,
folks. You have to keep making b'lieve all the
time."

"Martha doesn't like cats. And Jim would
torment it and plague you continually. And you
know I wouldn't let Jim's little dog come in the
house."

"But so many people do have cats."

"There's hardly room with so many folks. You wait until Christmas and see what Santa Claus brings you," said her mother cheerily.

There came a little snow and the boys brought out their sleds. For two days the air was alive with shouts and snowballing, and then it was like a drift of gray sand alongside of the street gutter. But winter had fairly set in. Stoves were up.

In the back room at the Underhills' they had a fire of logs on the hearth, and it was delightful.

Ben was tormented more and more. The boys knocked off his cap in the gutter and made up rhymes about him which they sang to any sort of tune. This was one:

> "Benjamin Franklin Underhill,
> Was a little boy too awfully still:
> Forty bears came out of the wood,
> And ate up the boy so awfully good."

"Come out from under that hill," while some boy would reply, "Oh, he dassent! He's afraid his shadder'll meet him in the way."

One day he came home with his pocket all torn out. Perkins had slipped a crooked stick in it and given it what the boys called a "yank."

"Go in and ask your mother for a needle and thread. You'll make a good tailor!" he jeered.

"What is all this row about?" asked his mother, who was in the front basement.

Ben held out his jacket ruefully, and said, " Perkins never would leave him alone."

Jim had complained and said Ben always showed the white feather. Mrs. Underhill couldn't endure cowards. She was angry, too, to see his nice winter jacket in such a plight.

" Benny Frank, you just march out and thrash that Perkins boy, or I'll thrash you! I don't care if you are almost as tall as I am. A great boy of fifteen who can't take his own part! I should be ashamed! March straight out!"

She took him by the shoulder and turned him round, whisked him out in the area before he knew where he was. She would not have him so meek and chicken-hearted.

Ben stood a moment in surprise. Jim had been scolded for his pugnacity. Perkins was always worse when Jim wasn't around.

" Go on!" exclaimed his mother.

Ben walked out slowly. The boys were down the street. If they would only go away. He passed the Whitneys and halted. He could rescue hounded cats and tormented dogs, and once had saved a little child from being run over. But to fight—in cold blood!

" Oh, here comes my Lady Jane!" sang out some one.

> "She's quite too young—
> To be ruled by your false, flattering tongue."

"Sissy, wouldn't your mother mend your coat? Keep out of the way of the ragman!"

Perkins was balancing himself on one foot on the curbstone.

"Come on, Macduff!" he cried tragically.

Macduff came on with a quick step. Before the boys could think he strode up to Perkins and with a well-directed blow landed him in the sloppy débris of snow and mud, where the children had been making a pond. And before he could recover Ben was upon him, roused to his utmost. The boys were nearly of a size. They rolled over and over amid the plaudits of their companions, and Ben, who hated dirt and mud and all untidiness, didn't mind now. He kept his face pretty well out of the way, and presently sat on his adversary and held one hand, grasping at the other.

The boys cheered. A fight was a fight, if it was between the best friends you had.

"Beg," said Ben.

"I'll see you in Guinea first!"

Ben sat still. The kicks were futile. With such a heavy weight breathing was a difficult matter.

"You — you — if you'd said fight I'd a-known——" and Perkins gasped.

"Oh, let up, Ben. You've licked him! We didn't think 'twas in you. Come—fair play."

"There's a good deal in me," cried Ben sturdily. "And I'm going to sit here all night till Perkins begs. I've a good seat. You boys keep out. 'Tisn't your fight. And you all know I hate fighting. It may do for wild animals in a jungle."

Ben's lip was swelling a little. A tooth had cut into it. But his eyes were clear and sparkling and his whole face was resolute. Perkins' attempts at freeing his hands grew more feeble.

"Boys, can't you help a fellow?"

"'Twas a fair thing, Perk. You may as well own up beat. Come, no snivelling."

Quite a crowd was gathering. There was no policeman to interfere.

Perkins made a reluctant concession. Ben sprang up and was off like a shot. His mother met him at the door.

"Go up-stairs and put on your best clothes, Ben," she said, "and take those down to the barn." She knew he had come off victor.

"I s'pose I'd had to do it some time," Ben thought to himself. "Mother's awful spunky when she's roused. I hope I won't have to go on and lick the whole crew! I just hate that kind of work."

As he came down his mother kissed him on the white forehead, but neither said a word.

When he went in to see Mr. Theodore that

evening he told him the story. It was queer, but he would not have admitted to any one else his mother's threat. Mr. Theodore laughed and said boys generally had to make their own mark in that fashion. Then he thought they would try a game of chess, as Ben knew all the moves.

Jim was surprised and delighted to hear the story the next day. He nodded his head with an air of satisfaction.

"Ben's awful strong," he said. "He could thrash any boy of his size. But he isn't spoiling for a fight."

A few days later there came a real snow-storm of a day and a night. Jim sprung the old joke on Hanny "that they were all snowed up, and the snow was over the tops of the houses." She ran to the window in her night-dress to see. Oh, how beautiful it was! The red chimneys grew up out of the white fleece, the windows were hooded, the trees and bushes were long wands of soft whiteness, the clothes-line posts wore pointed caps.

"Don't stand there in the cold," said Margaret.

They all turned out to shovel snow. The areas were full. The sidewalks all along were being cleared, and it made a curious white wall in the street. Mr. Underhill insisted that the boys should level theirs. Some wagons tried to get through and made an odd, muffled sound. Then there was the joyful jingle of bells. The sun came out setting the world in a vivid sparkle, while the sky grew as blue as June.

Not to have snow for Christmas would have spoiled the fun and been a bad sign. People really did believe "a green Christmas would make a fat graveyard." It was so much better in the country to have the grain and meadows covered with the nice warm mantle, for it was warm to them.

Father Underhill took the little girl to school, for all the walks were not cleared. Men and boys were going around with shovels on their shoulders, offering their services.

"I could earn a lot of money if I didn't have to go to school to-day," said Jim, with a longing look at the piles of snow. "If it only *was* Saturday!"

But there was no end of fun at school. The boys began two snow-forts, and the snowballing was something tremendous. The air was crisp and cold, and it gave everybody red cheeks.

Before night the stage sleighs were running, for the omnibuses really couldn't get along. Steve came home early to take the boys and Hanny out. Hanny still wore the red cloak and a pretty red hood and looked like a little fairy.

They went over to the Bowery. You can hardly imagine the gay sight it was. Everything that could be put on runners was there, from the dainty cutter to the lumbering grocery box wagon. And oh, the bells on the frosty air! It was enough to inspire a hundred poets.

There were four horses to the long sleigh. Steve found a seat and took the little girl on his lap, covering her with an extra shawl. The boys dropped down on their knees in the straw. It was a great jam, but everybody was jolly and full of good-natured fun. Now and then a youngster threw a snowball that made a shower of snow in the sleigh, but the passengers shook it off laughingly.

They went down to the Battery and just walked across. Castle Garden was a great white mound. Brooklyn looked vague and ghostly. The shipping was huddled in the piers with fleecy rigging, and only a few brave vessels were breasting the river, bluer still than the sky. And here there was such a splendid turnout it looked like a pageant.

They came up East Broadway. The street lamps were just being lighted. They turned up Columbia Street and Avenue D, and stopped when they came to Houston Street. A man on the corner was selling hot waffles as fast as half a dozen men could bake them, and a colored woman had a stand of hot coffee that scented up the air with its fragrance.

They had to walk up home, but Steve carried Hanny over all the crossings. It was a regular carnival. The children decided snow in New York was ever so much more fun than snow in the country.

But after a few days they settled to it as a regular thing, though the sleighs were flying about in their tireless fashion, making the air musical with bells. And Christmas was coming.

It really *was* Christmas then. Not to have hung up your stocking would have been an insult to the sweetest, merriest, wisest, tenderest little man in the world. There were some fireplaces left for him to come down, and he was on hand promptly.

And such appetizing smells as lurked in every corner of the house! Fruit cake, crullers and doughnuts, and mince pies! Everybody was busy from morning till night. When Hanny went to the kitchen some one said, " Run up-stairs, child, you'll be in the way here," and Margaret would hustle something in her apron and say, " Run down-stairs, Hanny dear," until it seemed as if there was no place for her.

The Dean children were busy, too. But Nora Whitney didn't seem to have anything to do but nurse dear Old Gray and read fairy stories. Delia told them Ophelia was to be married Christmas morning, and " they were going over to *his* folks in Jersey to spend a week."

" But it won't make a bit of difference," Delia

announced. "Frank has a steady beau now and they'll take the parlor. And then, I suppose, it'll be my turn. I shall just hate to be grown up and have long skirts on and do up my hair, and be so fussy about everything. When I think of that I wish I was a boy."

The little girl wondered if Margaret would get married next Christmas. Her gowns were quite long now, and she did have a grown-up air. It seemed years since last Christmas. So many things had happened.

The cousins were to come down from Tarry-town and make a visit, and Aunt Patience and Aunt Nancy were to come up from Henry Street for the Christmas dinner. If they only *could* bring the cat!

"Merry Christmas! Merry Christmas!" some one shouted while it was still dark. Hanny woke out of a sound sleep. "Merry Christmas," said Margaret with a kiss.

"Oh dear, I shan't get ahead of anybody," she sighed. "Do you think I could get up, Peggy?"

"I must light a candle," Margaret said.

"Come down and see what's in your stocking, Han!" shouted Jim.

Margaret sprang out of bed and put on the little girl's warm woollen wrapper and let her go down. She ran eagerly to her mother's room, and her father made believe asleep that she might

wake him up. She wanted to wish some one
Merry Christmas the first of all.

Two wax candles were burning in the back
room and the fire was crackling. There were
stockings and stockings, and hers were such little
mites that some one had hung a white bag on the
brass nail that held the feather-duster, and
marked it "For Hanny." And a box lay in a
chair.

There was a cruller man with eyes, nose, and
mouth. There were candies galore, the clarified
ones, red and yellow, idealized animals of all
kinds. There was an elegant silver paper cor-
nucopia tied with blue ribbons. There was a box
of beautiful pop-corn that had turned itself inside
out. Ribbon for her hair, a paint-box, a case of
Faber pencils, handkerchiefs, a lovely new pink
merino dress, a muff that purported to be ermine,
a pair of beautiful blue knit slippers tied with
ribbons. These didn't come from Santa Claus,
for they had on a card—"With best love and a
Merry Christmas, from Dolly." That was Dolly
Beekman. Hanny laid them up against her face
and kissed them, they were so soft and beautiful.

She drew a long breath before she opened the
box. Of course it couldn't be a real live kitty.
John and Steve were coming in at the door.

"Merry Christmas!" she shouted with the boys.
They were not so very far ahead of her.

Steve caught her under the arms and held her almost up to the ceiling, it seemed. She was so little and light.

"Ten kisses before you can come down."

She paid the ten kisses, and would have given twice the number.

"I'm trying to guess what is in the box." She looked perplexed and a crease came between her eyes.

"It's a chrononhontontholagosphorus!"

"A—what?" Her face was a study.

The boys shouted with laughter.

"Yes, Joe sent it. Santa Claus had given his all out, and Joe had to skirmish around sharp to get one."

"Is it alive?" she asked timidly, her eyes growing larger with something that was almost fright.

"Oh, Steve!" said Margaret, in an upbraiding tone. "Boys, you're enough to frighten one."

Steve untied the string and took off the cover. Hanny had tight hold of her sister's hand. Steve lifted some tissue paper and tilted up the box. There lay a lovely wax doll with golden hair, a smiling mouth that just betrayed some little teeth, eyes that would open and shut. She was dressed in light-blue silk and beautiful lace. Though her mother had said she was too big to have a doll, Joe knew better.

She was almost speechless with joy. Then she knelt down beside it and took one pretty hand.

"Oh," she said, "I wish you could know how glad I am to have you! There's only one thing that could make me any gladder, that would be to have you alive!" Steve winked his eyes hard. Her delight was pathetic.

Then she had to see the boys' Christmas. Benny Frank had a new suit of clothes, Jim had a pair of boots, which was every boy's ambition then, and an overcoat. And lots of books, pencils, gloves, and the candy it would not have been Christmas without.

Mr. Underhill poked up the fire and took the little girl on his knee. Mrs. Underhill put out the candles, for it was daylight, and then went down to help get breakfast. Cousin Fannie and Roseann, as Mrs. Eustis was always called, came in and had to express their opinion of everything. Then breakfast was ready.

John went down in the sleigh for Aunt Patience and Aunt Nancy Archer. They were not own sisters but sisters-in-law and each had a comfortable income. It did not take very much to make people comfortable then. They owned their house and rented some rooms.

Hanny had to go in and see Josie and Tudie Dean's Christmas and bring them in to inspect hers. Then Dele and Nora Whitney were her next callers. Nora had a silk dress and a gold ring with a prettily set turquoise.

"The marriage was at ten," began Dele, "and it was just nothing at all. I wouldn't be married in such a doleful way. She just had on a brown silk dress with lots of lace, and white gloves, and the minister came and it was all over in ten minutes. There was wedding-cake and wine. I've brought you in some to dream on. Nora and I are going down to Auntie's in Beach Street where there's to be a regular party and a Christmas tree and lots of fun. After 'Phelia comes back she's going to have a wedding-party and wear her real wedding-dress."

Nora thought the doll beautiful. Hanny just lifted it out of the box and put it back. It seemed almost too sacred to touch.

Jim went out presently to get some Christmas cake. The grocers and bakers treated the children of their customers to what was properly New Year's cake, and the boys thought it no end of fun to go around and wish Merry Christmas.

The dinner was at two. Doctor Joseph came in to dine and to be congratulated by the cousins. The little girl's gratitude and delight was very sweet to him. He put up the piano stool and she played her pretty little exercises for him. Then about four he and Steve went down to the Beekmans', where there was a dancing party in the evening.

The elders sat and talked, to Benny Frank's great delight. The "old times" seemed so wonderful to the children. Aunt Patience was the elder of the two ladies, just turned seventy now, and had lived in New York all her life. She had seen Washington when he was the first President of the United States, and lived in Cherry Street with Mrs. Washington and the two Custis children. Afterward they had removed to the Macomb House. Everything had been so simple then, people going to bed by nine o'clock unless on very special occasions. To go to the old theatre on John Street was considered the height of fashionable amusement. You saw the Secretaries and their families, and the best people in the city.

But what amused the children most was the Tea Water Pump.

"You see," said Aunt Patience, "we had nice cisterns that caught rainwater for family use, and we think now our old cistern-water is enough better than the Croton for washing. There were a good many wells but some were brackish and poor, and people were saying then they were not fit to use. The Tea Water pump was on the corner of Chatham and Pearl, and particular people bought it at a penny a gallon. It was carried around in carts, and you subscribed regularly. My, how choice we were of it!"

"There's a pump down here at the junction that's just splendid!" said Jim, "I used to go for water last summer, it was so good and cold."

"We miss our nice spring at home," said Mrs. Underhill, with a sigh.

"And what else?" subjoined Ben.

"Oh, the milk did not go round in wagons. There were not half so many people to supply. We kept a cow and sold to our neighbors. The milkmen had what was called a yoke over their shoulders, with a tin can at each end. They used to cry, 'Milk ho! ye-o!' The garbage man rang his bell and you brought out your pail. A few huckster men were beginning to go round, but Hudson Market was the place to buy fresh vegetables that came in every morning. And, oh, there were the chimney-sweeps!"

"We had our chimney swept here," said Jim. "The man had a long jointed handle and a wiry brush at the end."

"But then there were little negro boys who climbed up and down and sometimes scraped them as they went. But several were smothered or stuck fast in London and it was considered cruel and dangerous. You'd hear the boys in the morning with their 'Sweep ho!' and you wouldn't believe how many variations they could make to it."

"Poor little boys!" said Hanny. "Didn't they get awful black and sooty?"

The boys laughed. "They were black to begin with," said Jim. "All they had to do was to shake themselves."

"And how do you suppose Santa Claus keeps so clean?" asked the little girl, nothing daunted.

That was a poser. No one could quite tell.

"We used to burn out our chimney," announced Aunt Patience.

"Burn it out?"

"Yes. We'd take a rather lowering day, or start in just as it was beginning to rain. We'd put a heap of straw in the fireplace and kindle it, and the soot would soon catch. Then some one would go up on the roof to see if the sparks caught anywhere. We never let it get very dirty. But presently they passed a law that no one should do it on account of the danger. But sometimes chimneys caught fire by accident," and Aunt Patience laughed.

"Why, it was like the wolf in little Red Riding Hood," declared Hanny.

Then they all talked of the old roads and streets and the Collect, which was a great marshy pond, and the canal through Lispenard's meadows over to the North River, where present Canal Street runs. In the Collect proper there was a beautiful clear lake where people went fishing. A great hill stood on Broadway, and had to be cut down more than twenty feet.

Father Underhill recalled his first visit to the city when he was nineteen, and going skating with some cousins. And now it was all graded and finished streets, houses, and stores.

But Aunt Patience said it was time to go home, and they planned for the Morgan cousins to come and spend the day. They were to bring the little girl with them.

They had a light supper and then John escorted the ladies home. Benny Frank wanted his father to tell some more incidents of the old times. The little girl was tired and sleepy and ready to go to bed, but she had one wish saved up for next Christmas already—a set of dishes.

Chapter Eleven.

A WHOLE week of holidays! Jim and Benny Frank had their mother almost wild, and Martha said "she would be dead in another week. If Christmas came twice a year there would be no money nor no people left. They would be all worn out."

It was splendid winter weather. Sunny and just warm enough to thaw and settle the snow during the day and freeze it up again at night. Then there came another small fall of snow to whiten up the streets and make the air gayer than ever with bells.

The Morgan cousins had to go down and call on Miss Dolly Beekman, and were very favorably impressed with her. The little girl went with them to Cherry Street and had "just a beautiful time with the kitty," she told her mother. Her blue woollen frock was full of white cat-hairs as a memento. She went to tea with the little Dean girls, she spent an afternoon with Nora, and had the little girls in to visit her. Margaret played on the piano and they had a charming dance, beside playing "Hot butter blue beans," which was no end of fun.

On New Year's Day everybody had "calls." Margaret was hardly considered a young lady, but Miss Cynthia came to help entertain. It was really very pleasant. A number of family relatives called in, some of whom they had not seen since they came to the city. They were all rather middle-aged, though Joe brought in his chum, a very handsome young man who had graduated with his class but was two years older. Margaret was quite abashed by Doctor Hoffman's attention to her, and his saying he should take her good wishes as a happy omen for his New Year. Indeed, she was very glad to have Miss Cynthia come to the rescue in her airy fashion.

Late in the afternoon the Odells drove down. The little girls went up-stairs to see the Christmas things and the lovely doll for whom no name had been good enough. John had a fire in his room and it was nice and warm, so he told them they might go up there. They played "mother" and "visiting," and wound up with a splendid game of "Puss in the Corner." There were only four pussies and they could have but three corners, but it was no end of fun dodging about, and if they did squeal, the folks down in the parlor hardly heard them.

Saturday was Saturday everywhere. It was "Ladies' day" too. But people had to clear up their houses and begin a new week, a new year, as well, for it was 1844.

The little girl wondered what made the years. Mrs. Craven explained that the recurrence of the four seasons governed them, and some rather learned reasons the child could not understand. But she said:

"It seems to me the year ought to begin in spring and not the middle of the winter."

Ophelia came home, she was Mrs. Davis now, and they had a grand party with music and dancing and a supper, and Nora wore her pretty new silk frock. Then Mrs. Davis went down-town to be near her husband's business, and started housekeeping in three rooms.

The next great event on the block was a children's party. They were children then until they were at least sixteen. Miss Lily Ludlow and her sister had ten dollars sent to each of them as a Christmas gift. Chris went out straightway and bought a new coat. Lily's was new the winter before. There were a great many things she needed, but most of all she wanted a party. She had been to two already.

"What a silly idea!" said her father.

But Lily kept tight hold of her idea and her money, and the last of January, with Chris' help, she brought it about. They took the bedstead out of the back parlor and changed the furniture around. And though her mother called it foolishness, she baked some tiny biscuits and made a batch of crullers and boiled a ham. Lily bought fancy cakes, mottoes, candies, and nuts, and a few oranges which were very expensive.

The Underhill boys were invited, of course. Benny said "he didn't believe he would go. He shouldn't know what to do at a party."

"Why, follow your nose," laughed Jim. "Do just as the rest do. Don't be a gump!"

"And I hate to be fooling round girls."

"You don't seem to mind Dele Whitney. You're just cracked about her."

I don't know how the boys of that day managed without the useful and pithy word "mashed."

"It's no such thing, Jim Underhill! She's always down-stairs with her mother. I go in to see Mr. Theodore;" yet Ben's face was scarlet.

"You know you like her," teasingly.

"I *do* like her. And it's awful mean not to ask her when she's in the same crowd and lives on the block. But she doesn't care. She wouldn't go."

"Sour grapes." Jim made a derisive face.

"You shut up about it."

"Don't get wrathy, Benjamin Franklin."

When his mother said "Benny Frank," he

thought it the best name in the whole world. Perhaps part was due to his mother's tone. And Ben was a splendid boy's name. But his schoolmates did torment him. They asked him if he had finished his roll, and if he had any to give away. They pestered him about flying his kite, and inquired what he said to the King of France when he went abroad—if it was "*parley vous de donkey.*" If there is anything the average schoolboy can turn into ridicule he does it. When Jim wanted to be exasperating he gave him his whole name. And then Ben wished he had been called plain John, even if there had been two in the family.

But the day of the party Jim coaxed him, and Jim could be irresistible. Then Margaret said: "Oh, yes, I think I would go. She fixed up both of the boys, and scented their handkerchiefs with her "triple extract," and hoped they would have a nice time, insisting that one needn't be afraid of girls.

Of course they did, especially Jim. He was in for all the fun and frolic, and the kissing didn't worry him a bit when the "forfeits" were announced. He didn't mind how deep he "stood in the well," nor how high the tree was from which they "picked cherries." Ben *could* rise to an emergency if he was not praying for it every moment.

Chris was a great card. She could not help wishing that she knew enough young people in her social round to ask to a party. There were enough young ladies, but a "hen party" wasn't much fun. She made herself very agreeable to the Underhill boys, and wished in the sweetest of tones "that she *did* know their sister Margaret."

There were a good many imperfect lessons the next day, but the party was the great topic. Hosts of girls were "mad."

"I couldn't ask everybody. The house wouldn't hold them," declared Lily. But she took great comfort in thinking she had "paid out" several girls against whom she had a little grudge. And the "left-outs" declared they wouldn't have gone anyhow. It must be admitted that the party did advance Lily socially.

The family had hardly recovered from this spasm of gayety when Stephen insisted that Margaret should go to a Valentine's ball at the Astor House, to be given to the ladies by a club of bachelors. He was going to take Dolly. Mrs. Bond would be there, and Dolly came up to coax her prospective mother-in-law. "Margaret had not gone into any society and was only a schoolgirl, altogether too young to have her head filled with such nonsense," with many more reasons and conjunctions. Dolly was so sweet and persuasive, and said the simplest white gown would do, young girls really didn't dress much. Then Margaret would have it ready for her graduation. They would be sure to send her home early and take the best of care of her.

Joe said: "Why, of course she must go. It wasn't like being among strangers with Dolly and her people." So the boys and Dolly carried the day. All the while Margaret's heart beat with an unaccustomed throb. She did not really know whether she wanted to go or not.

St. Valentine's Day was held in high repute then. You sent your best girl the prettiest valentine your purse could afford, and she laid it away in lavender to show to her children. Bashful young fellows often asked the momentous question in that manner. There were some lovely ones, with original verses written in, for there were young bards in those days who struggled over birthday and valentine verses, and who would have scorned second-hand protestations.

Though Margaret didn't get any valentines the little girl received three that were extremely pretty. She asked Steve if he didn't send one.

"Oh, dear," he answered, as if he were amazed at the question, "I had to spend all my money buying Dolly one." And Joe pretended to be so surprised. He had spent his money for Margaret's sash and gloves and bunch of flowers.

Even John would not own up to the soft impeachment and declared, "Your lovers sent them."

"But I haven't any lovers," said the little girl, in all innocence.

She used to read them to her mother, and ask her which she thought came from Steve, which from Joe and John. It was quite funny, though, that Nora Whitney had one exactly like one of hers. And even Mr. Theodore declared he didn't send them.

Margaret looked like an angel, the little girl thought. Her white cashmere frock was simply made, with a lace frill about the neck and at the edge of the short sleeves. Her broad blue satin sash was elegant. Miss Cynthia came and plaited her beautiful hair in a marvellous openwork sort of braid, and she had two white roses and a silver arrow in it. Her slippers were white kid, her gloves had just a cream tint, and Miss Cynthia brought her own opera cloak, which was light brocaded silk, wadded and edged with swansdown.

Joe looked just splendid, the little girl decided. If she could only have seen Dolly!

The Beekman coach was sent up for Margaret, who kissed her little sister and went off like Cinderella!

"Oh, do you suppose she will meet the king's son?" asked Hanny, all excitement.

"Oh, child, what nonsense!" exclaimed her mother.

It wasn't the king's son; but young Doctor Hoffman was there, and Margaret danced several times with him.   They talked so much about Joe that Margaret felt very friendly with him.

After that the world ran on in snow, in sunshine, and in rain.   The days grew longer.   March was rough and blowy.   Mother Underhill had to go up in the country for a week, for Grandfather Van Kortlandt died.   He had been out of health and paralyzed for a year or two.   Aunt Katrina had been staying there, and they would go on in the old house until spring.   She was grand-mother's sister.   Of course no one could feel very sorry about poor old Uncle Nickie, as he was called.   He had always been rather queer, and was no comfort to himself, for he had lost his mind, but everybody admitted that grandmother had done her duty, and the Van Kortlandt chil-dren, grown men and women, thanked her for all her good care.

Oh, what fun the children had on the first of April!   What rags were pinned to people—what shrieks of "My cat's got a long tail!"   And there on the sidewalk would lay a tempting half-dollar with a string out of sight, and when the pedes-trian stooped to pick it up—presto! how it would vanish.   When one enterprising wight put his foot on it and picked it up triumphantly the boys called out:

"April fool!   That's an awful sell, mister!   It's a bad half-dollar."

They watched and saw him bite it and throw it down.   Then they went after it and had their fun over and over again.   Stephen had given the half-dollar to Jim with strict injunctions not to attempt to pass it or he'd get a "hiding," which no one ever did in the Underhill family.   Mrs. Underhill declared "'Milyer was as easy as an old shoe, and she didn't see what had kept the children from going to ruin."   Joe always insisted "it was pure native goodness."

Then they called out to the carters and other wagoners: "Oh, mister, say!   Your wheel's goin' round!"   And sometimes without understanding the driver would look and hear the shout.

They had another trick they played out in the Bowery.   Boys had a reprehensible trick of "cutting behind," as the stages had two steps at the back, and the boys used to spring on them and steal rides.   It was such a sight of fun to dodge the whip and spring off at the right moment. Sometimes a cross-grained passenger who had been a very good boy in his youth would tell.

On this day they didn't steal the ride.   They called out with great apparent honesty: "Cuttin' behind, driver—two boys!"

Then the driver would slash his whip furiously, and even the passers-by would enjoy the joke. Of course you could only play that once on each driver.

Altogether it was a day of days. You were fooled, of course; no one was smart enough to keep quite clear. But almost everybody was good-natured about it. Martha found some eggs that had been "blown," and a potato filled with ashes, and there were inventions that would have done credit to the "pixies."

The little girl would not go out to play in the afternoon, and she didn't even run when Jim said, "Nora wanted her for something special." But she really had no conscience about fooling her father several times. He pretended to be so surprised, and said, "Oh, you little witch!" It was a day on which you had need to keep your wits about you.

Then with the long days and the sunshine came so many things. Little girls skipped rope and rolled hoops, their guiding-sticks tied with a bright ribbon. The boys had iron hoops and an iron guider, and they made a musical jingle as they went along. There were kites too, but you didn't catch Benny Frank flying one. And marbles and ball. In the afternoon the streets seemed alive with children. But what would those people have said to the five-story tenement-houses with their motley crew! Then Ludlow and Allen and many another street wore such a clean and quaint aspect, and the ladies sat at their parlor windows in the afternoon sewing and watching their little ones.

"Ring-a-round-a-rosy" began again. And dear me, there were so many signs! You must not step on a crack in the flagging or something dreadful would happen to you. And you mustn't pick up a pin with the point toward you or you would surely be disappointed. If the head was toward you, you could pick it up and make a wish which would be sure to come to pass. You must cut your finger-nails Monday morning before breakfast and you would get a present before the week was out. And if you walked straight to school that morning you were likely to have good lessons, but if you loitered or stopped to play or were late, bad luck would follow you all the week. And the little girls used to say:

> "Lesson, lesson, come to me,
> Monday, Tuesday, Wednesday, three,
> Thursday, Friday, then you may
> Have a rest on Saturday,"

So you see a little girl's life was quite a weighty matter.

That summer political excitement ran high. Indeed, it had begun in the winter. A new party had nominated Mr. James Harper for mayor, and in the spring he had been elected. Mr. Theodore used to pause and discuss men and measures now that it was getting warm enough to sit out on the stoop and read your paper. Country habits were not altogether tabooed. But what impressed his honor the mayor most strongly on the little girl's mind was something Aunt Nancy Archer, who was now an earnest Methodist, said when she was up to tea one evening.

"I did look to see Brother Harper set up a little. It's only natural, you know, and I can't quite believe in perfection. But there he was in class-meeting, not a mite changed, just as friendly and earnest as ever, not a bit lifted up because he had been called to the highest position in the city."

"There's no doubt but he will make a good mayor," rejoined Mr. Underhill. "He's a good, honest man. And all the brothers are capable men, men who are able to pull together. I'm not sure but we'll have to go outside of party lines a little. It ought to broaden a man to be in a big city."

The little girl slipped her hand in Aunt Nancy's.

"Is he your school-teacher?" she ventured timidly.

"School-teacher? Why, no, child!" in surprise.

"You said class——"

"You'll have to be careful, Aunt Nancy. That little girl has an inquiring mind," laughed her father.

"Yes. It's a church class. I belong to the same church as Brother Harper. We're old-fashioned Methodists. We go to this class to tell our religious experiences. You are not old enough to understand that. But we talk over our troubles and trials, and tell of our blessings too, I hope, and then Brother Harper has a good word for us. He comforts us when we are down at the foot of the hill, and he gives us a word of warning if he thinks we are climbing heights we're not quite fitted for. He makes a comforting prayer."

"I should like to see him," said the little girl.

"Well, get your father to bring you down to church some Sunday. Do, Vermilye."

"Any time she likes," said her father.

They talked on, but Hanny went off into a little dreamland of her own. She was not quite clear what a mayor's duty was, only he was a great man. And her idea of his not being set up, as Aunt Nancy had phrased it, was that there was a great handsome chair, something like a throne, that had been arranged for him, and he had come in and taken a common seat. She was to have a good deal of hero-worship later on, and be roused and stirred by Carlyle, but there was never anything finer than the admiration kindled in her heart just then.

After Aunt Nancy went away she crept into her father's lap.

"Aren't you glad Mr. Harper's our mayor?" she asked. "Did everybody vote for him? Do girls—big girls—and women vote?"

"No, dear. Men over twenty-one are the only persons entitled to vote. Steve and Joe and I voted. And it's too bad, but John can't put in his vote for President this fall."

"The mayor governs the city, and the governor, the State. What does the President do?"

Her father explained the most important duties to her, and that a President was elected every four years. That was the highest office in the country.

"And who is going to be our President?" She was getting to be a party woman already.

"Well, it looks as if Henry Clay would. We shall all work for him."

If it only wouldn't come bedtime so soon!

The little girl studied and played with a will. She could skip rope like a little fairy, but it had been quite a task to drive her hoop straight. She was unconsciously inclined to make "the line of beauty." I don't know that it was always graceful, either.

Some new people moved in the block. Just opposite there was a tall thin woman who swept and dusted and scrubbed until Steve said "he was afraid there wouldn't be enough dirt left to bury her with." She wore faded morning-gowns and ragged checked aprons, and had her head tied up with something like a turban, only it was grayish and not pretty. She did not always get dressed up by afternoon. Oh, how desperately clean she was! Even her sidewalk had a shiny look, and as for her door brasses, they outdid the sun.

She had one boy, about twelve perhaps. And his name was John Robert Charles Reed. He was fair, well dressed, and so immaculately clean that Jim said he'd give a dollar, if he could ever get so much money together, just to roll him in the dirt. His mother always gave him his full name. He went to a select school, but when he was starting away in the morning his mother would call two or three times to know if he had all of his books, if he had a clean handkerchief, and if he was sure his shoes were tied, and his clothes brushed.

And one day a curious sort of carriage went by, a chair on wheels, and a man was pushing it while a lady walked beside it. In the chair was a most beautiful girl or child, fair as a lily, with long light curls and the whitest of hands. Hanny watched in amazement, and then went in to tell her mother.   "She looks awful pale and sick," said Hanny.

Josie Dean found out presently who she was. She had come to one of the houses that had the pretty gardens in front.   She had been very ill, and she couldn't walk a step.   And her name was Daisy Jasper.

Such a beautiful name, and not to be able to run and play!   Oh, how pitiful it was!

The little girl had her new spring and summer clothes made.   They were very nice, but somehow she did not feel as proud of them as she had last summer.   Her father took her to Aunt Nancy's church one Sunday.   It was very large and plain and full of people.   Aunt Nancy sat pretty well up, but they found her.   There seemed a good many old men and women, Hanny thought, but the young people were up in the galleries.   She thought the singing was splendid, it really went up with a shout.   People sang in earnest then.

When they came out everybody shook hands so cordially.   Aunt Nancy waited a little while and then beckoned a tall, kindly looking man, who was about as old as her father, though there was something quite different about him.   He shook hands with Sister Archer, and she introduced him.   He said he was very glad to see Mr. Underhill among them, and smiled down at the little girl as he took her small hand. She came home quite delighted that she had shaken hands with the mayor. Then one day Steve took her and Ben down to Cliff Street, through the wonderful printing-house, small in comparison to what it is to-day. They met the mayor again and had a nice chat.

The next great thing to Hanny was Margaret's graduation. She had been studying very hard to pass this year, for she was past eighteen, and she was very successful. Even Joe found time to go down. She wore her pretty white dress, but she had a white sash, and her bodice had been turned in round the neck to make it low, as girls wore them then. Hanny thought her the prettiest girl there. She had an exquisite basket of flowers sent her, beside some lovely bouquets. Annette Beekman graduated too, and all the Beekman family were out in force.

There were some very pretty closing exercises in the little girl's school, and at Houston Street Jim was one of the orators of the day, and distinguished himself in "Marco Bozzaris," one of the great poems of that period.

After that people went hither and thither, and when schools opened and business started up the Presidential campaign was in full blast. There was Clay and Frelinghuysen, Polk and Dallas, and at the last moment the Nationals, a new party, had put up candidates, which was considered bad for the Whigs.   Still they shouted and sang with great gusto:

"Hurrah, hurrah, the country's risin'
For Harry Clay and Frelinghuysen!"

The Democrats, Loco-Focos, as they were often called in derision, were very sure of their victory. So were the Whigs.   The other party did not really expect success.   There were parades of some kind nearly every night.   Even the boys turned out and marched up and down with fife and drum.   There was no end of spirited campaign songs, and rhymes of every degree.   The Loco Foco Club at school used to sing:

"Oh, poor old Harry Clay!
Oh, poor old Harry Clay!
You never can be President
For Polk stands in the way."

Nora Whitney used to rock in the big chair with kitty in her arms, and this was her version:

"Oh, poor old pussy gray!
Oh, poor old pussy gray!
You never can be President
For Polk stands in the way."

This didn't tease the little girl nearly so much, for she knew no matter how sweet and lovely and good a cat might be, it could only aspire to that honor in catland. She did so hate to hear Mr. Clay called old and poor when he was neither. To her he was brave Harry of the West, the hero of battle-fields.

Jim had a rather hard time as well. He thought, with a boy's loyalty, his people must be right. But there was Lily, who, with all *her* people, was a rabid Democrat. He quite made up his mind he wouldn't keep in with her, but the two girls he liked next best had Democratic affiliations also.

Then the Whigs had a grand procession. Perhaps it would have been the part of wisdom to wait until the victory was assured, but the leaders thought it best to arouse enthusiasm to the highest pitch.

Stephen had joined with some friends and hired a window down Broadway. The little girl thought it a very magnificent display. Such bands of strikingly dressed men marching to inspiriting music, their torches flaring about in vivid rays, such carriage loads, such wagons representing different industries, and there was the grand Ship of State, drawn by white horses, four abreast, and gayly attired, in which Henry Clay was to sail successfully into the White House. After that imposing display the little girl had no fear at all. Jim was very toploftical to Miss Lily for several days.

Then came the fatal day. There were no telegraphs to flash the news all over the country before midnight. A small one connected Baltimore and Washington, but long distance was considered chimerical.

So they had to wait and wait. Fortunes varied. At last reliable accounts came, and Polk had stood in the way, or perhaps Mr. Binney, the third candidate, had taken too many votes. Anyhow, the day was lost to brave Harry of the West.

The little girl was bitterly disappointed. She would have liked all the family to tie a black crape around their arms, as Joe had once when he went to a great doctor's funeral. Dele teased her a good deal, and Nora sang:

> "Hurrah, old pussy gray!
> Hurrah, old pussy gray!
> We've got the President and all,
> And Polk has won the day."

Then the Democrats had *their* grand procession. The houses were illuminated, the streets were full of shouting children. Even the boys had a small brigade that marched up and down the street. And oh, grief, Jim marched with them!

"I wouldn't be such a turn-coat!" declared the little girl angrily. "I'm ashamed of you, James Underhill. I shall always feel as if you wasn't my brother any more."

14

"Sho!" returned Jim. "Half the boys turning out have Whig fathers! There wouldn't have been enough for any sort of procession without us. And they promised to cry quits if we would turn out. It don't mean anything but fun!"

She took her trouble to her father. "You are sorry we have been beaten?" she said excitedly.

"Yes, pussy, very sorry. I still think we shall be sorry that Clay isn't President."

"I'm sorry all the time. And when he was so good and splendid, why didn't they put him in?"

"Well, a great many people think Mr. Polk just as splendid."

"Oh, the Democrats!" she commented disdainfully.

"More than half the votes of the country went against our Harry of the West. One side always has to be beaten. It's hard not to belong to the winning side. But we won four years ago, and we did a big lot of crowing, I remember. We shouted ourselves hoarse over the announcement that:

> 'Tippecanoe and Tyler too!
> Were bound to rule the country through.'

We drove our enemies out of sight and erected Log Cabins on their ruins. We had a grand, good time. And then our brave and loyal Tippecanoe died, and some of us have been rather disappointed in Mr. Tyler. We will all hope for the best. There are a good many excellent men on both sides. I guess the country will come out all right."

There really were tears in her eyes.

"You see, my little girl, we must make up our minds to occasional defeat, especially when we go into politics," and there was the shrewd laughing twinkle in his eye. "It is supposed to be better for the country to have the parties about evenly divided. They stand more on their good behavior. And we will hope for better luck next time."

"But *you* couldn't turn round and be a Democrat, could you?" she asked, with a sad entreaty.

"No, dear," he replied gravely.

"I'm glad we have Mayor Harper left. Can the new President put him out?"

"No, my dear."

They kissed each other in half-sorrowful consolation. But alas! next year even Mayor Harper had to go out.

Chapter Twelve.

A REAL PARTY.

THE little girl would have felt a great deal better if Lily Ludlow had not been on the other side. Lily was growing into a very pretty girl. They were wearing pantalets shorter now, and she noticed that Lily wore hers very short. Then aprons were made without bibs or shoulder bands, and had ruffles on the bottom. They were beginning to go farther around, almost like another skirt. Lily had two white ones. She walked up and down the block with a very grand air. Then Miss Chrissy met Margaret at the house of a mutual acquaintance, and invited her very cordially to call on her, and Margaret did the same. Miss Chrissy lost no time, but came card-case in hand, and made herself very agreeable.

"Would you like to go down and call on Jim's girl?" Margaret asked smilingly. Ben always called her that.

"No," replied Hanny, with much dignity. "I don't like her. She called me 'queer' the first time she saw me, and I shouldn't think of calling

Nora queer, no matter how she looked.   If Jim
wants her he may have her, but I *do* hope they
won't live in New York."

The temper was so unusual and so funny that
Margaret let it go without a word.

Everything came back to its normal state.   Mr.
Theodore and her father and Steve remained the
same good friends.   The party transparencies
and emblems were taken down.   It seemed to
her that people had not been as deeply disappointed as they ought to be.   She was very loyal
and faithful in her attachments, and no doubt
you think quite obstinate in her dislikes.

But something else happened that aroused her
interest.   Indeed, there were things happening
all the time.   Miss Jane Underhill, up at Harlem,
was dead and buried, and Margaret had taken a
great interest in Miss Lois.   Cousins had been
going and coming.   Mrs. Retty Finch had a little
son, and Aunt Crete had come down and spent a
week with her sister-in-law.   But this distanced
them all—Steve and Dolly Beekman were going
to be married!   The Beekmans had been staying
up in the country house.   All the girls had been
married there.

There were to be five bridesmaids.   Annette
and Margaret were among them.   Joe was to be
best man and stand with Miss Annette.   Doctor
Hoffman was to stand with Margaret.   There

was a Gessner cousin, a Vandam cousin, and Dolly's dear friend, Miss Stuyvesant. All the bridesmaids were to be gowned in white India mull, and Dolly was to have a white brocaded silk, and a long veil that her grandmother had worn. Hosts and hosts of friends were invited. The house would be big enough to take them all in.

Miss Cynthia made the little girl a lovely dress. First she took her pink merino for a slip. Then there were lace puffs divided by insertion, a short baby waist, short sleeves, pink satin bows on her shoulders, with the long ends floating almost like wings, and a narrow pink ribbon around her waist with a great cluster of bows and ends. She was to have her hair curled all around, and to stand and hold Dolly's bouquet while she was being married. I suppose now we would call her a maid of honor.

No one could say that Mr. Peter Beekman had ever given a mean wedding. He liked Stephen very much, and Dolly could almost have wheedled the moon out of him if she had tried. He teased Annetje by telling her she would have to be an old maid, and stay home to take care of her father and mother.

Grandmother Van Kortlandt came down. She laid off her mourning and wore her black velvet gown with its English crown point lace. Grandmother Underhill came too, but she wore black silk with her pretty fine lace fichu that she had been married in herself. Uncle David, and Aunt Eunice, who wore a gray satin that had been made for her eldest son's wedding. There were Underhill cousins by the score, some Bounetts from New Rochelle, some Vermilyeas, for no one really worth while was to be slighted.

The day had been very fine and sunny. That was a sign the bride would be merry and happy and pleasant to live with. And when the evening fell the great · lawn was all alight with Chinese lanterns that a second cousin in the tea trade had sent Dolly. All the front of the big old house was illuminated. It was square, with a great cupola on top of the second story, and that was in a blaze of light as well.

The Underhills all went up early. Steve was very proud of his mother, who had a pretty changeable silk, lilac and gray, and Joe had given her a collar and cuffs of Honiton lace, to wear at his wedding, he said.

They went in to see the bride when she was dressed. Of course she was beautiful, a pretty girl couldn't look otherwise in her wedding gear. Her veil was put on with orange blossoms and buds, and delicately scented. There was a wreath of the same over one shoulder and across her bosom. Her hair was done in a marvellous fashion, and looked like a golden crown.

How the carriages rolled around and the silks rustled up and down the stairs. There were gay voices and soft laughs, and presently word was sent that the Reverend Dr. De Witt had arrived. Then the immediate family went down. Dolly stooped and kissed Hanny and told her she must not feel a mite afraid. The young men filed out. Stephen took Dolly, just putting her white-gloved hand on his arm as if it was the most precious thing in the world. Joe, smiling and really much handsomer than Stephen, though you couldn't persuade Dolly to any such heresy; then Doctor Hoffman and the others. They seemed to float down the broad stairs. The rooms were very large, but oh, how full they were! The procession walked through the back parlor; Stephen and Dolly and the little girl went straight up to Dr. De Witt, who stood there in his gown and bands, a sweet, reverential old man. The bridesmaids and groomsmen made a half-circle around. There was some soft beautiful music, then a silence. Dr. De Witt began. Dorothea Beekman and Stephen Decatur Underhill promised each other and all the world, to love and cherish, and live together according to God's holy ordinance all their lives.

The little girl held the flowers and listened attentively. She had an idea there must be a great deal more to it and was almost disappointed, for she could not understand that it included all one's life. Dr. De Witt bent over and kissed the bride with solemn reverence. Then Stephen kissed his wife. There was a great deal of kissing afterward, for the new husband kissed the bridesmaids, and the groomsmen had a right to kiss the bride. The mothers had their turn next, and afterward all was laughing confusion.

In the midst of this Philip Hoffman leaned over Margaret.

"I believe you kiss the bridesmaid, too," he said, in a serious fashion, and touched her soft red lips with his. Margaret's face was scarlet, and her breath seemed taken away.

They made a pretty semicircle afterward, and all the guests came up with good wishes. There were so many elegantly dressed people that the little girl was half dazed. I forgot to tell you that she wore her string of gold beads, and they always had a wedding flavor after that.

Presently the procession re-formed and went out to the dining-room, where the table ought to have groaned, if tables ever do. There were some immaculate black waiters who handed one thing after another. The bride cut the cake of both kinds—pound cake like gold, and fruit cake rich enough to give you indigestion. And this wasn't the regular supper.

The bride had to grace the head of every table.

What merry quips and jests there were! People were really gay and happy in those days. No one thought of being bored, they had better manners and kindlier hearts, and enjoyment was a duty as well as pleasure. The musicians were playing softly in the hall. By and by the elder people, who had a long drive to take and who had passed their dancing days long ago, began to say good-by to the bridal couple. In the upper hall a table was piled with white boxes tied with narrow white ribbon, containing a bit of the bride's cake, and a maid stood there handing them to the guests. You put some under your pillow and dreamed on it. If the dream was delightful you might look for it to come true. If it was disagreeable you felt sure you didn't believe in such nonsense.

Then the dancing commenced. There were three large rooms devoted to this. Several of the old men went up-stairs to Mr. Beekman's special room to have a smoke and a good game of cards. But oh, how merry they were down-stairs! They danced with the utmost zest because they really liked to.

The little girl danced, too. Steve took her out first, and she went through a quadrille very prettily. Then it was Joe, and after that Doctor Hoffman begged her mother to let her dance just once with him, and though she was a little afraid, she enjoyed it very much. Dolly introduced her to ever so many people, and said she was her little sister.

"Am I really?" said Hanny, a little confused.

"Why, yes," laughingly. "And one reason why I wanted to marry Stephen was because he had so many brothers. Now they are all mine, five of them."

The little girl studied a moment. "It's queer," she said with a smile, "but I have one more than you. And are you going to have Margaret, too?"

"Yes, and your mother and father. But I am going to be very good and not take them away. Instead, I shall come to see you and have my little piece. I'm quite in love with Benny Frank. And Jim's a regular mischief."

Jim did wish, when he saw all the pretty girls, that he was a grown man and could dance. Ben found some men to talk to, and Mr. Bond, who was in a large jewelry establishment, told him about some rare and precious stones. Old Mrs. Beekman made much of them and said she envied Mrs. Underhill her fine boys.

There was supper about midnight. Cold meats of all kinds, salads, fruits, and ice cream, to say nothing of the wonderful jellies. Tea and coffee, and in an anteroom a great bowl of punch.

After that Mrs. Underhill gathered her old people and her young people, and said they must go home. Joe promised he would look out for George, and Margaret was to stay to the bridesmaid's breakfast the next morning.

Dolly slipped a ring on the little girl's finger.

"That's a sign you are *my* little sister for ever and ever," she said, with a kiss.

"Can't I ever grow big?" asked Hanny seriously.

Mr. Beekman laughed at that.

"You must come *down* and see me," he exclaimed. "We're going to move next week, and we always take Katchina. Come and have a good time with us."

The little girl was asleep in grandmother's arms when they reached home. And the old lady gently took off her pretty clothes and laid her in the bed.

"She's by far the sweetest child you've got, Marg'ret," she said to Mrs. Underhill.

That was not the end of the gayeties. Relatives kept giving parties, and the bridesmaids were asked. Margaret began to feel as if she knew Doctor Hoffman very well. He liked Annette, too. Perhaps he would marry Annette. They had all been saying, "One wedding makes many."

It seemed so queer to be without Stephen. The little girl began to realize that they had somehow given him away, and she did not quite enjoy the thought. He and Dolly came down and stayed two days, and, oh, dear! Dolly was the sweetest and merriest and funniest being alive. She played such jolly tunes, she sang like a bird, and whistled like a bobolink, could play checkers and chess and fox and geese, and she brought Jim a backgammon board.

They talked a good deal about building a house way up-town. Mr. Beekman had offered Dolly a lot. John said it was going to be the finest part of the city. Stephen couldn't really afford to build, but they would like to begin in their own home. Property was getting so high down-town that young people like them, just beginning life, must look around and consider.

"You just g up-town, you can't miss it. And Mayor Harper is going to make a beautiful place of Madison Square. The firm I am with count on that being the fine residential part," declared John.

"We can't afford much grandeur on the start," says Dolly, with charming frankness. "When we get to be middle-aged people, perhaps——"

Mrs. Underhill is very glad to have her so prudent. She will make a fine wife for Stephen.

Stephen took his new wife up to Yonkers to spend a Sunday, so that Aunt Crete would not feel slighted. She seemed quite an old lady. And though it was cold and blustering they walked up on the hill where father's new house was to be built, by and by, a lovely place for the children and grandchildren to cluster around a hearthstone.

Meanwhile Margaret was learning to cook and bake and keep house. She practised her music diligently, she kept on with her French, and she began to read some books Dr. Hoffman had recommended. There were calls to make and invitations to tea, and a Christmas Eve party at one of her schoolmate's. Joe said she must let him know when she wanted an escort, and John was ready to go for her at any time.

It did not seem possible that Christmas *could* come around so soon. Santa Claus was not quite such a real thing this year, so many gifts came to the little girl by the way of the hall door. But she hung up her stocking all the same, and had it full to the topmost round. There was a beautiful set of dishes, and they came with best love from "Dolly and Stephen." There was cloth for a pretty new winter coat, blue-and-black plaid, some squirrel fur to trim it with, and a squirrel muff.

Among the gifts bestowed on Margaret was a box of lovely hothouse flowers. There was only "Merry Christmas" on the card.

Stephen and Dolly came to the Christmas dinner, but they strenuously denied any knowledge of it. Mrs. Underhill had all her family together, and she was a happy woman. In truth she was very proud of Stephen's wife.

Grandmother Van Kortlandt had come to make a visit. Aunt Katrina was down also staying with her son, as the two old ladies found it rather lonesome now that there were no active duties demanding their attention. And Grandmother Underhill had sent the little girl her Irish chain bedquilt, finished and quilted.

The Dean children came in during the afternoon to exchange notes and tell a grand secret. Their aunt and two cousins were coming from Baltimore. Bessy was quite a big girl, fourteen, and Ada was ten. Their mother had said they might have a real party of boys and girls, not just a little tea party and playing with dolls; but real plays with forfeits.

"You know I've just studied with all my might and main, and mother said if I had all my lessons and a good record that I could have the thing I wanted most, if it didn't cost too very much. And I said I wanted a real party."

"It will be just splendid!" declared Hanny.

"And we've been counting up. We have seven cousins to ask. And the girls at school—some of them. I wish we knew some more boys. Oh, do you think Jim would come?"

"I'll ask him if you would like."

"Oh, just coax him. I suppose Benny Frank

will feel that he's too old. But he's so nice. Oh, do you s'pose John Robert Charles' mother would let him come? Oh, there! I promised to call him Charles, but I think Robert's prettier, don't you? And mother said she'd write the invitations on note-paper. And she has some lovely little envelopes."

That did look like a party.

"I think John Robert Charles is real nice," said Hanny timidly. "But I am afraid of his mother."

"Oh, so is he, awful! Yet she isn't real ugly to him, only cross, and so dreadful particular. She makes him go out and wipe his feet twice, and wear that queer long cloak when it rains, and that red woollen tippet. She bought red because it was healthy; he said so. He wanted blue-and-gray. She lets him come over to our house sometimes, and he can sing just splendid. But the boys do make fun of him."

Poor John Robert Charles often thought his life was a burden on account of his name and his mother's great virtue of cleanliness. He was not allowed to play with the boys. Ball and marbles and hopscotch were tabooed. He could walk up and down and do errands, and that with going to school was surely enough. Then she exaggerated him. His white collars were always broader; if trousers were a little wide, his were regular sailor's. She bought his Sunday suit to grow into, so by the second winter it just fitted him. His every-day clothes she made. And oh, she cut his hair!

It is very hard to be the daughter of such a mother, a rigid, uncompromising woman with no sense of the fitness of things, of harmony or beauty, or indulgence in little fancies that are so much to a child. Quite as hard to be the son. Charles had everything needful to keep him warm, in good health, and books for study. When it rained hard he had six cents to ride in the omnibus. And he did have the cleanest house, and the cleanest clothes, and, his mother thought, a very nice time.

Luckily there were no boys this end of the block. They were quite grown up, or little children. But there were enough below to torment the poor lad. In the summer when the charcoal man went by they would sing out:

"John Robert Charles, what did you have for breakfast?" and the refrain would be, "Charcoal."

"What did you have for dinner?" "Charcoal."

"How do you keep so clean?" "Charcoal."

Early this autumn the boy had made a protest. Day after day he said it over to himself until he thought he had sufficient courage.

"Mother, why don't you call me just Charles, as my father does?"

His mother's surprise almost withered him.

15

"Because," when she had found her breath, "John is after *my* father, who was an excellent man, and Robert was for the only brother I ever had, and Charles for your grandfather Reed.   If you grow up as good as any of them you'll have no occasion to find fault with your name."

Yet boys at school called him Bob, and he really did enjoy it.   He went to a very nice, select school where there were only twenty boys.

He had made quite an acquaintance with the Dean girls.   He could play house, and they had such delightful books to read.

"And the party must be some time next week. Thursday, mother thought, would be convenient. I should give the invitations out on Monday," Josie said.   "And, oh, try to coax Jim."

The cousins came.   Hanny saw them on Sunday, and on Monday two little girls went round with a pretty basket and left pale-green missives at the houses of friends.   There was one for Ben also.

"H-m-m," ejaculated Jim.   "A baby party. Will they play with dolls?"

"Oh, Jim! it's going to be a real party with refreshments.   Of course there won't be dolls."

"Washington pie and round hearts."

The tears rushed to Hanny's eyes.

"Never mind about him," said Ben, "I'll go. I'll be your beau.   And see here, Hanny, it's polite to answer an invitation.   Now you write

yours and I'll write mine, and I'll leave them at
the door."

Hanny smiled and went up-stairs for her box of
paper.

Jim gave a whistle and marched off; but when
he saw the pretty Baltimore cousin, he reconsid-
ered, though he was afraid Lily Ludlow would
laugh at him when she heard of it.

Margaret dressed the little girl in her pretty
blue cashmere, and she felt very nice with her
two brothers. Most of the children were ten and
twelve, but the two cousins were older. Bessie
Ritter was quite used to parties and took the lead,
though the children were rather shy at first.

They played "Stage-coach," to begin with.
When the driver, who stood in the middle of the
room, said, "Passengers change for Boston,"
every one had to get up and run to another seat,
and of course there was one who could not find a
seat, and he or she had to be driver. That broke
up the stiffness. Then they had "Cross Questions," where you answered for your neighbor,
and he answered for you, and you were always for-
getting and had to pay a forfeit. Of course they
had to be redeemed.

Charles Reed came, though his mother couldn't
decide until the last moment. He looked very
nice, too. He had to sing a song, and really, he
did it in a manly fashion.

But the little girl thought "Oats, peas, beans,"
the prettiest of all.   It nearly foreshadowed kin-
dergarten songs.   The children stood in a ring
with one in the middle, and as they moved slowly
around, sang:

> "Oats, peas, beans, and barley grows,
>   'Tis you nor I nor nobody knows
>   How oats, peas, beans, and barley grows.
>   Thus the farmer sows his seeds,
>   Thus he stands and takes his ease,
>   Stamps his foot and claps his hands
>   And turns around to view his lands;
>   A-waiting for a partner,
>   A-waiting for a partner,
>   So open the ring and take one in,
>   And kiss her when you get her in."

The children had acted it all, sowing the seed,
taking his ease, stamping, clapping hands, and
whirling around.   They looked very pretty doing
it.   Bessy Ritter had asked Ben to stand in first
and he had obligingly consented.   Of course he
chose her.   Then the children sang again:

> "Now you're married you must obey,
>   You must be true to all you say,
>   You must be kind, you must be good,
>   And keep your wife in kindling-wood.
>   The oats are gathered in the barn,
>   The best produce upon the farm,
>   Gold and silver must be paid,
>   And on the lips a kiss is laid."

The two took their places in the ring, and Jim next sacrificed himself for the evening's good and chose another of Josie's cousins. Then John Robert Charles manfully took his place and chose Josie Dean. So they went on until nearly all had been chosen. Then Mrs. Dean asked them out to have some refreshments. They were all very merry indeed. Mr. Dean sang some amusing songs afterward, and they all joined in several school songs.

"I've just been happy through and through," admitted Charles. "I wish I could give a party. You should come and plan everything," he whispered to Josie.

It was time to go home then. There was a Babel of talk as the little girls were finding their wraps, mingled with pleasant outbursts of laughter. Mr. Dean was to take some of the small people home, and Jim obligingly offered his escort. It had not been so *very* babyish.

Ben wrapped his little sister up "head and ears," and ran home with her. How the stars sparkled!

"It's been just splendid!" she said to her mother. "Don't you think I might have a party some time, and Ben and all of us?"

"Next winter, may be."

Her father looked up from his paper and smiled. She seemed to have grown taller.

What if, some day, he should lose his little girl!

The very next day Mr. Whitney announced that he was going to take the Deans and their cousins and Nora to the Museum. He wanted the little girl to go with them. Delia was visiting in Philadelphia. He promised, laughingly, to have them all home in good season.

Chapter Thirteen.

NEW YEAR'S DAY was gayer than ever. The streets were full of throngs of men in twos up to any number, and carriages went whirling by. There were no ladies out, of course. Margaret had two of her school friends receiving with her, one a beautiful Southern girl whose father was in Congress, and who was staying on in New York, taking what we should call a post-graduate course now, perfecting herself in music and languages. Margaret was a real young lady now. Joe had taken her to several parties, and there had been quite a grand reception at the Beekmans'.

The little girl was dressed in her blue cashmere and a dainty white Swiss apron ornamented with little bows like butterflies. Miss Butler thought she was a charming child. She stood by the window a good deal, delighted with the stir and movement in the street, and she looked very picturesque. Her hair, which was still light, had been curled all round and tied with a blue ribbon instead of a comb. Her mother said " it was foolishness, and they would make the child as vain as a peacock." But I think she was rather proud of the sweet, pretty-mannered little girl.

There was one great diversion for her. About the middle of the afternoon two gentlemen called for her father. One was quite as old, with a handsome white beard and iron-gray hair, very stylishly dressed. He wore a high-standing collar with points, and what was called a neckcloth of black silk with dark-blue brocaded figures running over it, and a handsome brocaded-velvet vest, double-breasted, the fashion of the times, with gilt buttons that looked as if they were set with diamonds, they sparkled so. Over all he had worn a long Spanish circular which he dropped in the hall. The younger man might have been eighteen or twenty.

Ben was waiting on the door. He announced " Mr. Bounett and Mr. Eugene Bounett."

"We hardly expected to find any of the gentlemen at home," began the elder guest. "We are cousins, in a fashion, and my son has met the doctor——"

"Father is at home," said Margaret in the pause. "Hanny, run down-stairs and call him."

"Miss Underhill, I presume," exclaimed the young man. "I have seen your brother quite often of late. And do you know his chum, Phil Hoffman? Doctor, I ought to say," laughingly.

"Oh, yes," and Margaret colored a little.

Then her father came up. These were some of the Bounetts from New Rochelle, originally farther back from England and France in the time of the Huguenot persecution. Mr. Bounett's father had come to New York a young man seventy odd years ago. Mr. Bounett himself had married for his first wife a Miss Vermilye, whose mother had been an Underhill from White Plains. And she was Father Underhill's own cousin. She had been dead more than twenty years, and her children, five living ones, were all married and settled about, and he had five by his second marriage. This was the eldest son.

They talked family quite a while, and Mrs. Underhill was summoned. The young man went out in the back parlor where the table stood in its pretty holiday array, and was introduced to Margaret's friends. They hunted mottoes, which was often quite amusing, ate candies and almonds and bits of cake while the elder people were talking themselves into relationship. Eugene explained that his next younger brother was Louis; then a slip of a girl of fifteen and two young cubs completed the second family. But the older brothers and sisters were just like own folks; indeed he thought one sister, Mrs. French, was one of the most charming women he knew, only she did live in the wilds of Williamsburg. Francesca was married in the Livingston family and lived up in Manhattanville. How any one could bear to be out of the city—that meant below Tenth Street—he couldn't see!

"Is that little fairy your sister?" he asked. "Isn't she lovely!"

Margaret smiled. She thought Mr. Eugene very flattering. Then the others came out, and Mr. Bounett took a cup of black coffee and a very dainty sandwich. He left sweets to the young people. And now that they had broken the ice, he hoped the Underhills would be social. They, the Bounetts, lived over in Hammersley Street, which was really a continuation of Houston. And they might like to see grandfather, who was in his ninetieth year and still kept to his old French ways and fashions.

Miss Butler was very enthusiastic about the callers. "Why, you are quite French," she said, "only *they* show it in their looks."

"We have had so much English admixture," and Father Underhill laughed with a mellow sound. "But I've heard that my great grandmother was a useless fine lady when they came to this country, and had never dressed herself or brushed her hair, and had to have a lady's maid until she died. She never learned to speak English, or only a few words, but she could play beautifully on a harp and recite the French poets so well that people came from a distance to see her. But her daughters had a great many other things to learn, and were very smart women. My own grandmother could spin on the big wheel and the little wheel equal to any girl when she was seventy years old."

"How delightfully romantic!" cried Miss Butler.

"There's a big wheel in the garret at Yonkers, and a little wheel, and a funny reel," said Hanny, who was sitting on Miss Butler's lap, "and we used to play the reel was a mill, and make believe we ground corn."

"I've done many a day's spinning!" exclaimed Mrs. Underhill. "The Hunters raised no end of flax, and we spun the thread for our bed and table linen. One of our neighbors had a loom and did weaving. Cotton goods were so high we were glad to keep to linen. Ah, well, the world's changed a deal since my young days."

They were disturbed by an influx of guests. The fashionable young men came late in the afternoon and evening. The gilt candelabrum on the mantel was lighted up, and it had so many branches and prisms it was quite brilliant. Then there were sconces at the side of the wall to light up corners, and these have come around again, since people realize what a soft, suggestive light candles give. The Underhills had no gas in their house, it was esteemed one of the luxuries. Even the outskirts of the city streets were still lighted with oil.

Steve came in and teased the girls and begged them to eat philopenas with him. He seemed to find so many. And he said the best wish he could give them for 1845 was that they might all find a good husband, as good as he was making, and if they didn't like to take his word they were at liberty to go and ask his wife.

Quite in the evening the two doctors called, and Joe announced that he was going to have a Christian supper and a cup of tea, so that he would be able to attend to business to-morrow, as half the city would be ill from eating all manner of sweet stuff. After he had chaffed the girls a while he took Doctor Hoffman down-stairs, "out of the crowd," he said, and Mrs. Underhill gave them a cup of delicious tea. She and Martha were kept quite busy with washing dishes and making tea and coffee. Joe had requested last year that they should not offer wine to the callers.

He went out in the kitchen to have a talk with his mother about the Bounetts. Dr. Hoffman played with his spoon and would not have another cup of tea. Mr. Underhill wondered why he did not go up-stairs and have a good time with the girls. They could hear the merry laughter.

"Mr. Underhill——" he began presently.

"Eh—what?" said that gentleman, rather amazed at the pause.

Doctor Hoffman cleared his throat. There was nothing at all in it, the trouble was a sort of bounding pulsation that interfered with his breath, and flushed his face.

"Mr. Underhill, I have a great favor to ask." He rose and came near so that he could lower his voice. "I—I admire your daughter extremely. I should choose her out of all the world if I could——"

Father Underhill glanced up in consternation. He wanted to stop the young man from uttering another word, but before he could collect his scattered wits, the young man had said it all.

"I want permission to visit her, to see—if she cannot like me well enough to some day take me for a husband. I have really fallen in love with her. Joe will tell you all you want to know about me. I'm steady, thank Heaven, and have a start in the world beside my profession. I wanted you to know what my intentions were, and to give me the opportunity of winning her——"

"I never once thought——" The father was confused, and the lover now self-possessed.

"No, I suppose not. Of course, we are both young and do not need to be in a hurry. I wanted the privilege of visiting her."

"Yes, yes," in embarrassed surprise. "I mean——"

"Thank you," said the lover, grasping his hand. "I hope to win your respect and approval. Joe and I are like brothers already. I admire you all so much."

Hanny came flying in with pink cheeks and eager eyes.

"Where is Joe? Margaret wants him—she said I must ask them if they wouldn't please to like to dance a quadrille, and come up-stairs when they had finished their tea."

Joe was sitting astride a chair, tilting it up and down and talking to his mother.

"Oh, yes, your royal highness. Phil, if you have finished your tea——" and Joe laughed, inwardly knowing some other business had been concluded as well.

They had a delightful quadrille. Then Miss Butler sang a fascinating song—"The Mocking-Bird." Two of the gentlemen sang several of the popular airs of the day, and the party broke up. The little girl had gone to bed some time before, though she declared she wasn't a bit tired, and her eyes shone like stars.

The very next day it snowed, so the ladies could have no day at all. There was sleigh-riding and merry-making of all sorts. One day Dr. Hoffman came and took Margaret and her little sister out in a dainty cutter. Then he used to drop in St. Thomas' Church and walk home with her evenings. Father Underhill felt quite guilty in not forewarning his wife of the conspiracy, but one evening she mistrusted.

"Margaret is altogether too young to keep company," she declared in an authoritative way.

"Margaret is nineteen," said her father. "And you were only twenty when I married you."

"That's too young."

"Seems to me we were far from miserable. As I remember it was a very happy year."

"Don't be silly, 'Milyer. And you're so soft about the children. You haven't a bit of sense about them."

In her heart she knew she would not give up one year of her married life for anything the world could offer.

"Margaret knows no more about housekeeping than a cat," she continued.

"Well, there's time for her to learn. And perhaps she will not really like the young man."

"She likes him already. 'Milyer, you're blind as a bat."

"Well, if they like each other—it's the way of the world. It's been going on since Adam."

"It's simply ridiculous to have Margaret perking herself up for beaux."

"I guess you'll have to let the matter go.

Hoffman is well connected and a nice young fellow."

Yes, she had to let the matter go on. She was unnecessarily sharp with Margaret and pretended not to see; she was extremely ceremonious with the young man at first. She didn't mean to have him coming to tea on Sunday evenings, a fashion that still lingered. But Dolly was very good to the young lovers, and they had so many mutual friends. Then Margaret was quite shy, she hardly knew what to make of the attentions that were so reverent and sweet. She couldn't have discussed them with a single human being.

Mr. and Mrs. Underhill had called on their new cousins in Hammersley Street. And on Washington's Birthday he took the little girl and Ben over.

The street was still considered in the quality part of the town. The row was quite imposing, the stoops being high, the houses three stories and a half, with short windows just below the roof. The railing of the stoop was very ornate, the work around the front door and the fanlight at the top being of the old-fashioned decorative sort. They were ushered into the parlor by a young colored lad.

It was a very splendid room, the little girl thought, with a high, frescoed ceiling and a heavy cornice of flowers and leaves. The side walls were a light gray, but they were nearly covered with pictures. The curtains were a dull blue and what we should call old gold, and swept the floor. There was a mirror from floor to ceiling with an extremely ornamental frame, the top forming a curtain cornice over the windows. At the end of the room was the same kind of cornice and curtains, but no glass. The carpet had a great medallion in the center and all kinds of arabesques and scrolls and flowers about it. The furniture was rather odd, divans, chairs, ottomans and queer-looking tables, and the little girl came to know afterward that two or three pieces had been in the royal palace of Versailles.

A very sweet, dark-eyed, dark-haired woman came through the curtain.

. "I am Mrs. French," she said, in a soft tone, "and I am very glad to see you. Is this the little girl of whom I have heard so much? Be seated, please. Father is out, and he will be very sorry to miss you."

She dropped on an ottoman and drew the little girl toward her.

"Let me take off your hat and coat. There are some children who will be glad to see you. Mother will be up in a few moments. Do you know that I have been seriously considering a visit to you? Father and Eugene have talked so much about you."

16

"And your grandfather——"

"He is very well to-day.   I was in his room read-ing to him.   He will be pleased you have come."

Mrs. Bounett came in with her daughter, a rather tall, lanky girl of fifteen, very dark, and with a great mop of black hair that was tied at the back without being braided.   She looked as if she had outgrown her dress.

This was Miss Luella.   After a moment she came over to Ben, and asked him where he went to school, and if he had any pets.   They had a squirrel and some guinea-pigs and a parrot that could talk everything.   Didn't he want to see them?

Hanny looked eager as well.

"Can I take her?" asked Lu.

"The boys are down-stairs.   Don't be rough."

It was rather dark.   Lu caught Hanny in her arms and whisked her down to the dining-room. The boys were thirteen and eleven, and were playing checkers on the large dining-table. Every-thing looked so immensely big to Hanny.   The shelves of the sideboard were full of glass and silver and queer old blue china; the chairs had great high backs and were leather-covered.

"We want to see the guinea-pigs," said Lu. "But I'll take her out to see the parrots first."

There was a fat colored woman in the kitchen who suggested Aunt Mary.   They went through to a little room under the great back porch, made in the end of the area.

There were two parrots and a beautiful white paroquet. Polly was sulky. "Mind your business!" was all she would say. Dan soon began to be quite sociable, declaring "He was glad to see them, and would like to have some grapes."

"You shut up!" screamed Polly.

"I'll talk as much as I like."

"No, you won't.   I'll come and choke you."

"Do if you dare!"

Then they shrieked at each other with the vigor of fighting cats. Polly rustled around her cage as if she would be out the next moment. Hanny clung to Lu and was pale with fright.

"They can't get out. They'd tear each other to pieces when they're mad, and sometimes they're sweet as honey. Pa's going to sell one of them, but we can't decide which must go. Polly talks a lot when she's in the mood. I don't know what's ruffled her so. Polly, my pretty Polly, sing for me, and the first time I go out I'll buy you some candy with lots of peanuts in it—lots —of—peanuts," lingeringly.

"Polly sing! Oh, ho! ho! Polly can't sing no more'n a crow," squeaked out Dan.

"Can too, can too!"

"Pretty Polly! Polly want a cracker. Polly sing for her dear Dan. Oh, boo hoo!"

Polly screamed in a tearing rage.

The young colored lad entered. "Miss Lu, de birds disturb yer gramper. Lemme take Polly. You bad bird, you're goin' in a dungeon."

With that he whisked Polly off. Dan laughed gleefully. The boys came, and Dan went through his stock accomplishments, much to their delight.

"But Polly's a sight the funniest," declared Lu. "Only she has such a horrid temper and it just grows worse. We had a monkey and that got to be so awful bad. Now let's go and see the guinea-pigs."

They were up on the top floor. "We had them down cellar," explained one of the boys, "but some of them died. 'Gene said 'twas too dark and damp."

The children trudged up-stairs. There was a pen in a small room which seemed a receptacle for all sorts of broken toys. Ah, how pretty the little things were; black-and-yellow-spotted, bright-eyed, and soft-coated, with a tiny sort of squeak, and tame enough to be caught. Lu offered one to Hanny, but she drew back in half fear. Then they brought in the squirrel, and he was a handsome fellow with beady eyes and a bushy tail, and when they let him out he ran up on any one's shoulder.

"If it was only warm, we'd go out and have a

swing.   Oh, don't you want a ride?   Here's our horse.   We don't care much for it now, though in summer we have it out-of-doors."

Hanny was speechless with amaze.   She had never seen so large a one in the stores.   He was covered with real hair, had a splendid mane and tail and beautiful eyes.   His silver-mounted red trappings were extremely gorgeous.

"He's magnificent!" declared Ben.   "Hanny, just try him.   Don't be a little 'fraid-cat!" as she hung back.

"See here!" Lu sprang on and took an inspiriting gallop.   The horse worked with springs and seemed fairly alive.   Afterward Hanny ventured and found it exhilarating.   Oh, if she could only have one!

"I suppose it cost a good deal," she questioned timidly.

Jeffrey laughed.   "'Gene picked it up at an auction where people were being sold out, and he got it for a song," he said.   "But we've outgrown it. I'd like a real pony.   I wish pa'd keep a horse."

"We have two," said the little girl.

"Pshaw now! you're joking."

"No," rejoined Ben quietly.   "We brought them down from the farm.   Father and Steve needed them."

"Do you own a farm, too?" Jeffrey asked in amaze.   "Why, you must be all-fired rich!"

"No, we're not so very rich," said Ben soberly. "Our house in First Street isn't nearly as big and as handsome as this. But we did have a big one in the country. Uncle lives there now, and we have a hundred acres of land."

"Jiminy!" ejaculated the young boy.

"Chillen! Chillen, please bring de company down to your gramper."

"Oh, I'm 'fraid you're going away," said Lu. "You're awful sweet! I just wish I had a little sister. I wish you'd come and stay a week. But I s'pose you'd feel like a cat in a strange garret. I'd be real good to you, though."

She caught Hanny in her arms and fairly ran down-stairs with her.

"You're the littlest mite of a thing! Why, you're never nine years old! You're just like a doll!"

"Oh, please let me walk," entreated Hanny.

Their mother stood in the lower hall.

"You boys go down-stairs or in the parlor. So many children confuse grandpa. Lu, you look too utterly harum-scarum. Do go and brush your hair."

Between the parlor and the back room was a space made into a library on one side and some closets on the other. Sliding doors shut this from the back room. This was large, with a splendid, high-post bedstead that had yellow silk curtains around it, a velvet sofa, and over by the window some arm-chairs and a table. And out of one chair rose a curious little old man, who seemed somehow to have shrunken up, and yet he was a gentleman from head to foot. His hair was long and curled at the ends, but it looked like floss silk. His eyes were dark and bright, his face was wrinkled, and his beard thin. Hanny thought of the old man at the Bowling Green who had been in the Bastile. His velvet coat, very much cut away, was faced with plum-colored satin, his long waistcoat was of flowered damask, his knee-breeches were fasened with silver buckles, and his slippers had much larger ones. There really were some diamonds in them. His shirt frill was crimped in the most beautiful manner, and the diamond pin sparkled with every turn.

"This is grandpa," said Mrs. French. "We are all very proud of him that he has kept his faculties, and we want him to live an even hundred years."

The old man smiled and shook his head slowly. He took Hanny's hand, and his was as soft as a baby's. He said he was very glad to see them both; he and their father had been talking over old times and relationships.

His voice had a pretty foreign sound. It was a soft, trained voice, but the accent was discernible.

"And you were here through the War of the

Revolution," said Ben, who had been counting back.

"Yes. My father had just died and left nine children. I was the oldest, and there were two girls. So I couldn't be spared to go. The British so soon took possession of New York. But in 1812 I was free to fight for liberty and the country of my adoption. We were never molested nor badly treated, but of course we could give no aid to our countrymen. It was a long, weary struggle. No one supposed at first the rebels could conquer. And all that is seventy years ago, seventy years."

He leaned back and looked weary.

"You must come down some Saturday morning when he feels fresh and he will tell you all about it," said Mrs. French. "His memory is excellent, but he does get fatigued."

"I wonder if you ever saw the statue of King George that was in Bowling Green," Hanny asked, with a little hesitation. "They made bullets of it."

"Ah, you know that much?" He smiled and leaned over on the arm of the chair. "Yes, my child. The soldiers met to hear the Declaration of Independence read for the first time. Washington was on horseback with his aides around him. The applause was like a mighty shout from one throat. Then they rushed to the City Hall and tore the picture of the king from its frame, and then they dragged the statue through the streets. Yes, its final end was bullets for the rebels, as they were called. As my daughter says, come and see me again, and I will tell you all you want to hear. You are a pretty little girl," and he pressed Hanny's hand caressingly.

Then they said good-by to him and went back to the parlor.

"He always dresses up on holidays," said Mrs. French smilingly, "though he continues to wear the old-fashioned costume. He has had a number of calls to-day. People are still interested in the old times. And believe me, I shall take a great deal of pleasure in continuing the acquaintance. You may expect me very soon."

Luella kissed Hanny with frantic fervor and begged her to come again. She was so used to boys, she cared nothing about Ben.

The little girl had so much to tell Jim, who had been skating. The quarrelling parrots, the beautiful house, the queer little guinea-pigs, and the splendid hobby-horse that they didn't seem to care a bit about. "And Lu is a good deal like Dele, only not so nice or so funny, and her hair is awful black. She ran down-stairs with me in her arms and I was 'most frightened to death. I don't believe I would want to be her little sister. And the grandpa is like a picture of the old French

people.   And to think that he doesn't read Eng‧
lish very well and always uses his French Bible.
There were so many foreign people in New York
at that time, I s'pose they couldn't all talk English."

"And they had preaching in Dutch after 1800
in the Middle Dutch Church," said Jim.   "And
even after the sermons were in English the singing had to be in Dutch.   Aunt Nancy said the
place used to be crowded just to hear the people
sing."

"It's queer how they could understand each
other.   Do you suppose the children had to learn
every language?"

Jim gave a great laugh at that.

Chapter Fourteen.

JOHN ROBERT CHARLES.

THE new President was inaugurated on the fourth of March. The little girl sighed to think how many Democratic people there were on her block. They put out flags and bunting, and illuminated in the evening. They had tremendous bonfires, and all the boys waived personal feeling and danced and whooped like wild Indians. No healthy, well-conditioned boy could resist the fragrance of a tar barrel.

Miss Lily Ludlow wore a red, white, and blue rosette with a tiny portrait of Mr. Polk in the centre. The public-school girls often walked up First Avenue and met Mrs. Craven's little girls going home. Lily used to stare at Hanny in an insolent manner. She and her sister could not forgive the fact that Miss Margaret had not called.

And now the talk was that Miss Margaret Underhill had a beau, a handsome young doctor.

"They do think they're awful grand," said Lily to some of her mates. "But they take up with that Dele Whitney, who sometimes does the washing on Saturdays.   It's a fact, girls; and the sister works in an artificial-flower place down in Division Street.   And the Underhills think they're good enough to company with."

But the fact remained that the Underhills kept a carriage, and that Mr. Stephen had married in the Beekman family, and Chris had heard that Dr. Hoffman was considered a great catch.   She was almost twenty and had never kept company yet.   Young men called at the house, to be sure, and attended her home from parties, but the most desirable ones seemed unattainable.

Her mother fretted a little that she didn't get to doing something.   Here were girls earning five or six dollars a week, and her father's wages were so small it was a pinch all the time.

"I'm sure I make all our dresses and sew for father, and do lots of housework," replied Chris, half-crying.

There were people even then who considered it more genteel not to work out of the house.   And since servants were not generally kept, a daughter's assistance was needed in the household.

And to crown the little girl's troubles her dear mayor was retired to private life and a Democrat ruled in his stead.

But there were the new discoveries to talk about, and the reduction of postage due to the old administration. Now you could send a letter three hundred miles for five cents. Hanny wrote several times a year to her grandmother Under-hill. so this interested her. At the end of the century we are clamoring for penny postage, and our delivery is free. Then they had to pay the carrier.

The electro-magnetic telegraph was coming in for its share of attention. Scientific people were dropping into the old University of New York, where Mr. Morse was working it. The city had been connected with Washington. There were people who believed "there was a humbugging fellow at both ends," and that the scheme couldn't be made to work. It was cumbersome compared to modern methods. And Professor John W. Draper took the first daguerreotype from the roof of that famous building. That was the greatest wonder of the day. What was more remarkable, a picture or portrait could be copied in a few moments. Then there was a hint of war with Mexico, and the Oregon question was looming up with its cabalistic figures of "54, 40, or fight." Indeed, it seemed as if war was in the air.

Children too had trials, especially John Robert Charles. He had been allowed to go to Allen Street Sunday-school with the Dean children, and he went over on Saturday afternoon to study the lesson. Hanny used to come in, and occasionally they had a little tea. They played in the yard and the wide back area. The boys did tease him; the target was too good to miss. Hanny sympathized with him, for he was so nice and pleasant. They couldn't decide just what name to call him. Bob did well enough for the boys, but it was a little too rough for girls.

His mother still made him put on a long, checked pinafore to come to meals. His father used a white napkin. And he did wipe dishes for her, and help with the vegetables on Saturday. He could spread up a bed as neatly as a girl, but he kept these accomplishments to himself.

There was another excitement among the small people. Mr. Bradbury, who for years was destined to be the children's delight, was teaching singing classes and giving concerts with his best pupils. Mrs. Dean decided to let the girls go to the four o'clock class. Hanny would join them. They could study the Sunday lesson before or afterward.

"If I only could go," sighed the boy. The tears came into his eyes.

"And you can sing just lovely!" declared Tudie.

Josie stood up with a warmly flushing face.

"I do believe I'd raise an insurrection. It isn't as if you wanted to do anything wicked, like swearing or stealing. And my father said God gave beautiful voices to people to sing with."

"But if I asked mother she wouldn't let me go. And—I couldn't run away. You see that would be just for once. Perhaps then I wouldn't be let to come over here, afterward," the boy replied sadly.

"Couldn't you coax?" asked Hanny.

"I could just ask, and she'd say no."

Hanny felt so sorry for him. He was very fair and had pretty, but rather timid eyes.

"You can't raise an insurrection when you know for certain it'll be put down the next moment," the boy added.

"Well," Josie drew a long breath and studied.

"I'd ask my father," said Hanny.

"And he'd say, 'Ask your mother; it's as she says.' Most everything *is* as mother says."

"Then I'd put my arms around his neck and coax. I'd tell him I wanted to be like other boys. They think it's queer——"

Hanny stopped, very red in the face.

"Oh, you needn't mind. I know they laugh at me and make fun of me. But mother's so nice and clean, only I wish she'd dress up as your mothers do, and take a walk sometimes and go to church. And she cooks such splendid things and makes puddings and pies, and she lets me sit and read when I'm done my lessons. I have all the Rollo books, and father has Sir Walter Scott, that he's letting me read now. It's only that mother thinks I'll get into bad things and meet bad boys and get my clothes soiled. Oh, sometimes I'm so tired of being nice! Only you wouldn't want me to come over here if I wasn't."

That was very true.

"But there are a great many nice boys. Ben's just lovely, only he is growing up so fast," said the little girl, with a sigh. "And though Jim teases, he is real good and jolly. He doesn't keep his hands clean, and mother scolds him a little for that."

They could not decide about the insurrection. Presently it was time for Charles to go home. He was always on the mark lest he should not be allowed the indulgence next time. The poor boy had been moulded into the straight line of duty.

The girls went out to swing. They could all three sit in at once. And they often talked all at once.

"It's just awful mean!"

"If we only could do something!"

"Girls!" Josie put her foot so firmly on the ground it almost tipped them out. "Girls, let *us* see Mr. Reed and ask him."

They all looked at each other with large eyes.

"It couldn't be wrong," began Josie; "because I've asked *your* father, Hanny, to let you come up to our stoop."

"No, it couldn't be," said the chorus in firm approval.

"Then let's do it. He always comes up First Avenue about half-past five on Saturdays. Now if we were to walk down——"

"Splendid!" ejaculated Tudie.

"And I'll ask mother if we can't go out for a little walk."

"We mustn't wait too late."

Tudie ran in to look at the kitchen clock. It was twenty minutes past five.

"I'll go and ask."

"Why, isn't your own sidewalk good enough?" was Mrs. Dean's inquiry. "Well—yes, you may do an errand for me down at the store. I want a pound of butter crackers. Don't go off the block."

They put on their bonnets. Hanny's was a pretty shirred and ruffled blue lawn. They twined their arms around each other's waists, with Hanny in the middle and walked slowly down to the store. Tudie kept watch while her sister was making the purchase. Then they walked up, then down, looking on the other side lest they should not see him. Up and down again—up with very slow steps. What if they *should* miss him!

They turned. "Hillo!" cried a familiar voice.

"Oh, Mr. Reed!" They blocked his way in a

manner that amused him. He looked from one to the other, and smiled at the eager faces.

"Oh, Mr. Reed—we wanted to—to——"

"To ask you——" prompted Tudie.

Josie's face was very red. It was different asking about a boy. She had not thought of that.

"We want Charles to go to singing-school with us next Saturday. Mr. Bradbury said we might ask all the *nice* children we knew."

Hanny had crossed the Rubicon in a very lady-like manner.

Mr. Reed laughed pleasantly, but they knew he was not making fun of them.

"Why, yes; I haven't any objection. It will be as his mother says."

They all looked blank, disappointed.

"If *you* would say it," pleaded Josie. "Then we should be sure."

"Well, I will say it. He shall go next Saturday. He has a nice voice, and there is no reason why he should not be singing with the rest of you."

"Oh, thank you a thousand times."

"It's hardly worth that." Mr. Reed was a little nettled. Had Charles put them up to this?

They were at the corner and turned down their side of the street, nodding gayly.

"You see it was just as easy as nothing," remarked Josie complacently.

Mr. Reed entered his own area, wiped his feet, and hung up his hat. He went out in the back area and washed his hands. Every other day a clean towel was put on the roller. The house was immaculate. The supper-table was set. Mrs. Reed was finishing a block of patchwork, catch-up work, when she had to wait two minutes. She went out in the hall taking the last stitch, and called up the stairway:

"John Robert.Charles!"

Meals were generally very quiet. Charles had been trained not to speak unless he was spoken to. Once or twice his father looked at him. A pinafore was rather ridiculous on such a big boy. How very large his white collar was! His hair looked too sleek. He was a regular Miss Nancy.

He helped his mother take out the dishes and wiped them for her.

"Come out on the stoop, Charles," said his father afterward, as he picked up his paper.

Mrs. Reed wondered if Charles had committed some overt act that she knew nothing about. *Could* anything elude her sharp eyes?

Mr. Reed pretended to be busy with his paper, but he was thinking of his son. In his early years the child had been a bone of contention. His mother always knew just what to do with him, just what was proper, and would brook no interference. What with her cleanliness, her inordinate love of regularity and order, she had become a domestic tyrant. He had yielded because he loved peace. There was a good deal of comfort in his house. He went out two or three evenings in the week, to the lodge, to his whist club, and occasionally to call on a friend. Mrs. Reed never had any time to waste on such trifling matters. He had not thought much about his boy except to place him in a good school.

"Charles, couldn't you have asked me about the singing-school?" he said rather sharply.

"About—the singing-school?" Charles was dazed.

"Yes. It wasn't very manly to set a lot of little girls asking a favor for you. I'm ashamed of you!"

"Oh, father—who asked? We were talking of it over to Josie Dean's. I knew mother wouldn't let me go. I—I said so." Charles' fair face was very red.

"You put them up to ask!"

"No, I didn't. They never said a word about it. Why, I wouldn't have asked them to do it."

Mr. Reed looked suspiciously at his son.

"You don't care to go?"

"Yes, I do, very much." The boy's voice was tremulous.

"Why couldn't *you* ask me?"

"Because you would leave it to mother, and she would say it was not worth while."

"Was that what you told them?" Mr. Reed was truly mortified. No man likes to be considered without power in his own household.

"I—I think it was," hesitated the boy. The girls had started an insurrection, sure enough. Well, the poor lad had no chance before. It was not a hope swept away, there had been no hope. But now he gave up.

"Don't be a fool nor a coward," exclaimed his father gruffly. "Here, get your hat and go straight over to the Deans'. Tell them your *father* says you can go to singing-school next Saturday afternoon, that he will be very glad to have you go. And next time you want anything ask me."

If the boy had only dared clasp his father's hand and thank him, but he had been repressed and snipped off and kept in leading-strings too long to dare a spontaneous impulse. So he walked over as if he had been following some imaginary chalk line. The Deans were all up in the back parlor. He did his errand and came back at once, before Josie and Tudie had recovered from their surprise.

Nothing else happened. Mrs. Reed went out presently to do the Saturday-night marketing.

She preferred to go alone. She could make better bargains. When she returned Mr. Reed lighted his cigar and took a stroll around the block. There was no smoking in the house, hardly in the back yard.

Saturday noon Mrs. Reed said to her son:

" You are to go to singing-school this afternoon. If I hear of your loitering with any bad boys, or misbehaving in any way, that will end it."

The poor lad had not felt sure for a moment. Oh, how delightful it was! though a boy nudged him and said, " Sissy, does your mother know you're out," and two or three others called him " Anna Maria Jemima Reed."

However, as Mr. Bradbury was trying voices by each row, the sweetness of Charles' struck him, and he asked him to remain when the others were dismissed. One other boy and several girls were in this favored class, and next week they had the seats of honor.

The next great thing for all the children was the May walk. All the Sunday-schools joined in a grand procession and marched down Broadway to Castle Garden. There was a standard-bearer with a large banner, and several smaller ones in every school. The teachers were with the classes, the parents and friends were to be at the Garden. Most of the little girls had their new white dresses, the boys their summer suits and caps.

For May was May then, all but Quaker week, when it was sure to rain.

A pretty sight it was indeed. The bright, happy faces, the white-robed throng, and almost every girl had her hair curled for the occasion. There was a feeling among some of the older people that curls were vain and sinful, but they forgave them this day.

The audience was ranged around the outside. The little people marched in, and up the broad aisle, singing:

> "We come, we come, with loud acclaim,
> To sing the praise of Jesus' name;
> And make the vaulted temple ring
> With loud hosannas to our King."

The platform—they called it that on such occasions—was full of clergymen and speakers for the festival. Some of the older eminent divines, some who were to be eminent later on, some of the high dignitaries of the city; and they could hardly fail to be inspired at the sight of the sweet, happy, youthful faces.

And how they sang! The most popular thing of that day was:

> "There is a happy land—
> Far, far away."

It was fresh then and had not been parodied to

everything. No doubt it would have shocked some of the sticklers if they had known that the words and tune were, in a measure, adapted from a pretty opera song:

> "I have come from a happy land,
> Where care is unknown;
> And first in a joyous band
> I'll make thee mine own."

There were many other hymns that appealed to the hearts of the children of those days. "I Think When I Read that Sweet Story of Old," and "Jesus Loves Me, this I Know."

There were speeches, short and to the point, some with a glint of humor in them, and then hymns again. Perhaps we have done better since, but the grand enthusiasm of that time has not been reached in later reunions.

It seemed to the little girl that this really was the crowning glory of her life. She could not have guessed under what circumstances she was to recall it, indeed this day had no future to her. At first her mother had insisted the walk was too long, but Steve said he and Dolly would bring her home in the carriage. Margaret promised to get her new white dress done, and it was to be tucked almost up to the waist. Her mother gave in at last, and went down to see the children, being delighted herself.

Aunt Eunice was there, too. She had come to the city for the long-talked-of visit, and next week was to be Quaker Meeting. She had not been to one in years. Indeed, she could hardly call herself a Friend. She had married out of the faith and said *you* oftener than *thee*, but she kept to the pretty, soft gray attire and plain bonnet.

Hanny and the Deans and Nora thought her "just lovely." Hanny went to the Friends' Meeting-House with her on Sunday afternoon, down in Hester Street. It was severely plain, and the men sat on one side, the women on the other, while a few seats were reserved for any of the world's people that might stray in. The men looked odd, Hanny thought, with their long hair just "banged" across the forehead and falling over their collars. The coats were queer, too, and they kept on their hats, which shocked her a little at first.

Oh, how still it was! Hanny waited and waited for the minister, but she could not see any pulpit. There was no singing, only that solemn silence. If she had been a little Quaker girl she would have been thinking of her sins, and making new resolves. Instead she watched the faces. Some were very sweet; many old and wrinkled.

Suddenly an old gentleman arose and talked a few moments. When he sat down a tall woman laid off her hat and, standing up, began to speak in a more vigorous manner than the brother.

She seemed almost scolding, Hanny thought. After her, another silence, then a lovely old lady with a soft voice told of the blessings she had found and the peace they ought all to seek.

Everybody rose and went out quietly.

"It doesn't seem a real church, Aunt Eunice," said Hanny. "And there was no minister."

"Oh, child, it isn't! It's just a meeting. It did not seem very spiritual to-day."

"If they only had some singing."

Aunt Eunice smiled, but made no reply. Hanny decided she did not want to be a Friend.

They went down to visit Aunt Nancy and Aunt Patience, and Margaret took Aunt Eunice up to see Miss Lois Underhill, who had gone on living alone. She said she could never take root in any other place, and perhaps it was true. Her kindly German neighbor looked after her, but she was very grateful for a visit.

Steve was building his new house and they thought to get in it by the fall. It was on the plot Dolly's father had given her at Twentieth Street near Fifth Avenue. The Coventry Waddells, who were really the leaders of fashionable society, were erecting a very handsome and picturesque mansion on Murray Hill, between Fifth and Sixth avenues on Thirty-eighth Street. The grounds took the whole block. There were towers and gables and oriels, and a large conservatory that was to contain all manner of rare plants, native as well as foreign. But everybody thought it quite out in the country.

Steve laughingly said they would have fine neighbors. The Waddells were noted for their delightful entertaining.

They took Aunt Eunice a walk down Broadway to show her the sights. The "dollar side" had become the accepted promenade. Already there were some quite notable people who were pointed out to visitors. You could see Mr. N. P. Willis, who was then at the zenith of his fame. When a Sunday-school entertainment wanted to give something particularly fine, the best speaker recited his poem, "The Leper," which was considered very striking. There was Lewis Gaylord Clark, of *The Knickerbocker*, who wrote charming letters, and these two were admitted to be very handsome men. There was George P. Morris, whose songs were sung everywhere, and not a few literary ladies. There was the Broadway swell in patent-leather boots and trousers strapped tightly down, in the style the boys irreverently called pegtops. He had a high-standing collar, a fancy tie, a light silk waistcoat with a heavy watch-chain and seal, a coat with large, loose sleeves, a high hat, and carried his cane under his arm, while, as one of the writers of the day said, "he ambled along daintily."

Then you might meet the Hammersley carriage with its footman and livery that had made quite a talk. Young and handsome Mrs. Little, whose marriage to an old man had been the gossip of the season, sat in elegant state with her coachman in dark blue. Now one hardly notes the handsome equipages, or the livery either.

But the "Bowery boy" was as great a feature of the time as the Broadway swell. He, too, wore a silk hat, and it generally had a three-inch mourning band. His hair was worn in long, well-oiled locks in front, combed up with a peculiar twist. He wore a broad collar turned over, and a sailor tie, a flashy vest with a large amount of seal and chain, and wide trousers turned up. His coat he carried on his arm when the weather permitted, and he always had a cigar in the lower corner of his mouth. He walked with a swagger and a swing that took half the sidewalk. He ran " wid de machine," and a fire was his delight; to get into a fight his supreme happiness. He really did not frequent the Bowery so much as the side streets. There were little stores where cigars and beer were sold, something stronger perhaps, and they were generally kept by some old lady who could also get up a meal on a short notice after a fire. On summer nights they had chairs out in front of the door, and tilting back on two legs would smoke and take their comfort. For diversion

they went to Vauxhall Garden or the pit of the
Bowery Theatre. Yet they were quite a picturesque feature of old New York. .

Bowery and Grand Street were the East Side's
shopping marts. Stewart was building a marble
palace at the corner of Broadway and Chambers
Street. You went to Division and Canal streets
for your bonnets. There were a few private
milliners who made to order and imported.

There were sails and short journeys to take
even then. Elysian Fields had not lost all its
glory. And yet the little girl was quite disappointed in her visit to it. She had lived in the
country, you know, she had looked off the Sound
at Rye Beach and seen the Hudson from Tarrytown and Sleepy Hollow, and really there were
lovely spots up the old Bloomingdale road. And
she had pictured this as beyond all.

Aunt Eunice was very much struck with the
changes. Her surprise really delighted the little
girl. They took her over in Hammersley Street.
Old Mr. Bounett seemed quite feeble, and though
he was not in his court attire, he had a ruffled
shirt-front and small-clothes. Aunt Eunice
thought him delightful. It seemed queer to
think of a French quarter in New York in the
old part of the last century where people met
and read from the French poets and dramatists,
and almost believed when civilization set in ear-

nestly, French must be the polite language of the day.

The little girl felt quite as if she was one of the hostesses of the city. She knew so many strange things and could find her way about so well. And yet she was only ten years old.

Aunt Eunice thought her a quaint, delightful little body, and wise for her years. But she *was* small. Nora Whitney had outgrown her, and the Dean children were getting so large. As for the boys, they grew like weeds, and the trouble now was what to do with Ben. There was no free academy in those days, but the public school gave you a good and thorough education in the useful branches.

Chapter Fifteen.

A PLAY IN THE BACK YARD.

THE pretty block in First Street that had been so clean and genteel, a word used very much at that time, was fast changing. The lower part on the south side was filling up with undesirable people, some foreigners who crowded three families into a house. Houston Street was growing gaudy and common with Jew stores. And oh, the children! There was a large bakery where they sold cheap bread, and in the afternoon there really was a procession coming in and going out.

Chris and Lily Ludlow had teased their mother to move. The place was comfortable and near their father's business, so why should they? But the girls Lily was intimate with had moved away, and she hated to go around Avenue A to school.

There were changes at the upper end as well. The Weirs had gone from next door, and two families with small children had taken the house. The babies seemed so pudgy and untidy that the little girl did not fancy them much. Frank Whitney was married with quite a fine wedding-party, and had gone to Williamsburg to live.

Mrs. Whitney had rented two rooms in the house to a dressmaker. Delia was almost grown up. She had shot into a tall girl, though she would have her dresses short; she despised young lady-hood. She was smart and capable. She helped with the meals; often, indeed, her mother did not come down until breakfast was ready, when she had had a "bad night." That was when she read novels in bed until two or three o'clock. Delia swept the house—she often did wash on Saturday, though her brother scolded when she did it. She was the same jolly, eager, careless girl, and de-lighted in a game of tag, but she could so easily outrun the smaller children. She and Jim some-times raced round the block, one going in one direction, one in the other, and Jim didn't always beat, either.

Then she would sit out on the stoop with a crowd of children and tell wonderful stories. She didn't explain that they were largely made up "out of her own head." Next door above the Deans two new little girls had come, very nice children, who played with dolls. There was quite an array when five little girls had their best dolls out. Nora generally brought Pussy Gray, and they were always entertained with her talking.

Some boys had invaded the Reed's side of the block. Charles had strict injunctions not to parley with them. But one went in an office as errand boy, and the other quite disdained Jane Robertine Charlotte, as he called him. It did begin to annoy Mr. Reed to have his son made the butt of the street. He was a nice, obedient, upright, orderly boy. What was lacking? In some respects he was very manly. Mr. Reed suddenly concluded that a woman wasn't capable of bringing up boys, and he must take him in hand.

For two weeks Mrs. Reed had been threatening to cut his hair. The boys said, "Sissy, why don't your mother put your hair up in curl papers?" It looked so dreadful when it was first cut that Charles always spent these weeks between Scylla and Charybdis. He knew all about the rock and the whirlpools. But something had been happening all the time, even to this Saturday afternoon, when all the silver had to be scoured. Mr. Reed inspected his son as he sat at the supper-table. He had a rather poetical appearance with his long hair curling at the ends, but it was no look for a boy.

"Don't you want to take a walk down the street with me?" said his father.

Charles started as if he had been struck.

"I'm dead tired and I want him to wipe my dishes. I haven't been off my feet since five o'clock this morning only at meal-time. Then he must go to the store."

"I'll wait until then."

Mrs. Reed looked sharply at them. Had Charles done something that had escaped her ali-sided vision and was his father going to take him to task? Or was there a conspiracy?

"What do you want him for?" she inquired sharply.

"Oh, I thought we'd walk down the street."

"Smoking a cigar, of course," as Mr. Reed took one out of his case. "It certainly won't be your fault if the child hasn't every bad tendency under the sun. I've done *my* best. And you know smoking is a vile habit."

Mr. Reed had long ago learned the wisdom of silence, which was even better than a soft answer.

Charles put on a pinafore that hung in the kitchen closet. He could dry dishes beautifully.

"You've been cutting behind on stages," said his mother. "Some one has told your father."

"No, I haven't. Upon my word and honor."

"That's next to swearing, John Robert Charles. How often have I told you these little things lead to confirmed bad habits."

John Robert Charles was silent.

"Well, you've done something. And if your father does once take you in hand——"

The boy trembled. This awful threat had been held over him for years. Nothing *had* come of it, so it couldn't as yet be compared to Mrs. Joe Gargery's "rampage."

Mr. Reed sat comfortably on the front stoop smoking and reading. The wind drove the smoke straight down the street, and not into the house. How it could get in with the windows shut down was a mystery, but it seemed to sometimes.

Charles brushed his hair and washed his hands.

"I *must* cut your hair. I ought to do it this very night, tired as I am. Now brush your clothes and go out to your father. I'll be thinking up what I want. Pepper is one thing. Go down to the old man's and get some horseradish. If there is anything else I'll come out and tell you."

Charles went reluctantly out to the front stoop.

"Hillo!" said his father cheerfully. "You through?"

That did not sound very threatening.

"We are to get pepper and horseradish."

Mr. Reed nodded, folded his paper and, slipping it into his pocket, settled his hat.

"Mother may think of something else."

She positively couldn't. She considered that it saved time to do errands when you were going out, and she spent a great deal of time trying to think how to save it.

They walked down First Avenue past Houston

Street. Almost at the end of the next block there was a barber-pole with its stripes running round. The barber-pole and the Indian at the cigar shops were features of that day, as well.

"Wouldn't you like to have your hair cut, Charles?" inquired his father.

The world swam round so that Charles was minded to clutch the barber-pole, but he bethought himself in time that it was dusty. He looked at his father in amaze.

"Oh, don't be a ninny! No one will take your head off. Come, you're big enough boy to go to the barber's."

The palace of delight seemed opening before the boy. No one can rightly understand his satisfaction at this late day. The mothers, you see, used to cut hair as they thought was right, and nearly every mother had a different idea except those whose idea was simply to cut it off.

They had to wait awhile. Charles sat down in a padded chair, had a large white towel pinned close up under his chin, his hair combed out with the softest touch imaginable. The barber's hands were silken soft; his mother's were hard and rough. Snip, snip, snip, comb, brush, sprinkle some fragrance out of a bottle with a pepper-sauce cork—bulbs and sprays had not been invented. Oh, how delightful it was! He really did not want to get down and go home.

Mr. Reed had been talking to an acquaintance. The other chair being vacant, he had his beard trimmed. He was not sure whether he would have it taken off this summer, though he generally did. He turned his head a little and looked at his son. He wasn't as poetical looking, but really, he was a nice, clean, wholesome, and—yes —manly boy. But he blushed scarlet.

"That looks something like," was his father's comment. What a nice broad forehead Charles had!

"He's a nice boy," said the barber in a low tone. "Boy to be proud of. I wish there were more like him."

Mr. Reed paid his bill and they went to the store. Then they strolled on down the street. But Charles was in distress lest the pungent berry and odoriferous root should take the barber's sweetness out of him. He was puzzled, too. It seemed to him he ought to say something grateful to his father. He was so very, very glad at heart. But it was so hard to talk to his father. He always envied Jim and Ben Underhill their father. He had found it easy to talk to him on several occasions.

"I must say you are improved," his father began presently. "You mother has too much to do bothering about household affairs. And you're getting to be a big boy. Why don't you find

some boys to go with? There are those Underhills. You're too big to play with girls."

"But mother doesn't like boys," hesitatingly.

"You should have been a girl!" declared his
father testily. "But since you're not, do try to be
a little more manly."

The father hardly knew what to say himself.
And yet he felt that he did love his son.

They were just at the area gate. Charles
caught his father's hand. "I'm so glad," breathlessly. "The boys have laughed at me, and you—
you've been so good."

Mr. Reed was really touched. They entered
the basement. Mrs. Reed, like Mrs. Gargery,
still had on her apron. Charles put the pepper in
the canister, his mother took care of the horseradish. Then he sat down with his history.

"For pity's sake, Abner Reed, what have you
done to that child! He looks like a scarecrow!
He's shaved thin in one place and great tufts left
in another. I was going to cut his hair this very
evening. And I'll trim it to some decency now."

She sprang up for the shears.

"You will let him alone," said Mr. Reed, in a
firm, dignified tone. "He is quite old enough to
look like other boys. When I want him to go to
the barber's I'll take him. You will find enough
to do. Charles, get a lamp and go up to your
own room."

"I don't allow him to have a lamp in his room. He will set something a-fire."

"Then go up in the parlor."

"The parlor!" his mother shrieked.

"I'll go to bed," said Charles. "I know my lesson."

There was a light in the upper hall. On the second floor were the sleeping-chambers. Charles' was the back hall room. He could see very well from the light up the stairway.

What happened in the basement dining-room he could not even imagine. His father so seldom interfered in any matter, and his mother had a way of talking him down. But Charles was asleep when they came to bed.

Still, he had a rather hard day on Sunday. His mother was coldly severe and captious. Once she said:

"I can't bear to look at you, you are so disfigured! If *that* is what your father calls style——" and she shook her head disapprovingly.

He went to church and Sunday-school, and then his father took him up to Tompkins Square for a walk. It seemed as if they had never been acquainted before. Why, his father was real jolly. And it was a nice week at school after the boys got done asking him "Who his Barber was?" He could see the big B they put to it.

On Saturday afternoon Mrs. Reed had to go out shopping with a cousin. She was an excellent shopper. She could find flaws, and beat down, and get a spool of cotton or a piece of tape thrown in. When Charles came home from singing-school he was to go over to the Deans and play in the back yard. He was not to be out on the side-walk at all.

They were going to have a splendid time. Elsie and Florence Hay would bring their dolls. Even Josie envied the pretty names, though she confessed to Hanny that she didn't think Hay was nice, because it made you think of "hay, straw, oats" on the signs at the feed stores. But the girls were very sweet and pleasant. Nora had come in with the cat dressed in one of her own long baby frocks.

Hanny ran in to get her doll. It was still her choice possession, and had been named and un-named. Her mother began to think she was too big to play with dolls, but Margaret had made it such a pretty wardrobe.

Ben sat at the front basement window reading. Mr. and Mrs. Underhill had gone up to see Miss Lois, who was far from well. Margaret was out on "professional rounds," which Ben thought quite a suggestive little phrase. Martha was scrubbing and of course he couldn't talk to her. He had cut the side of his foot with a splinter of glass, and his mother would not allow him to put on his shoe.

Hanny brought down her doll.   Ben looked rather wistfully at her.

"I wish you'd come in too.   We're going to have such a nice time," she said in a soft tone.

"I'd look fine playing with dolls."

"But you needn't really play with dolls.   Mrs. Dean doesn't.   She's the grandmother.   We go to visit her, and she tells us about the old times, just as Aunt Nancy and Aunt Patience do.   Of course she wasn't there really, she makes believe, you know.   And you might be the—the——"

"Grandfather who had lost his leg in the war."

Ben laughed.   He had half a mind to go.

"Oh, that would be splendid.   And you could be a prisoner when the British held New York. There'd be such lots to talk about.   You could wear John's slipper, you see——"

She smiled so persuasively.   She would never be as handsome as Margaret, but she had such tender, coaxing eyes, and such a sweet mouth.

"Well, I'll bring my book along."   It was one of Cooper's novels that boys were going wild over just then.   "Do you really think they'd like to have me?"

"Oh, I know they would,"eagerly

Ben had to walk rather one-sided.   Joe said he

must not bear any weight on the outside of his foot to press the wound open.

"I've brought Ben," announced the little girl. "And he's going to be a Revolutionary soldier."

"We are very glad to see him," and Mrs. Dean rose. She had a white kerchief crossed on her breast, and a pretty cap pinned up for the occasion.

The yard was shady in the afternoon. There was a piece of carpet spread on the grass, and some chairs arranged on it, and two or three rugs laid around. On the space paved with brick stood the table, and two boxes were the dish closets. There were some cradles, and a bed arranged on another box. It really was a pretty picture.

Josie and Charles were generally the mother and father of one household. Charles blushed up to the roots of his hair. He liked playing with the girls, when he was the only boy, with no one to laugh at him.

"Now you mustn't mind me or I shall go back home and stay all alone," said Ben. That appealed to everybody's sympathy. "I'm coming over here to talk to grandmother about what we did when we were young."

Grandmother had some knitting. People even then knit their husband's winter stockings because they wore so much better. "And Mrs. Pennypacker, you might come and call on us."

Nora laughed.   That was Ben's favorite name for her when she had the cat.

The soft gray head and the gray paws looked rather queer out of the long white dress.   Pussy Gray had a white nose and his eyes were fastened in with a black streak that looked like a ribbon.

"How is your son to-day?" Ben inquired.

"He is pretty well, except he's getting some teeth.   Ain't you, darling?" and Nora hugged him up.

"Wow," said Kitty softly.

"Have you had the doctor?"

"No-o," answered Kitty, looking up pathetically.

"I'm afraid I've neglected him," explained Mrs. Pennypacker.   "You poor darling!   But your mother has been so busy."

"Meaow," said Kitty resignedly.

"Are you hungry, dear?   Would you like a bit of cold chicken?   He has to have something to keep up his strength.   Teething is so hard on children."

"Me-e-a-ow," returned Kitty, with plaintive affirmation.

Mrs. Pennypacker went over to the table and gave him a mouthful of something.   If it wasn't chicken it answered the purpose.   Then she sat down to rock him to sleep and asked Ben in what battle he had lost his leg.

Ben thought it was the battle of White Plains. He was very young at the time.

"How hard it must be to have a wooden leg," sighed Nora. "And of course you can't dance a bit."

"Oh, no, indeed!"

"Did they treat you very badly when you were a prisoner?"

"Dreadful," answered Ben. "They didn't give us half enough to eat."

"That was terrible. I hope you'll be contented here, where everything is so nice and cheerful. I am going to see Mr. and Mrs. Brown now."

"Please give them my compliments and tell them I should be very happy to have them call."

Charles had been watching Ben furtively with an apprehension that the real enjoyment of the afternoon would be spoiled. And no doubt he would tell the Houston Street boys "all about it." He was hardly prepared to see Ben enter so into the spirit of the "make believe."

Then Ben and Mrs. Dean had a little talk that might have been considered an anachronism, since it was about the foot still fast to his body. He had stepped on a piece of glass in the stable, and it had gone through the old shoe he had on for that kind of work. But Joe had seen it that morning and thought it would get along all right.

They were talking very eagerly over the other

side of the city. And presently quite a procession came to call on the old veteran. Ben and Charles fell into a discussion about some battles, and the misfortune it was to the country to lose New York so early in the contest. They compared their favorite generals and discussed the prospect of war with Mexico that was beginning to be talked about. And Mr. Brown said he had some cousins who were very anxious to see an old soldier of the Revolution. Could he bring them over?

Then Elsie and Florence Hay came. Mrs. Brown and Mrs. Pennypacker asked him to tea and he said he should be glad to accept.

Mrs. Dean thought they had better have their tea in the dining-room, but Josie said let them spread the cloth on the coping of the area, and bring the chairs and benches just inside. Charles said that would be a sort of Roman feast and the guests would make believe there were couches. They put down papers and then a cloth, and Josie brought out her dishes. Grandmother held the Pennypacker baby, who certainly was the best cat in the world and settled himself down, white dress and all.

Ben asked Charles if he was studying Roman history, and found he was reading the Orations of Cicero in Latin, and knew a great deal about Greece and Rome. He had read most of Sir

Walter Scott's novels, and liked "Marmion" beyond everything.

"What was he going to do—enter college?"

"Mother wants me to. Father says I may if I like."

He colored a little, but did not say his mother had set her heart on his being a minister because his Uncle Robert, who died, had intended to enter that profession. Ben said the boys, John and the doctor, wanted him to go, but he wished he could be a newspaper man like Nora's father. His mother thought it a kind of shiftless business. They talked over their likes and dislikes in boy fashion, and Charles enjoyed it immensely. He thought it would be just royal to have a big brother who was a doctor, and a little sister like Hanny.

Meanwhile the little women had been very much engrossed with their children and their tea party, and the prospect of a grandmother and an old soldier coming to visit them.

"And Mr. Brown is so heedless," said Mrs. Brown. "He ought to be here to go to the store, but he's off talking and men are *so* absent-minded."

Elsie said she'd go to the store, which was the closet in the basement.

Then the company came, and the old soldier limped dreadfully. Mrs. Brown scolded her husband a little, and then excused him, and everybody was seated in a row. There was a plate of thin bread-and-butter, some smoked beef cut in small pieces, some sugar crackers, quite a fad of that day, and a real cake. Mrs. Dean had given them half of a newly baked one.

It was quite a tea. Mr. Dean came home in the midst of it and sympathized warmly with the hero of 1776, and was extremely courteous to grandmother. The little girls cleared away the dishes, put their children to bed, had a fine swing and played "Puss in the Corner" with two sets.

Mr. Reed came in for Charles.

"I wish you'd come over and see my boy," he said to Ben. "He's a rather lonely chap, having no brothers or sisters."

"Let him come over to our house," returned Ben cordially. "We have a good supply."

Then everybody dispersed. They'd had such a good time, and were eager in their acknowledgments.

"Why, I quite like John Robert Charles," said Ben. "He's a real smart fellow."

"If you would please not call him all those names," entreated Hanny. "He doesn't like them."

"Well, I should say not. I'd like just plain Bob. He wants the girlishness shaken out of him."

"But he's so nice.   And if he should come over please don't let Jim plague him."

"Oh, I'll look out."

It was a week before Ben could put on his shoe, and of course it was not wisdom for him to go to school.   He went downtown in the wagon and did some writing and accounts for Steve, and read a great deal.   Mr. Reed and Charles sauntered over one evening.   Hanny was sitting out on the stoop with "father and the boys," and gave Charles a soft, welcoming smile.   Margaret was playing twilight tunes in a gentle manner, and the dulcet measures fascinated the boy, who could hardly pay attention to what Ben was saying.

"Do you want to go in and hear her?" Hanny asked, with quick insight as she caught his divided attention.

"Oh, if I could!" eagerly.

"Yes."   Hanny rose and held out her hand, saying: "We are going in to Margaret."

The elder sister greeted them cordially.   After playing a little she asked them if they would not like to sing.

They chose "Mary to the Saviour's Tomb" first. It was a great favorite in those days.   The little girl liked it because she could play and sing it for her father.   She was taking music lessons of Margaret's teacher now, and practised her scales and exercises with such assiduity that she had been allowed to play this piece. She did sometimes pick out tunes, but it was after the real work was done.

"Your boy has a fine voice," said John to Mr. Reed.

The father was not quite sure singing was manly. He had roused to the fact that Charles was rather "girly," and he wanted him like other boys.

"He is a good scholar," his father returned in half protest. "Stands highest in his class."

"Going to send him to college?"

"I don't just know," hesitatingly.

"Has he any fancy for a profession? He'd make an attractive minister."

"I don't know as I have much of a fancy for that."

Mr. Reed knew it was his wife's hope and ambition, but it had never appealed to him.

"The boys want Ben to go to college," said John, the "boys" standing for the two older brothers.

"I don't want to be a lawyer nor a doctor," subjoined Ben decisively. "And I shouldn't be good enough for a minister. There ought to be some other professions."

"Why, there are. Professorships, civil engineering, and so on.

While the men discussed future chances, the

19

children were singing, and their sweet young voices moved both fathers curiously. Mr. Reed decided that he would cultivate his neighbor, even if Charles had not made much headway with Ben and Jim.

Chapter Sixteen.

WHAT to do with Ben was the next question of importance. He was fond of books, an omnivorous reader, in fact, a very fair scholar, and, with a certain amount of push, could have graduated the year before. He really was not longing for college.

There was only one line of horse-cars, and that conveyed the passengers of the Harlem Railroad from the station on Broome Street to the steam-cars uptown. Only a few trains beside the baggage and freight cars were allowed through the city. Consequently a boy's ambition had not been roused to the height of being a " car conductor" at that period. A good number counted on "running wid de machine" when they reached the proper age, but boys were not allowed to hang around the engine-houses. Running with the machine was something in those days. There were no steam-engines. Everything was drawn by a long rope, the men ranged on either side. The force of the stream of water was also propelled by main strength, and the " high throwing" was something to be proud of. There was a good deal of rivalry among the companies to see who could get to a fire the first. Sometimes, indeed, it led to quite serious affrays if two parties met at a crossing. "Big Six" never gave up for any one. "Forty-one" was another famous engine on the East side. Indeed they had a rather menacing song they sometimes shouted out to their rivals, which contained these two blood-curdling lines:

"From his heart the blood shall run
By the balls of Forty-one."

Later on the fights and disturbances became so bitter that the police had to interfere, and as the city grew larger some new method of expediting matters had to be considered. But the "fire laddies" were a brave, generous set of men, who turned out any time of day or night and dragged their heavy engines over the rough cobble-stones with a spirit and enthusiasm hard to match. They received no pay, but were exempt from jury duty, and after a number of years of service had certain privileges granted them. Jim counted strongly on being a fireman. John had sometimes gone to fires but was not a "regular."

But all differences were forgotten in the "great fire," as it was called for a long time. There had been one about ten years before that had devastated a large part of the city. And in February of this year there had been quite a tragic one in the Tribune Building. There was a fierce drifting snowstorm, so deep it was impossible to drag the engines through it, and some of the hydrants were frozen. Men had jumped from the windows to save their lives, and there had been quite a panic.

Early in the gray dawn of July nineteenth, a watchman discovered flames issuing from an oil store on New Street. A carpenter shop next door was soon in flames. A large building in which quantities of saltpetre was stored caught next. A dense smoke filled the air, and a sudden explosive sound shot out a long tongue of flame that crossed the street. At intervals of a few moments others followed, causing everybody to fly for their lives. And at last one grand deafening burst like a tremendous clap of thunder, and the whole vicinity was in a blaze. Bricks and pieces of timber flew through the air, injuring many people. Then the fire spread far and wide, one vast, roaring, crackling sheet of flame. One brave fireman and several other people were killed, and Engine 22 was wrecked in the explosion.

It was said at first that powder had been stored in the building, but it was proved on investigation that the saltpetre alone was the dangerous agent. Three hundred and forty-five buildings were destroyed, at a loss, it was estimated, of ten millions of dollars. For days there was an immense throng about the place. The ruins extended from Bowling Green to Exchange Place.

A relic of Revolutionary times perished in this fire. The bell of the famous Provost prison, that had been used by the British during their occupancy of the city, had been removed when the building was remodelled and placed on the Bridewell at the west of the City Hall, and used for a fire-alarm bell. When the Bridewell had been destroyed it was transferred to the cupola of the Naiad Hose Company in Beaver Street. It rang out its last alarm that morning, for engine house and bell perished in the flames.

Stephen had been very fortunate in that he was out of the fire district. He took Margaret and Hanny down to view the great space heaped with blackened débris, and when a fire alarm was given the little girl used to shiver with fright for months afterward.

And now schools were considering their closing exercises, and parents of big boys were puzzled to know just where to start them in life. Ben declared his preference at last—he wanted to be some sort of a newspaper man.

They called Mr. Whitney in to council. He was not quite sure he would recommend beginning there. It would be better to learn the trade thoroughly at such a place as the Harpers'.

Then there would always be something to fall back upon. Steve did not cordially approve, and Dr. Joe was quite disappointed. He was ready to help Ben through college.

Newspaper people did not rank as high then as now. There was a good deal of what came to be called Bohemianism among them, and it was not of the artistic type. For the one really good position there were a dozen precarious ones.

Aunt Nancy Archer rather amused them with another objection. She wasn't at all sure the publishing of so many novels was conducive to the advancement of morals and religion. She never could quite understand how so good a man as Brother Harper could lend it countenance. When she was young the girls of her time were reading Hannah More. And there was Mrs. Chapone's letters, and now Charlotte Elizabeth and Mrs. Sigourney.

"Did you know Hannah More wrote a novel?" inquired John, with a half smile of his father's humor. "And Mrs. Barbauld and Mrs. Edgeworth and Charlotte Elizabeth's stories are in the novel form."

"But they have a high moral. And there are so many histories for young people to read. They ought to have the real truth instead of silly make-believes and trashy love stories."

"There are some histories that would be rather terrible reading for young minds," said John. "I think I'll bring you two or three, Aunt Nancy."

"But histories are *true*."

"There are a great many sad and bitter truths in the world. And the stories must have a certain amount of truth in them or they would never gain a hearing. Do we not find some of the most beautiful stories in the Bible itself?"

"Well, I can't help thinking all this novel reading is going to do harm to our young people. Their minds will get flighty, and they will lose all taste and desire for solid things. They are beginning to despise work already."

"Aunt Nancy," said Ben, with a deprecating smile, "the smartest girl I know lives just below here. She does most all the housekeeping, she can wash and iron and sweep and sew, and she reads novels by the score. She just races through them. I do believe she knows as much about Europe as any of our teachers. And I never dreamed there had been such tremendous conquests in Asia, and such wonderful things in Egypt until I heard her talk about them; and she knows about the great men and generals and rulers who lived before the Christian era, and at the time Christ was born——"

Aunt Nancy gasped.

"Of course there were Old Testament times," she returned hesitatingly.

"And I am not sure but Mayor Harper is doing a good work in disseminating knowledge of all kinds. I believe we are to try all things and hold fast to that which is good," said John.

He brought Aunt Nancy the history of Peter the Great and the famous Catharine of Russia, but she admitted that they were too cruel and too terrible for any one to take pleasure in.

Mrs. Underhill and Margaret went to the closing exercises of Houston Street school. Jim as usual had a splendid oration, one of Patrick Henry's. Ben acquitted himself finely. There was a large class of boys who had finished their course, and the principal made them an admirable address, in which there was much good counsel and not a little judicious praise as well as beneficial advice concerning their future.

But at Mrs. Craven's there was something more than the ordinary exercises. The front parlor was turned into an audience-room, and a platform was raised a little in the back parlor almost like a stage. There was a dialogue that was a little play in itself, and displayed the knowledge as well as the training of the pupils. Some compositions were read, and part of a little operetta was sung quite charmingly by the girls. Then there was a large table spread out with specimens of needlework that were really fine; drawing, painting, and penmanship that elicited much praise from the visitors.

The crowning pleasure was the little party given in the evening, to which any one was at liberty to invite a brother or cousin, or indeed a neighbor of whom their mother approved. And strange to relate, there were a good many boys who were really pleased to be asked to the "girls' party." Charles Reed came and had a delightful time. Josie had waylaid Mr. Reed again and told him all about it, and hoped he would let Charles come, and he said he would be very happy to. Mrs. Reed did not approve of parties for children, and Charles had been but to very few.

Mr. Underhill and Dr. Joe went down to the Harpers', having decided to place Ben there to learn a trade. Thinking it all over, he resolved to acquiesce, though he told Hanny privately that some day he meant to have a newspaper of his own and be the head of everything. But he supposed he would have to learn first.

Margaret and Hanny went with them, and found many changes since their first visit. The making of a book seemed a still more wonderful thing to the child, but how one could ever be written puzzled her beyond all. A composition on something she had seen or read was within the scope of her thought, but to tell about people and make them talk, and have pleasant and curious and sad and joyous happenings, did puzzle her greatly.

Ben was not to go until the first of September. So he would help Steve, go to the country for a visit, and have a good time generally before he began his life-work. Stephen's house was approaching completion, and it was wonderful to see how the rows of buildings were stretching out, as if presently the city would be depleted of its residents. One wondered where all the people came from.

John Robert Charles had grown quite confidential with his father and began to think him as nice as Mr. Underhill—not as funny, for Mr. Underhill had a way of joking and telling amusing stories and teasing a little, that was very entertaining, and never sharp or ill-natured.

He had carried off the honors of his class and was proud of it. Mr. Reed showed his satisfaction as well. Mrs. Reed was rather doubtful and severe, and thought it her duty to keep Charles from undue vanity. She was in a fret because she had to go away and leave the house and waste a whole month.

"I don't want to go," said Charles to his father. "It's awful lonesome up there in the mountains, and there's no one to talk to. Aunt Rhoda's deaf, and Aunt Persis hushes you up if you say a word.

And the old gardener is stupid. There are no books to read, and I do get so tired."

"Well, we'll see," replied his father.

To his wife Mr. Reed said: "Why do you go off if you don't want to?"

"I won't have Charles running the streets and getting into bad company, and wearing out his clothes faster than I can mend them," she replied shortly.

It would not be entertaining for Charles in his office, and he didn't just see what the boy could do. But he met a friend who kept a sort of fancy toy store, musical instruments and some curios, down Broadway, and learned that they were very much in want of a trusty, reliable lad who was correct in figures and well-mannered. A woman came in the morning to sweep the store and sidewalk, to wash up the floor and windows, and do the chores. So there was no rough work.

"I'll send my boy down and see how you like him. I think he would fancy the place, and during the month you might find some one to take it permanently. There seems to be no lack of boys."

"You can't always find the right sort," said Mr. Gerard. "Yes, I shall be glad to try him."

Mr. Reed did not set forth the matter too attractively to his wife, not even to Charles, who had learned to restrain his enthusiasm before his mother.   And though she made numerous objections, and the thought of bad company seemed to haunt her, she reluctantly decided to let him try it for a week.   He would go down in the morning with his father, so he could not possibly begin his day in mischief.

Charles was delighted.   The city was not overcrowded then.   The Park gave "downtown" quite a breathing space.

Now a boy would think it very hard not to have any vacation after eleven months of study.   He would be so tired and worn and nervous that ten weeks would be none too much.   The children then studied hard and played hard and were eager to have a good time, and generally did have it. And now Charles was delighted with the newness of the affair.   He walked up at night fresh and full of interest, and was quite a hero to the girls over on Mrs. Dean's stoop.

"I hope you will bring them down even if you shouldn't want to buy anything.   Mr. Gerard said the stock was low now, as it is the dullest season of the year.   But there are such beautiful articles for gifts, china cups and saucers and dainty pitchers and vases, and sets like yours, Josie, some ever so much smaller, and a silver knife and fork and spoon in a velvet case, and lovely little fruit-knives and nut-picks and ever so many things I have never heard of.   And musical instruments, flutes and flageolets and violins, and oh, the accordeons! There are German and French. Oh, I wish I *could* own one. I know I could soon learn to play on it!" declared Charles eagerly.

In that far-back time an accordeon really was considered worth one's while. A piano was quite an extravagance. A good player could evoke real music out of it, and at that period it had not been handed over to the saloons. In fact, saloons were not in fashion.

The children listened enchanted. It was a great thing to know any one in such a store. Mrs. Dean promised to take them all down.

Hanny had a new source of interest. Dr. Joe had told her a very moving story when he was up to tea on Sunday evening, about a little girl who had been two months in the hospital and who had just come home for good now, who lived only a little way below them. It was Daisy Jasper, whom they had seen a little while last summer in a wheeling chair, and who had disappeared before any one's curiosity could be satisfied. She was an only child, and her parents were very comfortably well off. When Daisy was about six years old, a fine, healthy, and beautiful little girl, she had trodden on a spool dropped by a careless hand and fallen down a long flight of stairs. Beside a broken arm and some bruises she did not seem seriously injured. But after a while she began to complain of her back and her hip, and presently the sad knowledge dawned upon them that their lovely child was likely to be a cripple. Various experiments were tried until she became so delicate her life appeared endangered. Mr. Jasper had been attracted to this pretty row of houses standing back from the street with the flower gardens in front. It seemed secluded yet not lonely. She grew so feeble, however, that the doctors had recommended Sulphur Springs in Virginia, and thither they had taken her. When the cool weather came on they had gone farther south and spent the winter in Florida. She had improved and gained sufficient strength, the doctors thought, to endure an operation. It had been painful and tedious, but she had borne it all so patiently. Dr. Mott and Dr. Francis had done their best, but she would always be a little deformed. The prospect was that some day she might walk without a crutch. Joe had seen a good deal of her, and at one visit he had told her of his little sister who was just her age, as their birthdays were in May.

Hanny had cried over the sorrowful tale. She thought of her early story heroine, " Little Blind Lucy," whose sight had been so marvellously restored. But Daisy could never be quite restored to straightness.

After supper Joe had taken her down to call on Daisy. . Oh, how pretty the gardens were, a beautiful spot of greenery and bloom, such a change from the pavements! A narrow brick walk ran up to the house, edged with rows of dahlias just coming into bloom. On the other side there were circles and triangles and diamond-shaped beds with borders of small flowers, or an entire bed of heliotrope or verbena. The very air was fragrant. Up near the house was a kind of pavilion with a tent covering to shield one from the sun.

Daisy, with her mother and aunt, were sitting out here when Dr. Joe brought his little sister. Daisy's chair was so arranged that the back could be adjusted to any angle. It was of bamboo and cane with a soft blanket thrown over it, a pretty rose color that lighted up the pale little girl whose languor was still perceptible.

After a little Mrs. Jasper took Dr. Joe into the house, as she wanted to question him. Then Hanny and Daisy grew more confidential. Daisy asked about the children in the neighborhood and thought she would like to see Nora and Pussy Gray. She was very fond of cats, but theirs, a very good mouser, was bad-tempered and wanted no petting. And then the Dean girls and Flossy and Elsie Hay, and last but not least of all, Charles Reed with his beautiful voice.

"I do so dearly love music," said Daisy longingly. "Auntie plays but she doesn't sing. Mamma knows a good many old-fashioned songs that are lovely. When I am tired and nervous she sings to me. I don't suppose I can ever learn to play for myself," she ended sadly.

Hanny told her she was learning and could play "Mary to the Saviour's Tomb" for her father. And there were the boys and Stephen and her lovely married sister Dolly and her own sister Margaret.

"Oh, how happy you must be!" cried Daisy. "I should like such a lot of people. I never had any brothers or sisters, and I *do* get so lonesome. And the doctor is so pleasant and sweet; you must love him a great deal."

"I can't tell which one is best. Steve teases and says funny things, and is—oh, just as nice as any one can be! And John is splendid, too. And Ben is going to learn to make books, and I can have all the books I want."

Daisy sighed. She was very fond of reading, but it soon tired her.

"I should so like to see you all. You know I've never been much with children. And I like live people. I want to hear them talk and sing and see them play. One gets tired of dolls."

"If you would like I will bring Nora and Pussy Gray. And I know Josie's mother will let them

20

come.   If you could be wheeled up on our side-walk"

"Oh, that would be delightful!" and the soft eyes glowed.

Hanny had taken Nora the very next afternoon, and Pussy Gray had been just too good for anything.   Daisy had to laugh at the conversations between him and Nora.   It really did sound as if he said actual words.   And they told Daisy about the time they went to the Museum and had a double share for their money.   Daisy laughed heartily, and her pale cheeks took on a pretty pink tint.

"You are so good to come," said Mrs. Jasper. "My little girl has had so much suffering in her short life that I want her to have all the pleasure possible now."

Josie and Tudie Dean had been out spending the day, and really, there was so much to tell that it was nine o'clock before it was all discussed. Charles was very much interested in Daisy Jasper.

"You know I can tell just how she feels about not having any brothers and sisters," he exclaimed.   "I've wished for them so many times. And I *do* think Hanny is the luckiest of the lot; she has so many.   It is like a little town to yourself."

"I'm so glad it is vacation," declared Josie.

"If we were going to school we wouldn't have half time for anything."

Mr. Underhill came for his little girl. While he was exchanging a few words with Mr. Dean Hanny caught one hand in both of hers and hopped around on one foot. She was so glad she could do it. Poor Daisy, with her beautiful name, who could never know the delight of exuberant spirits.

Hanny's thoughts did not take in the long word, but that was what she felt in every fibre of her being.

Charles wondered how she dared. He was frightened when he caught his father's hand with an impulse of gratitude. But in pure fun!

There was quite a stir with the little clique in the upper end of the block. Mrs. Underhill, Mrs. Dean, and Margaret called on their neighbor, and the wheeled chair came up the street a day or two after. It had to go to the corner and cross on the flagging, as the jar would have been too great on cobble stones. They had a young colored lad now who kept the garden in order, did chores, and waited upon "Missy" as he called her.

The sidewalk was generally sunny in the afternoon, but this day it was soft and gray without being very cloudy. The chariot halted at the Underhills'. The little girls brought their dolls to show Daisy, their very best ones, and Nora dressed up Pussy Gray in the long white baby dress, and pussy was very obliging and lay in Daisy's arms just like a real baby. The child felt as if she wanted to kiss him.

What a pretty group of gossips they were! If Kate Greenaway had been making pictures then, she would have wanted them, though their attire was not quite as quaint as hers. They went up and down the steps, they told Daisy so many bright, entertaining things, and the fun they had with their plays. Josie's party was described, the closing exercises at school, and the many incidents so important in child life. Sometimes two or three talked together, or some one said, "It's my turn, now let me." They referred to Charles so much it really piqued Daisy's curiosity.

"Jim calls him a 'girl-boy,' because he plays with us," said Hanny, "and in some ways I like girl-boys best. Ben is a sort of girl-boy. I'm going to bring him over to see you. Jim's real splendid and none of the boys dare fight him any more," she added loyally.

"And first, you know," began Tudie in a mysteriously confidential manner, "we thought it so queer and funny. His mother called him John Robert Charles. And she used to look out of the window and ask him if he had his books and his handkerchief, and tell him to come straight home from school, and lots of things. Oh, we thought we wouldn't have her for our mother, not for a world!"

"How did he come by so many names?" Daisy smiled.

"Well, grandfather and all," replied Tudie rather ambiguously. His father calls him Charles. It sounds quite grand, doesn't it? We all wanted to call him Robert. And Hanny's big sister sings such a lovely song—"Robin Adair." I'd like to call him that."

"I should so like to hear him sing. I'm so fond of singing," said Daisy plaintively.

"Now if we were in the back yard we could all sing," rejoined Josie. "But of course we couldn't in the street with everybody going by."

"Oh, no!" Yet there was a wistful longing in Daisy's face, that was beginning to look very tired.

There were not many people going through this street. Houston Street was quite a thoroughfare. But the few who did pass looked at the merry group of girls and at the pale invalid whose chair told the story, and gave them all a tender, sympathetic thought.

All except Lily Ludlow. She was rather curious about the girl in the chair and made an errand out to the Bowery. When Hanny saw who was coming she turned around and talked very eagerly to Elsie Hay, and pretended not to know it.   Lily had her President, and Jim admired her, that was enough.

"You're very tired, Missy," Sam said presently.

"Yes," replied Daisy.   "I think I'll go home now.   And will you all come to see me to-morrow? Oh, it is so nice to know you all! And Pussy Gray is just angelic.   Please bring him, too."

They said good-by.   For some moments the little girls looked at each other with wordless sorrow in their eyes.   I think there were tears as well.

Chapter Seventeen.

SOME OF THE OLD LANDMARKS.

"Yes, all of us," said Ben. "We can tuck in the Deans. I only wish Charles could go. Well, the house won't run away. And Mr. Audubon has travelled all over the world. Mr. Whitney wrote an article about him. That's the work I'd like to do—go and see famous people and write about them."

Interviewing was not such a fine art in those days. Ben had enough of it later on.

Dr. Joe had asked Mr. Audubon's permission to bring a crowd of children to see him and his birds. He was getting to be quite an attraction in the city.

When they packed up they found a crowd sure enough. But Dr. Hoffman took Margaret and the little girl with him, as Charles had been allowed a half day off for the trip. The drive was so full of interest. They went up past the old Stuyvesant place and took a look at the pear-tree that had been planted almost two hundred years ago and was still bearing fruit. Then they turned into the old Bloomingdale Road, and up by

Seventy-fifth Street they all stopped to see the house where Louis Philippe taught school when he was an emigrant in America. And now he was on the throne, King of the French people, a grander and greater position, some thought, than being President of the United States.

"For of course," said Jim, "he can stay there all his life, and the President has only four years in the White House. After all, it is a big thing to be a king."

And in a little more than two years he was flying over to England for refuge and safety, and was no longer a king. Mr. Polk was still in the White House.

It was an odd, low, two-story frame house where royalty had been thankful to teach such boys as Ben and Jim and Charles. There was a steep, sloping roof with wide eaves, a rather narrow doorway in the middle of the front, carved with very elaborate work, and an old knocker with a lion's head, small but fierce. The large room on one side had been the schoolroom, and the board floor was worn in two curious rows where the boys had shuffled their feet. The fireplace was what most people came to see. It was spacious and had a row of blue and white Antwerp tiles with pictures taken from the New Testament. They were smoked and faded now, but they still told their story. The mantelpiece and the doors were a mass of the most elaborate carving.

There were still some old houses standing in New York that had been built with bricks brought from Holland.   Charles was very much interested in these curiosities and had found one of the houses down in Pearl Street.

Then they drove up through McGowan's Pass, where Washington had planned to make a decisive stand at the battle of Harlem Heights.   There was the ledge of rock and the pretty lake that was to be Central Park some day.   It was all wildness now.

There was so much to see that Dr. Joe declared they had no more time to spend following Washington's retreat.

"But it was just grand that he should come back here to be inaugurated the first President of the United States," said Charles.   "I am proud of having had that in New York."

"The city has a great many famous points," said Dr. Joe; "but we seem to have lost our enthusiasm over them.   Beyond there," nodding his head over east, "is the Murray House that can tell its story.   Handsome Mrs. Murray, and she was a Quaker, too, made herself so charming in her hospitality to the British generals that she detained them long enough for Silliman's brigade to retreat to Harlem.   Washington was awaiting them at the Apthorpe House, and they had left that place not more than fifteen minutes when the British came flying in the hot haste of pursuit. So but for Mrs. Murray's smiles and friendliness they might have captured our Washington as well as the city."

"That was splendid," declared Charles enthusiastically.

"And maybe as a boy Lindley Murray might have thought up his grammar that he was to write later on to puzzle your brains," continued Dr. Joe.

"Well, that is odd, too. I'll forgive him his grammar," said Ben, with a twinkle in his eye.

"And if we don't go on we will have no time for Professor Audubon and the birds. But we could ramble about all day."

"I didn't know there were so many interesting things in the city. They seem somehow a good ways off when you are studying them," replied Charles.

He really wished Hanny was in the carriage. She was so eager about all these old stories.

Then they went over to Tenth Avenue. There was the old Colonial house, with its broad porch and wide flight of steps. It was country then with its garden and fields, its spreading trees and grassy slopes.

And there was Professor Audubon on the lawn

with his wife and two little grandchildren. He came and welcomed the party cordially. He had met both doctors before. He was tall, with a fine fair face and long curling hair thrown back, now snowy white. Once with regard to the wishes of some friends while abroad he had yielded and had it cut "fashionable," to his great regret afterward, and the reminiscence was rather amusing. His wide white collar, open at the throat, added to his picturesque aspect. Then he had a slight French accent that seemed to render his hospitality all the more charming.

Ben and Charles knew that he had been nearly all over the Continent, and had hardships innumerable and discouragements many, and had in spite of them succeeded in writing and illustrating one of the most magnificent of books. And when they trooped into the house and saw the stuffed birds and animals, the pictures he had painted, and the immense folio volumes so rich with drawings, it hardly seemed possible that one brain could have wrought it all.

Everything, from the most exquisite hummingbird to an eagle and a wild turkey. There was no museum of natural history then. Mr. Barnum's collection was considered quite a wonder. But to hear this soft-voiced man with his charming simplicity describe them, was fascination itself.

The little girl really wavered in her admiration for Mayor Harper. He had been her hero *par excellence* up to this time. A man who could govern a city and make books had seemed wonderful, but here was a man who could keep the birds quite as if they were alive. You almost expected them to sing.

He was very fond of children and Mrs. Audubon was hardly less delightful. They could not see half the treasures in such a brief while, and they were glad to be invited to come again. Ben did find his way up there frequently, and Charles gleaned many an entertaining bit of knowledge. When the little girl went again, the tender, eager eyes had lost their sight, and the enthusiasm turned to a pathos that was sorrow itself. But there was no hint of it this happy day, which remained one of their most delightful memories.

Now that they were so near, Margaret said they must go and see Miss Lois. Dr. Joe was quite a regular visitor, for Miss Lois was growing more frail every week. Josie and Tudie thought they would like to see another old house, and a harp "taller than yourself." Charles was much interested. Jim had his mind so full of birds and hunting adventures he could think of nothing else, and said he would rather walk around.

Miss Lois was quite feeble to-day, and said Margaret must be the hostess. They went into the old parlor and examined the quaint articles and some of the old-fashioned books. Josie wished they might try the harp and see how it . would sound, but no one would propose it if Miss Lois was so poorly.

"It's very queer," said Hanny. "She played for me once. The strings are rusted and broken, and it sounds just like the ghost of something, as if you were going way, way back. I didn't like it."

The German woman was out in the kitchen and gave them each a piece of cake. There was a quaint old dresser with some pewter plates and a pitcher, and old china, and a great high mantel.

"You seem way out in the country," said Charles. "But it's pretty, too. And the trees and the river and Fort Washington. Why, it's been like an excursion. I am so glad you asked me to come."

Margaret entered the room. "She wants to see you, Hanny," she said quietly. "And when she is stronger she would like the little girls to come again."

Hanny went into the chamber. Miss Lois was sitting up in the big rocker, but her face was as white as the pillow back of her head. And oh, how thin her hands were! strangely cold, too, for a summer day.

"I'm very glad you came again, little Hanny,'

she said. "I had been thinking of you and Margaret all day, and how good it was of your father and you to hunt me up as you did. You've given me a deal of happiness. Tell him I am thankful for all his kindness. Will you kiss me good-by, dear? I hope you'll be spared to be a great comfort to every one."

Hanny kissed her. The lips were almost as cold as the hands. And then she went out softly with a strange feeling she did not understand.

It was late enough then to go straight home. Dr. Joe had a little talk with his mother, and the next day he took her up to Harlem. The children went over to Daisy's in the afternoon and told her about "everything." Mrs. Jasper insisted upon keeping them to supper.

Her mother had not returned when the little girl went to bed. It seemed so strange the next morning without her. Margaret was very quiet and grave, so the little girl practised and sewed, and then read a while. In the afternoon her mother came, home and said Miss Lois had gone to be with her sister and her long-lost friends in the other country.

A feeling of awe came over her. No one very near to her had died, and though she had not seen so very much of Miss Lois, for her mother had gone up quite often without her, the fact that she had been there so lately, had held her poor nerveless hand, had kissed her good-by in an almost sacred manner when she was so near death, touched her.   Did she know? Hanny wondered. What was death?   The breath went out of your body—and her old thoughts about the soul came back to her.   It was so different when the world was coming to an end.   Then you were to be caught up into heaven and not be put into the ground.   She shrank from the horrible thought of being buried there, of being so covered that you never could get out.   She decided that she would not so much mind if the world did come to an end.

"Margaret," she said, "was it dreadful for Miss Lois to die?"

"No, dear," returned her sister gently.   "If we were all in another country, the beautiful heaven, and you were here all alone, would you not like to come to us?   That was the way Miss Lois felt. It is so much better than living on here alone. And then when one gets old—no, dear, it was a pleasant journey to her.   She had thought a great deal about it, and had loved and served God. This is what we all must do."

"Margaret, what must I do to serve Him?"

"I think trying to make people happier is one service.   Being helpful and obedient, and taking up the little trials cheerfully, when we have to do the things we don't quite like."

"I wish you would tell me something hard that I do not like to do."

"Suppose I said I would not go out and play with the girls this afternoon."

"I'd rather not of myself," said Hanny. "I feel like being still and thinking."

Margaret smiled down in the sweet, serious face. There was no trial she could impose.

"Then think of the beautiful land where Miss Lois has gone, where no one will be sick or tired or lonely, where the flowers are always blooming and there is no winter, where all is peace and love."

"But I don't understand—how you get to heaven," said the puzzled child.

"No one knows until the time comes. Then God shows us the way, and because He is there we do not have any terror. We just go to Him. It is a great mystery. No one can quite explain it."

Elsie Hay came for her, but she said she was not going out, that she did not feel like playing. She brought her sewing, and in her mind wandered about heaven, seeing Miss Lois in her new body.

They did not take her to the funeral. She went over to Daisy Jasper's and read to her, wondering a little if Daisy would be glad to go where she would be well and strong and have no more pain.

But then she would have to leave her father and mother who loved her so very much.

Miss Lois had left some keepsakes to Margaret. Two beautiful old brocaded silk gowns that looked like pictures, some fine laces, and a pretty painted fan that had been done expressly for her when she was young. A white embroidered lawn for Hanny, a pearl ring and six silver spoons, besides some curious old books. Mrs. Underhill was to take whatever she liked, and dispose of the rest. The good German neighbor was to have the house and lot for the care she had taken of both ladies. Mr. Underhill had arranged this some time before, so there would be no trouble.

Everything in the house was old and well worn. There was a little china of value, and the rest was turned over to the kindly neighbor.

Margaret and Hanny went up to visit grandmother, both grandmothers, indeed. The old Van Kortlandt house was a curiosity in its way, and though Hanny had seen it before she was not old enough to appreciate it. The satin brocade furniture was faded, the great gilt-framed mirrors tarnished, and all the bedsteads had high posts and hanging curtains, and a valance round the lower part. Aunt Katrina was there and a cousin Rhynders, a small, withered-up old man who played beautifully on a jewsharp, and who sang, in a rather tremulous but still sweet voice, songs that seemed quite fascinating to Hanny, pathetic old ballads such as one finds in "The Ballad Book" of a hundred years ago. There was an old woman in the kitchen who scolded the two farmhands continually; a beautiful big dog and a cross mastiff who was kept chained, as well as numerous cats, but Grandmother Van Kortlandt despised cats.

It was delightful to get home again, though now Elsie and Florence had gone to see their grandmother, and the Deans were away also. But Daisy Jasper kissed her dozens of times, and said she had missed her beyond everything and she would not have known how to get along but for Dr. Joe. Hanny had so much to tell her about the journey and her relatives.

"And I haven't even any grandmother," said Daisy. "There is one family of cousins in Kentucky, and one in Canada. So you see I am quite destitute."

Both little girls laughed at that.

Dr. Joe said Daisy was really improving. She walked about with her crutch, but they were afraid one leg would be a little short.

Charles came over to see Hanny that very evening. He certainly had grown taller, and had lost much of his timidity. He really "talked up" to Jim. He was so fair and with the sort of sweet expression that was considered girlish, and kept himself so very neat, that he was different from most boys. I don't suppose his mother ever realized how much mortification and persecution it had cost him.

She still toiled from morning to night. Charles began to wish she would wear a pretty gown and collar and a white apron at supper time instead of the dreadful faded ginghams. Everything had a faded look with her, she washed her clothes so often, swept her carpets, and scrubbed her oil-cloths so much. The only thing she couldn't fade was the window-glass.

Charles and his father had grown quite confidential. They had talked about school and college.

"Though I am afraid I don't want to be a minister," said Charles, drawing a long breath as if he had given utterance to a very wicked thought.

"You shall have your own choice about it," replied his father firmly. "And there's no hurry."

It had been such a pleasure to walk down-town every morning with his father. Broadway was fresh and clean, and the breeze came up from the river at every corner. There were not so many people nor factories, and there were still some lots given over to grassy spaces and shrubs. Walking to business was considered quite the thing then.

He had a great deal to tell Hanny about "our"

store, and what "we" were doing. The new beautiful stock that was coming in, for then it took from twelve to sixteen days to cross the ocean, and you had to order quite in advance. He had learned to play several tunes on the accordeon, and he hoped his father would let him take his four weeks' wages and buy one. And Mr. Gerard had said he should be very happy to have all the girls and their mothers come down some afternoon.

"And if Daisy only could go!"

"Isn't she beautiful?" said Charles. "She looks like an angel. Her short golden hair is like the glory they put around the saints and the Saviour, an aureole they call it."

"What a beautiful word."

"I thought at first she would die. But your brother is sure she will live now. Only it's such a pity——" the boy's voice faltered a little from intense sympathy.

Hanny sighed too. She knew what he meant to say. But the children refrained from giving it a name. "Hanny, I think it's just splendid to be a doctor. To help people and encourage them when you can't cure them. He said one night when he stopped at the Deans that she might have been dreadfully deformed, and now it will not be very bad, that when her lovely hair gets grown out again it will not show much. I'm so glad."

They had cut the golden ringlets close to her head, for she could not be disturbed during those critical weeks in the hospital.

When the Deans came home there was great rejoicing.   And since there was such a little time left for Charles to stay in the store they could not wait for Elsie and Flossie.

"If we *could* take Daisy," Hanny said to Joe. He dropped in nearly every evening now.   The city was very healthy in spite of August weather, and young doctors were not wont to be overrun with calls.

"I don't see why you shouldn't.   It would be the best thing in the world for her to go out, and to be with other children and have some interests in common with them.   Yes, let us go down and see."

The family were all out on the stoop and the little paved court.   They were so screened from observation.   Dr. Joe came and stood by Daisy's chair, while Hanny sat on a stool and held the soft hand.   Then he preferred the children's request.

"Oh, it would be lovely!"   Then the pale face flushed.   "I don't believe I—could."

"Why not?" asked Dr. Joe.

There was no immediate answer.   Mrs. Jasper said hesitatingly: "Would it be wise, doctor?   One cannot help being—well, sensitive."

"Yet you do not want to keep this little girl forever secluded. There are so many enjoyable things in the world. It is not even as if Daisy had brothers and sisters who were coming in hourly with all manner of freshness and fun."

"I can't bear people to look at me so. I can almost hear what they say——"

Daisy's voice broke in a short sob.

"My dear child," Dr. Joe took the other hand and patted it caressingly. "It is very sad and a great misfortune, but if you had to remember that it came from the violence of a drunken father, or the carelessness of an inefficient mother, it would seem a harder burden to bear. We can't tell why God allows some very sad events to happen, but when they do come we must look about for the best means of bearing them. God has seen fit to make a restoration to health and comparative strength possible. I think He means you to have some enjoyment as well. And when one gets used to bearing a burden it does not seem so heavy. Your parents are prosperous enough to afford you a great many indulgences, and you must not refuse them from a spirit of undue sensitiveness. And then, my little girl, God has given you such a beautiful face that it cannot help but attract. Can't you be brave enough to take the pleasures that come to you without darkening them by a continual sense of the misfortune?"

Daisy was crying now. Dr. Joe pressed the small figure to his heart, and kissed her forehead. He had been unusually interested in the case, but he knew now some effort must be made, some mental pain endured, or her life would drop to weariness. Mrs. Jasper was very sensitive to comment herself.

Mr. Jasper began to walk up and down the path.

"Yes, doctor," he exclaimed; "what you say is true. You have been such a good friend to my little girl. We want her to be happy and to have some companionship. The children up your way have been very kind and sympathetic. I like that young lad extremely. It is only at first that the thing seems so hard. Daisy, I think I would go."

He came and kissed his unfortunate little girl.

"Oh, do!" entreated Hanny softly. "You see, it will be like the ladies of long ago when they went out in their chairs. There's some pictures in the old books Miss Lois sent us, and the funny clothes they wore. I'll bring them over some day. I read about a lady going to Court in her chair. And there were two or three pretty maids to wait on her. We'll make believe you are the Countess Somebody, and we are the ladies in waiting. And we'll all go to the Palace. The King will be out; they're always on hunting expeditions, and the Prince, that will be Charles, there was a bonnie Prince Charlie once, will take us about and show us the lovely things in the Palace——"

Hanny had talked herself out of breath and stopped.

Mr. Jasper laughed. "Upon my word, Miss Hanny, you would make a good stage manager. There, could you have it planned out any nicer, Daisy? I shall have to be on hand to see the triumphal procession as it goes down Broadway."

Hanny's imagination had rendered it possible.

Joe swung her up in his strong arms.

"We think a good deal of our Hanny," he said laughingly. "If she was smaller she might be exhibited along with Tom Thumb, but she's spoiled that brilliant enterprise, and yet she stays so small that we begin to think she's stunted."

"Oh, Joe, do you really?" she cried.

"We shall have to call her the little girl all her life. And you know she's bothered a good deal about her name, which isn't at all pretty, but she takes it in good part, and puts up with it."

"I call her Annie sometimes," said Daisy.

> "Ann is but plain and common,
> And Nancy sounds but ill;
> While Anna is endurable,
> And Annie better still,"

repeated Dr. Joe. "So you see we all have some trials. To be a little mite of a thing and to be called Hanneran is pretty bad. And now, little mite, we must go back home. When will the cavalcade start? I must be on hand to see it move."

"About three, Charles said. Oh, it will be just delightful!"

Now that Hanny had been put down she hopped around on one foot for joy.

They said good-night and walked up home.

"Don't you think I *will* grow some, Joe?" she asked, with a pretty doubt in her tone. "I did grow last year, for mother had to let down my skirts."

"I don't want you to grow too much. I like little women," he answered.

The cavalcade, as Dr. Joe called it, did start the next day. Daisy's mother and her Aunt Ellen went, Mrs. Dean and Margaret, and four little girls, including Nora Whitney, who was growing "like a weed." They went out to Broadway and then straight down. Of course people looked at them. The children were so merry, and really, Daisy in her chair with her colored attendent was quite an unusual incident. Aunt Ellen had let her carry her pretty dove-colored sunshade. It was lined with pink and had a joint in the handle that turned it down and made a shelter from too curious eyes.

There were a good many people out. It was not necessary then to go away for the whole summer in order to be considered fashionable. People went and came, and when they were home they promenaded in the afternoon without losing caste.

Stores were creeping up Broadway. "Gerard & Co." was on the block above the Astor House, a very attractive notion and fancy store. The window was always beautifully arranged, and the cases were full of tempting articles. There were seats for customers, and across the end of the long store pictures and bijou tables and music-boxes were displayed. In a small anteroom there was a workshop where musical instruments, jewelry and, trinkets were repaired.

Sam lifted out his young mistress and carried her in. Charles came forward to receive his guests, and though he flushed and showed some embarrassment, acquitted himself quite creditably. Mr. Gerard, with his French politeness, made them very welcome and took a warm interest at once in Daisy. She sat by the counter with Sam at her back, and looked quite the countess of Hanny's description. Mr. Gerard brought her some rare and pretty articles to examine. The others strolled around, the children uttering ejaculations of delight. Such elegant fans and card cases and mother-of-pearl *portemonnaies* bound with silver and steel! Such vases and card receivers—indeed, all the pretty bric-a-brac, as we should term it nowadays.

But the greatest interest was aroused by the music-boxes. The children listened enchanted to the limpid tinkle of the tunes. It was like fairyland.

"Oh," cried Daisy, with a long sigh of rapture; "if I only could have a music-box! Then I could play for myself. And it is so beautiful. Oh, mamma!"

Mrs. Jasper inquired prices. From twenty-four dollars to beyond one hundred. There was one at forty dollars that played deliciously, and such a variety of tunes.

"And when you tire of them you can have new music put in," explained Mr. Gerard.

"And you don't have to learn all the tiresome fingering," commented Hanny.

"If I had a piano I shouldn't ever think it tiresome," said Charles.

"Oh, yes, you would, even when you loved it and tried to learn with all your might. Tunes give you a joyful sort of feeling," and Hanny's eyes sparkled.

"And you could dance to this," Tudie whispered softly, while her eyes danced unmistakably.

Mrs. Jasper examined several of them and listened to the tunes. They came back to that for forty dollars.

"We will have to talk to papa. He thought he might drop in."

The children did not tire of waiting. Hanny thought she might spend a whole day looking over everything, and listening to the dainty, enchanting music. But Mrs. Dean said she *must* go.

Just at that instant Mr. Jasper arrived, having been detained. His wife spoke in a little aside, and he showed his interest at once. Why, yes, a music-box could not fail to be a great delight to Daisy.

Mr. Gerard wound up two or three of them again. Then the ladies decided they would ride up in the stage with the children. Mr. Jasper and Sam would see to Daisy's safety.

And the result was that Mr. Jasper bought the music-box, ordering it sent home the next day. Daisy was speechless with joy. Sam carried her out and put her into her chair.

"I don't believe I shall ever be afraid to go out again," she said eagerly. Indeed she did not mind the eyes that peered at her now. Some were very pitying and sympathetic.

As Charles was putting away many of the choice articles for the night Mr. Gerard slipped a dollar into his hand.

"That's your commission," he said smilingly,

"on unexpected good fortune.   And I shall be so sorry to lose you.   I wish it was the first of August instead of the last, or that you didn't want to go back to school."

Chapter Eighteen.

SUNDRY DISSIPATIONS.

THE schools were all opened again. Hanny wasn't too big to go to Mrs. Craven's, indeed her school commenced with some girls two or three years older. Ben went to work, starting off in the morning with John. Jim felt rather lonely.

His best girl had been undeniably "snifty" to him. Something *had* happened to her at last. Through a friend her father had secured a position in the Custom House. It was not very high, but it had an exalted sound. And instead of the paltry five hundred dollars he earned at the shoe store, the salary was a thousand. They were going to move around in First Avenue. Hanny was sorry that it was a few doors above Mrs. Craven's. If Lily had only gone out of the neighborhood!

Of course she disdained the public school. She was going to Rutgers. She held her head very high as they went back and forth during the removal, and stared at Hanny as if she had never known her.

But there were so many things to interest

Hanny. Sometimes she read the paper to her father, and it was filled with threats and excitements. In the year before, the independence of Texas had been consented to by Mexico on condition that her separate existence should be maintained. But on the Fourth of July, at a convention, the people had accepted some terms offered by the United States, and declared for annexation. For fear of a sudden alarm General Zachary Taylor had been sent with an army of occupation, and Commodore Connor with a squadron of naval vessels to the Gulf of Mexico. The talk of war ran high.

Then we were in a difficulty with England about some Oregon boundaries. "The whole of Oregon or none," was the cry. England was given a year's notice that steps would be taken to bring the question to a settlement. Timid people declared that wild land was not worth quarrelling about.

If you could see an atlas of those days I think you would be rather surprised, and we are all convinced now that geography is by no means an exact science. The little girl and her father studied it all out. There was big, unwieldy Oregon. There were British America and Russian America. There were Nova Zembla and Spitzbergen, and though there were dreams of an open Polar Sea, no one was disturbing it. We had a great American Desert, and some wild lands the other side of the Rocky Mountains. An intrepid young explorer, John Charles Frémont, had discovered an inland sea which he had named Salt Lake, and then gone up to Fort Vancouver on the Columbia River.

He had started again now to survey California and Oregon. We thought Kansas and Nebraska very far West in those days, and the Pacific coast was an almost unknown land. We had just ratified a treaty with China, after long obstinacy on their part, and Japan was still The Hermit Kingdom and the Mikado an unknown quantity.   .

And so everybody was talking war. But then it was so far away one didn't really need to be frightened unless we had war with England.

There were various other matters that quite disturbed the little girl. It had not seemed strange in the summer to have Dr. Hoffman come and take Margaret out driving, or for an evening walk. But now he began to come on Sunday afternoon and stay to tea. Mrs. Underhill was very chatty and pleasant with him. She had accepted the fact of Margaret's engagement, and to tell the truth was really proud of it. Already she was beginning to "lay by," as people phrased it, regardless of Lindley Murray, for her wedding outfit. There were a few choice things of Cousin Lois' that she meant for her. Pieces of muslin

came in the house and were cut up into sheets
and pillow-cases. They were all to be sewed overseam and hemmed by hand. A year would be
none too long in which to get ready.

Josie one day said something about Margaret
being engaged. Hanny made no reply. She
went home in a strange mood. To be sure, Steve
had married Dolly, but that was different. How
could Margaret leave them all and go away with
some one who did not belong to them! She could
not understand the mystery. It was as puzzling
as Cousin Lois' death. She did not know then it
was a mystery even to those who loved, and the
poets who wrote about it.

Her mother sat by the front basement window
sewing. Martha was finishing the ironing and
singing:

> "O how happy are they
> Who their Saviour obey
> And have laid up their treasure above."

Martha had been converted the winter before
and joined the Methodist church in Norfolk
Street. The little girl went with her sometimes
to the early prayer-meeting Sunday evening, for
she was enraptured with the singing.

But she went to her mother now, standing
straight before her with large, earnest eyes.

"Mother," with a strange solemnity in her tone,

"are you going to let Margaret marry Dr. Hoffman?"

"Law, child, how you startled me!" Her mother sewed faster than ever. "Why, I don't know as I had much to do with it any way. And I suppose they'd marry anyhow. When young people fall in love——"

"Fall in love." She had read that in some of the books. It must be different from just loving.

"Don't be silly," said her mother, between sharpness and merriment. "Everybody falls in love sooner or later and marries. Almost everybody. And if I had not fallen in love with your father and married him, you mightn't have had so good a one."

"Oh, mother, I'm so glad you did!" She flung her arms about her mother's neck and kissed her so rapturously that the tears came to her mother's eyes. Why, she wouldn't have missed the exquisite joy of having this little girl for all the world!

"There, child, don't strangle me," was what she said, in an unsteady voice.

"But Dr. Hoffman isn't like father——"

"No, dear. And Margaret isn't like me, now. They are young, and maybe when they have been married a good many years they will be just as happy, growing old together. And since Margaret loves him and he loves her—why, we are all delighted with Dolly. She's just another daughter."

" But we have a good many sons," said the little girl, without seeing the humor of it.

" Yes, we didn't really need him, just yet. But he's Joe's dear friend and a nice young man, and your father is satisfied. It's the way of the world. Little girls can't understand it very well, but they always do when they're grown up. There, go hang up your bonnet, and then you may set the table."

Yes, it was a great mystery. Margaret seemed suddenly set apart, made sacred in some way. Hanny's intensity of thought had no experience to shape or restrain it. All the girls had liked Charles,—perhaps if there had been several boys and spasms of jealousy between the girls, she might have been roused to a more correct idea. But though they had made him the father, a lover had been quite outside of their simple category.

Margaret came down presently. She had on her pretty brown merino trimmed with bands of scarlet velvet, and at her throat a white bow just edged with scarlet. Her front hair was curled in ringlets.

" Mother, can't we have supper quite soon, or can't I? The concert begins at half-past seven and we want to be there early and get a good seat. Dr. Hoffman is coming at half-past six."

Father came in. Mrs. Underhill jumped up and brought in the tea. Jim came whistling down the area steps. They did not need to wait for John and Benny Frank.

Hanny looked at her sister quite as if she were a new person, with some solemn distinction. How had she come to love Dr. Hoffman?

She had not settled it when she went to bed alone. There was a dreary feeling now of years and years without Margaret.

That was Friday, and the following Sunday Dr. Hoffman marched into the parlor with a vital at-home step. Margaret was up-stairs. Hanny sat in her little rocker reading her Sunday-school book. He smiled and came over to her, took away her book, and clasping both hands drew her up, seated himself, and her on his knee before she could make any resistance.

"Hanny," he began, "do you know you are going to be my little sister? I can't remember when I had a *little* sister, mine always seemed big to me. And I am very glad to have you. You are such a sweet, dear little girl. Won't you give me a word of welcome?"

Something in his voice touched her.

"I wasn't glad on Friday," she said slowly. "I don't want Margaret to go away——"

"Then you will have to take me in here."

"There's Stephen's room," she suggested naïvely.

"Yes, that would do. But I'm not going to take Margaret away in a long, long time."

"Oh!" She was greatly relieved.

"But I want you to love me," and he gave her a squeeze, wondering how she could have kept so deliciously innocent. "Won't you try? You will make Margaret ever so much happier. We should be sad if you didn't love us, and now if you love one, you must love the other."

Then Margaret came down, and she said the same thing, so what could Hanny do but promise. And it seemed not to disturb any one else. When she spoke of the prospect to her father, he said with a laugh and a hug: "Well, I have my little girl yet."

Dolly and Stephen took possession of their new abode and had a "house-warming," a great, big, splendid party almost as grand as the wedding. And what a beautiful house it was! There was a bathroom and marble basins, and gas in every room, and pretty light carpets with flowers and green leaves all over them. There was music and dancing and a supper, and old Mr. Beekman walked round with her and told her Katschina wasn't well at all, and he was afraid he should lose her. Dolly said she was to come up on Friday after school and stay until Monday morning.

Would Margaret and Dr. Hoffman have a house like this some time?

She had more lessons to learn now. And grammar was curiously associated with Mrs. Murray being so sweet and attentive to the British officers while the Federal soldiers stole along—she could fairly see them with her vivid imagination. History began to unfold the great world before her. Another thing interested her, and this was that every pleasant day Daisy Jasper came to school for the morning session. She was very backward, of course, for she had never been to school at all. She could walk now without her crutch, but Sam was always very careful of her. The Jasper house became the rendezvous for the girls, as the Deans' had been. Even bonnie Prince Charlie was allowed to go there. Daisy loved so to see them dance to the music of her wonderful box. But Charles had not been able to buy his accordeon. He needed a new suit of clothes if he had any money to throw away, and Mrs. Reed insisted this should be put in the bank when his father said he could buy him all the clothes he needed.

Some of the girls at school were making pretty things for a fair to be held in the basement of the Church of the Epiphany in Stanton Street, and they begged Hanny to help. They were to have a fair at Martha's church also, and the little fingers flew merrily. Hanny had found a new accomplishment, and she was very proud to bring it into the school. This was crocheting. Next door to the stable in Houston Street lived a very tidy German family with a host of little children. The man did cobbling, mending boots and shoes. His wife did shoe binding and stitching leather "foxings" on cloth tops for gaiters. Button shoes had not come in. They either laced in front or at the side. And very few ladies wore anything higher than the spring heel, as it was called. To be sure, some of them did wear foolishly thin shoes, but there were rubbers unless you disdained them; and they were real India-rubber, and no mistake, rather clumsy oftentimes, but they lasted two or three years.

The little German girls, Lena and Gretchen, took care of the babies and did the work. It seemed to Hanny they were always busy. Lena knit stockings and mittens and caps, and her small fingers flew like birds. One day she was doing something very beautiful with pink zephyr and an ivory needle with a tiny hook at the end.

"Oh, what is it?" cried Hanny eagerly.

"Lace. Crocheted lace. A lady on Grand Street will give me ten cents a yard. It is for babies' petticoats. And you can make caps and hoods and fascinators. It plagued me a little at first, but now I can do it so fast, much faster than knitting it. And I am to have all the work I can do."

"Oh, if I could learn!" cried Hanny.

"I'll show you because you are so good to us. Your boy brought mother such a package of clothes. But I am not going to teach the girls around here. They will be wanting to do it for the stores. You can make lace with cotton thread and oh! elegant with silk. That is worth a good deal."

Hanny bought her needle and worsted. At first she was "bothered" as well. But she was an ingenious little girl, and when you once had the "knack" there were such infinite varieties to it. And oh, it was so fascinating! She hardly had time to study her lessons, and one day she did actually miss in her definitions. But she begged Mrs. Craven to let her study them over and recite after school, for she knew her father would feel badly about the imperfect mark.

When she had made two yards of beautiful pink lace she showed it to Margaret. She meant to make two yards of blue and give them both to Katy Rhodes for her table at the Fair. Margaret was very much pleased and said she must learn herself. Daisy Jasper did a little, too. She was learning very rapidly and had a wonderful genius for drawing.

Oh, dear! how busy they were. They were

happy and interested, and almost forgot to take out their dolls, or read their story-books. Martha said: "You might do something for my fair, too," and Margaret promised.

Jim *did* feel a little sore that Lily Ludlow did not ask him to her party, which was quite a grand affair. She announced that she had broken with the public-school crowd, and was going to have all new friends. But the very next week she met Jim at another party, and he was so handsome and manly that she really regretted her haste. Jim was very proud and dignified, and never once danced with her nor chose her in any of the games.

Dolly and Stephen came home to the Thanksgiving dinner. If Hanny had not been so much engrossed she might have considered herself left out of some things, only her father never left her out. And Ben brought home such tempting books that she did wish she could sit up like the others and not have to go to bed at nine.

The Epiphany fair came first, the week before Christmas. The Sunday-school room was all dressed with greens, and tables arranged over the tops of the seats with long boards, covered with white cloths. And oh, the lovely articles! Everything it seemed that fingers could make, useful or ornamental, from handsomely dressed dolls to pincushions, from white aprons with lace and ribbon bows on the dainty pockets down to unromantic holders. Everybody laughed and chatted and were as gay as gay could be.

In the back room that was rented out for a day school—indeed, the little girl had come quite near being sent here—there were tables for refreshments. The coffee and tea had a delightful fragrance, and the different dishes looked wonderfully tempting.

It was Hanny's first fair, but people didn't expect to take children out everywhere then, or indeed to go themselves. There was more home life, real family life. Her father was her escort, and her mother had said: " Now don't make the child sick by feeding her all kinds of trash, or she can't go out again this winter." So you see they had to be careful. But they had some delightful cake and cream, and he bought her a pound of candy tied up in a pretty box, and the loveliest little work-basket with a row of blue silk pockets around the inside.

Katy Rhodes was waiting at a table with her mother, but she found an opportunity to whisper to Hanny "that her lace had sold the very first thing, and there had been such a call for it she just wished they had had a hundred yards."

That pleased the child very much.

" It was like a store," said Hanny to her mother; "only everybody seemed to know everybody, and there were all kinds of things. So many people came for their suppers they must have made lots of money. And I'm as tired as I can be, only it *was* beautiful."

Martha's church was to have their Christmas Sunday-school anniversary, and Charles Reed was to sing a solo with a chorus of four voices. The Deans and half the people in the street went. Margaret and Dr. Hoffman, and this time John and Ben took the little girl. Mother had been up at Steve's all day.

There was a large platform at the end of the church, and crowds of pretty children dressed in white, ranged in tiers one above another. After a prayer and singing by the congregation the real exercises began. The body of children sang some beautiful hymns, then there were several spirited dialogues, and separate pieces, very well rendered indeed. When it came "bonnie Prince Charlie's" turn, he seemed to hesitate a moment. Hanny thought she would be frightened to death before all the people. I think Charles would have been a year ago.

The piano began the soft accompainment. After the first few notes the sweet young voice swelled out like the warble of a bird. People were silent with surprise and admiration. The fair, boyish face and slim figure looked smaller there on the platform. The face had a youthful sweetness that nowadays would be pronounced artistic.

The chorus came in beautifully. There were three verses in the solo, and really, I do not know as the audience were to blame for applauding. The boy had to come out and sing again, this time a pretty Christmas carol that they had practised at singing-school.

When the exercises were finished the children were all taken down-stairs and they looked very pretty flitting about. There was another surprise, one that greatly interested the little girl. In one prettily arranged booth were two curious small beings who had a history. They had already been in Sunday-school on two occasions. A missionary to China, seeing these little girls about to be sold, had rescued them by buying them himself. He had brought them back on his return, and now kindly disposed people were making up a sum to provide them with a home and educate them.

Hanny pressed forward holding John's hand tightly. They were so strange-looking. The larger and older one was not at all pretty, but the younger one had a sweet sort of shyness and was not so stolid. Their yellow-brown skins, oblique dark eyes, black brows, and black hair done up in a remarkable fashion with some long pins, and their Chinese attire seemed very curious. The gentleman with them said there were hundreds of little girls sold in China, and that women bought them for future wives for their sons, and treated them like bond slaves. These children's feet had not been cramped, this was done mainly to the higher orders. He had some Chinese shoes worn by grown women, and they were such short, queer things, like some of the pincushions made for the Fair.

We didn't suppose then the Chinese would come and. live with us and have a Chinatown in the heart of the city; do our laundry work and take possession of our kitchens; that the blue shirts and queer pointed shoes would be a common sight in our streets. So the Chinese children were a curiosity. Indeed, several years elapsed before Hanny saw another inhabitant of the Flowery Kingdom.

"Don't you want to put something in the box?" John held out a quarter to the little girl.

Her eyes sparkled with pleasure. Then she shook hands with the small Chinese maidens, and she felt almost as if she had been to a foreign country.

If Mrs. Reed had been present she would have marched Charles home in short order. She did not believe in praising children, or anybody else for that matter. Everybody, in her opinion, needed a strict hand. She hardly approved of the singing-school, and if she had really understood that Charles would stand out alone facing the audience, and then be applauded for what he had done, and go into the fair and be praised and "treated," she would have been horrified and put him on the strictest sort of discipline for the next month.

Charles had endeavored to persuade his mother to go, but she wanted to get the turkey ready for the Christmas dinner, and had no time for such trifling things.   No woman had who did her duty by her house and her family.   The harder and stonier and more rigid the discipline was, the more virtue it contained, she thought.   There was no especial end in view with her; it was the way all along that one had to be careful about and make as rough as possible.

Mr. Reed was secretly proud of his boy.   He had a misgiving that all this praise and attention was not a good thing, but the boy looked so happy, and it was Christmas Eve, with the general feeling of joy in the air.   He was curiously moved himself.   Perhaps happiness wasn't such a weak and sinful thing after all.   It did not seem to ruin the Underhill faimly.

But he said to Charles as they were nearing home: "I wouldn't make much fuss about the evening.   Your mother thinks such things rather foolish."

They all returned in a crowd, laughing and

talking and saying merry good-nights. Martha had the key of the basement and they trooped in. Indeed, Martha was so much one of the family that Dr. Hoffman paid her a deal of respect.

Father was up-stairs in the sitting-room reading his paper. He glanced up and nodded.

"Oh!" cried Hanny, "where's mother? The house looks so dark and dull and not a bit Christmassy. It was all so splendid, and oh, Father! Charles sung like an angel, didn't he, Margaret? They made him sing over again, and he looked really beautiful. And there were two Chinese girls at the fair, such queer little things," she flushed, for the word recalled Lily Ludlow. "Their hands were as soft as silk, and when they talked—well, you can't imagine it! It sounded like knocking little blocks all around and making the corners click. But where *is* mother?"

"Mother is going to stay up to Steve's all night. They wanted her to help them."

"Oh, dear! It won't be any Christmas without her," cried the little girl ruefully.

"Oh, she'll be home in the morning, likely."

"Hanny, it is after eleven, and you must go to bed," said Margaret.

"I'd just like to stay up all night, once. And can't I hang up my stocking?"

"I'll see to that. Come, dear. And boys, go to bed."

WHEN CHRISTMAS BELLS WERE RINGING.

THE boys tried to be merry with a big M to it, on Christmas morning. But something was lacking. The stockings hung in a row, and there were piles of gifts below them. Books and books and books! They were all too old for playthings now. Hanny had two white aprons ruffled all round, and a pretty pair of winter boots. They were beginning to make them higher in the ankle and more dainty, and stitching them in colors. These were done with two rows of white. She had a set of the Lucy books that all little girls were delighted with. Oh, I do wonder what they would have said to Miss Alcott and Susan Coolidge and Pansy! But they were very happy in what they had. Jim was delighted with two new volumes of Cooper. Ben had a splendid pair of high boots, and three new shirts Margaret and the little girl had made for him.

But, oh, dear! what was it all without mother! They missed her bright, cheery voice, her smile and her ample person that had a warm buoyant atmosphere. They would have been glad to hear her scold a little about the litter of gifts around, and their lagging so when breakfast was ready.

To make the little girl laugh her father told her that once a man was driving along a country road when he saw seven children sitting on the door-step crying, and seven more on the fence. Startled at so much grief he paused to inquire what had happened, and with one voice they answered:

"Our mother's gone away and left us all alone!"

"There's only seven of us with Martha, and I am not crying," said the little girl spiritedly.

Joe dropped in just as they were seated at the table, and whispered something to his father and Margaret. He seemed very merry, and Mr. Underhill gave a satisfied nod. He brought Margaret a beautiful cameo brooch, which was considered a fine thing then, and put a pretty garnet ring on Hanny's finger.

Hanny guessed what the word had been. Mother was going to bring Steve and Dolly down to dinner. Dolly had changed her mind, for she had said she could not come. That was what they were smiling about.

At ten Stephen brought mother down in the sleigh, and they were more mysterious than ever.

Peggy and the little girl must bundle up and go back with him, for he had such a wonderful Christmas present to show them.

"But why didn't you bring Dolly and stay to dinner? And oh, Mother! Christmas morning wasn't splendid at all without you!" said the little girl, clinging to her.

Mrs. Underhill stooped and kissed her and said in a full, tremulous sort of voice:

"Run and get your hood, dear, and don't keep Stephen waiting."

The horses tossed their heads and whinnied as if they too, said, "Don't keep us waiting." The sun was shining and all the air seemed infused with joy, though it was a sharp winter day. The weather knew its business fifty years ago and didn't sandwich whiffs of spring between snow-banks. And the children were blowing on tin and wooden horns, and wishing everybody Merry Christmas as they ran around with the reddest of cheeks.

Steve took Hanny on his lap. What did make him so laughing and mysterious? He insisted that Hanny should guess, and then kept saying, "Oh, you're cold, cold, cold as an icehouse! You should have put on your guessing cap," and the little girl felt quite teased.

They stopped down-stairs to get good and warm and take off their wraps. Then Stephen led them up to the front room. It was a kind of library and sitting-room, but no one was there. In the window stood a beautiful vase of flowers. Hanny ran over to that. Roses at Christmastide were rare indeed. "Here," said Stephen, catching her arm gently.

She turned to the opposite corner. There was an old-fashioned mahogany cradle, black with age, and polished until it shone like glass. It was lined overhead with soft light-blue silk, and had lying across it a satin coverlet that had grown creamy with age, full of embroidered flowers dull and soft with their many years of bloom.

On the pillow lay her brother's Christmas gift that had come while the bells were still ringing out their message first heard on the plains of Judea.

"Oh!" with a soft, wondering cry. She knelt beside the cradle that had come from Holland a century and a half ago, and held many a Beekman baby. A strange little face with a tinge of redness in it, a round broad forehead with a mistiness of golden fuzz, a pretty dimpled chin and a mouth almost as round as a cherry. Just at that instant he opened the bluest of eyes, stared at Hanny with a grave aspect, tried to put his fist into his mouth and with a soft little sound dropped to sleep again.

A wordless sense of delight and mystery stole over the little girl. She seemed lifted up to Heaven's very gates. She reached out her hand and touched the little velvet fist, not much larger than her doll's, but oh, it had the exquisite inspiration of life and she felt the wonderful thrill to her very heart. Something given to them all that could love back when its time of loving came, when it knew of the fond hearts awaiting the sweetness of affection.

"That's my little boy," said Stephen, with the great pride and joy of fatherhood. "Dolly's and all of ours. Isn't it a Christmas worth having?"

"Oh!" she said again with a wordless delight in her heart, while her eyes were filled with tears, so deeply had the consciousness moved her. There was a sort of poetical pathos in the little girl, sacred to love. She had never known of any babies in the family save Cousin Retty's, and that had not appealed with this delicious nearness.

Stephen bent over and kissed her. Margaret came to look at the baby.

"He's a fine fellow!" said the new father. "We wanted to surprise you," looking at Hanny and smiling. "We made Joe promise not to tell you. And now you are all aunts and uncles, and we have a grandmother of our very own."

"Oh!" This time Hanny laughed softly. There were no words expressive enough.

"And now you will have to knit him some little boots, and save your money to buy him Christmas gifts. And what's that new work—crochet him a cap. Dear me! how hard you will have to work."

"There were such lovely little boots at the Epiphany Fair. If I only had known! But I'm quite sure I can learn to make them;" her eyes lighting with anticipation. "Oh, when will he be big enough to hold?"

"In a month or so. You will have to come up on Saturdays and take care of him."

"Can I? That will be just splendid."

He was silent. He could not tease the little girl in the sacredness of her new, all-pervading love.

The nurse entered. She had a soft white kerchief pinned about her shoulders, and side puffs of hair done over little combs. She nodded to Margaret and said " the baby was a very fine child, and that Mrs. Underhill was sleeping restfully. They had been so glad to have Mr. Underhill's mother." Then she patted the blanket over the baby, and said " it had been worked for his great, great grandmother, and they put it over every Beekman baby for good luck."

Margaret declared they must return. Mother was tired, and the Archers were coming up to dinner after church.

"Could I kiss it just once?" asked Hanny timidly.

"Oh, yes." The nurse smiled and turned down the blanket, and the baby opened his eyes.

Hanny felt that in some mysterious manner he

knew she loved him. Her lips touched the soft little cheek, the tiny hands.

"He's very good now," said the nurse; "but he can cry tremendously. He has strong lungs."

Stephen took them back and then went down to Father Beekman's. There was so much to do, the little girl and the big girl were both busy enough, helping mother. The boys and her father had gone out, but they had all heard the wonderful tidings.

Hanny ran back and forth waiting on Martha and carrying dishes to the table, so there would be no flurry at the last.

"Hello, Aunt Hanny!" laughed Jim, bouncing in with the reddest of cheeks. "You'll have to grow fast now to keep up with your dignity. Well, is he Beekman Dutch or Underhill English?"

"He's just lovely. His eyes are blue as the sky."

"Hurrah for Steve! Well, that was a Christmas!"

Her father was coming with the two cousins, and she ran up-stairs to wish them Merry Christmas and tell her father what she thought of the baby. The baby and the Christmas sermon and the rheumatism and cold weather seemed to get jumbled all together, and for a little while everybody talked. Then John and Joe made their appearance, and Martha rang the bell, though the savory odors announced that all was ready.

They had a very delightful dinner. Mrs. Underhill had a pretty new consequence about her, and was not a bit teased by being called grandmother. Dolly's advent into the family had been a source of delight, for she fraternized so cordially with every member. And of late she and Mother Underhill had been tenderly intimate, for Mrs. Beekman was kept much at home by her husband's failing health.

When they had lingered over the mince pies which certainly were delicious, and finished their coffee, they went upstairs to chat around the fire. After the dishes were dried Hanny ran into the Deans' to interchange a little Christmas talk and tell the girls about Stephen's baby. She was so excited that all other gifts seemed of little moment.

Daisy Jasper had been confined to the house for a week with a severe cold.

"I began to think you had forgotten me," she said, as Hanny entered the beautiful parlor. "And Doctor Joe said you had something special to tell me. Oh, what is it?" for the little girl's face was still in a glow of excitement.

"I can never have any nieces or nephews because there is only one of me," said Daisy, with a sad little smile. "I *almost* envy you. If I could have one of your brothers out of them all I should choose Dr. Joe. He is so tender and sweet and patient. He used to take me in his arms and let me cry when crying wasn't good for me either. I was so miserable and full of pain, and he always understood."

Hanny was so moved by pity for Daisy that she felt almost as if she could give him away—she had so much. Not quite, however, for he was very dear to her. And when she looked into Daisy's lovely face and remembered her beautiful name and glanced at the elegant surroundings, it seemed strange there should be anything to wish for. But health outweighed all.

Daisy was delighted with the Christmas Eve anniversary, the singing of "bonnie Prince Charlie," the fair, and was wonderfully interested in the little Chinese girls. She meant to send some money toward their education.

Mr. Bradbury was to give a concert in February with the best child singers of the different schools. Charles was to take part, his father had promised him that indulgence.

"I hope I shall get strong enough to go," began Daisy wistfully. "It is the sitting up straight that tires my back, but last year it was so much worse. Doctor Joe says I shall get well and be almost like other girls. See how much I have gone to school. It is so splendid to learn for your own very self. You don't feel so helpless."

Daisy's Christmas had been a beautiful Geneva watch. We had not gone to watchmaking then and had to depend on our neighbors over the water for many choice articles. And a watch was a rare thing for a little girl to possess.

When she went home Hanny had to get out her pretty new work and show the visitors. She had nearly four yards of lovely blue edging she was making for Margaret, but she had not hinted at its destination.

"Why," exclaimed Aunt Nancy, "I've seen mittens knit with a hook something like that. Not open work and fancy, but all tight and out of good stout yarn. They're very lasting."

"I do believe they're like what Uncle David makes," said John. "Don't you remember, he used to give us a pair now and then?"

"Well, I declare, there's nothing new under the sun!" laughed Aunt Patience.

Hanny was quite sure there could not be any connection between her delicate lace and stout yarn mittens, and she meant to ask Uncle David the next time they made a visit. Both ladies praised her a good deal, especially when they heard of the shirts she had been making with Margaret.

"It used to be a great thing," said Aunt Patience. "When I was six years old I had knit a pair of stockings by myself, and when I was eight I had made my father a shirt. All the gussets were stitched, just as you do a bosom. My, what a sight of fine work there was then!"

"I'll tell you something I read the other day in a queer old book I picked up down at the office," began Ben. "When little Prince Edward was two years old, the Princess Elizabeth who was afterward queen made him a shirt or smock, as it was called, with drawn work and embroidery. And she was only six."

"Children have more lessons to study now," said Mrs. Underhill, half in apology. "And Hanny has done some drawn work for me, and embroidered some aprons."

"And Queen Elizabeth spent enough time later on with gay gallants," remarked Aunt Nancy. "So I do not know as her early industry held out."

"I'd rather have had her splendid reign than to have made shirts for an army," declared Ben.

"Well, we all have our duties in this world," sighed Aunt Patience. "I learned to make shirts, but I never had a husband or boys to make them for."

They all laughed at that. But what would a little girl say now if she had to stitch down the middle of a shirt bosom, following a drawn thread, and taking up only two threads at every stitch?

There certainly was great need of Elias Howe.

The visitors declared they must get home by dark.   There was the poor cat, and the fires must need looking after.   Mrs. Underhill was fain to keep them to tea, but instead packed them up a basket of cold turkey and some delicious boiled ham, a dozen or two crullers, and a nice mince pie. John was to see the old ladies home.

When they were gone Hanny went up to the "spare" room, for in one drawer of the best bureau she had kept her beautiful doll, which had never been permanently named.   She opened it and kneeling down raised the napkin that covered her, as one tucks in a little child.

Yes, she was lovely, really prettier than Stephen's baby, she felt, though she would not say it.   But when you came to kiss on the cold wax— ah, that was the test.   And Stephen's baby would grow and walk and talk, and have cunning little teeth and curly hair, maybe.   She did so love curly hair.

"Dolly," she began gravely, "I am going to put you away.   I shall be eleven next May, and though I shall always be father's little girl, I shall be growing up and too old to play with dolls.   Then I shall have so much to do.   And I should love the real live baby best.   That would hurt your feelings.   Sometime there may be another little girl who will be as glad to have you come on Christmas Day as I was.   I shall love you just the same, but you have a different kind of love for something that is human and can put truly arms around your neck and kiss you. When girls are little they don't mind the difference so much. You won't feel real lonesome, for dolls don't. We only make believe they do. And now I shall not make believe any more, because I am getting to know all about real things. There are so many real and strange things in the world that are lovely to think about, and I seem to have learned so much to-day. I can't feel quite as I did yester-day."

She put on the wadded satin cloak and the dainty hood and laid it back in the box. There was room for the muff and the travelling shawl. She put the cover on softly. She folded the pretty garments and packed them in the corner, and spread the towel over them all.

There was no morbid feeling of sacrifice or sense of loss. A great change had come over her, a new human affection had entered her soul. She had a consciousness that could not be put into words. She had outgrown her doll.

Margaret was going to an oratorio with Dr. Hoffman. The boys were to attend the Christmas celebration at Allen Street church with the Deans. Hanny had not cared to go. Her mother kept watching her with a curious feeling as if she saw or suspected some change in her.

The room settled to quiet. The fire burned drowsily. Mrs. Underhill took the big rocking-chair at one side, and Hanny came and settled herself on a footstool, leaning her arms on her mother's knee.

"I shall not hang up my stocking next Christmas," she said, in a soft, slow tone. "It is very nice when you believe in it, and real fun afterward when you don't believe in it but like it; when you seem little to yourself."

"You do grow out of it," replied her mother; but at heart she was half-sorry. "You get just the same things. At least you get suitable things."

Was she glad to have them all growing up?

"Dear me, there's no little children," she continued, with a sigh. "You'll be eleven next May, Hanny."

"But there's Stephen's lovely little baby. Doesn't it seem just as if God had sent him at the right time, when we were all growing big?"

She took the little girl's hands in hers and said dreamily, "You were sent that way, at the right time. I was so glad to have you. I can recall it so plainly. Old Mother Tappan was there. I was so afraid you'd be a boy, and we had boys enough. And she said, 'Oh, what a nice little girl. You'll be glad enough, Mrs. Underhill.' And so I was."

"As glad as Stephen?" said Hanny, with shin‧ing eyes.

"Yes, dear.   Even if it wasn't Christmas. You were a welcome little May flower."

In Bethlehem of Judea the other child had been born with the mighty significance of a great gift to the world, a gift that had made Christmas pos‧sible for all time to come.   Just how the world was redeemed no little girl of ten or so could un‧derstand.   But it was redeemed because the little child of Bethlehem bore the sins of the whole world in His manhood.   Ah, no wonder they wrote under the picture of His mother, when He was gone, "*Mater Dolorosa.*"   But the years of His childhood must have been sweet to remember. "The young child and His mother."   The wise men coming with their gifts.   The sweet song going around the world, the great love.

Her mother's hands relaxed from their clasp. She was very tired and had fallen asleep.   Her father folded his paper and looked over at her wistfully.   Hanny came and dropped softly on his knee and his strong, tender arms enclosed her.

Was there any child quite like the little girl? They had been so proud and happy over Stephen, so delighted with Margaret.   He had loved them all, and they were a nice household of children. But they were growing up and going their ways. They would be making new homes.   Ah, it would be many a long year before the little girl would think of such a thing.   They would keep her snug and safe, "to have and to hold," and he smiled to himself at the literal rendering.

The chime of the clock roused Mrs. Underhill. It was Hanny's bedtime, and she had been so busy all day, so full of excitement, too, that her cheeks had bloomed with roses.   She glanced across.   The fair flaxen head was on the shoulder half hidden by the protecting arm.   The other head, showing many silver threads now, drooped over a little.   The picture brought a mist to her eyes, and there was a half sob in her throat.   The same thought came into her mind.   She would be their "little girl" when the other one had gone to her new home.

She could not disturb them.   It was "good will and peace" everywhere.